Presumption of Guilt

BOOKS BY TERRI BLACKSTOCK

Newpointe 911
Private Justice
Shadow of Doubt
Trial by Fire
Word of Honor

Sun Coast Chronicles
Evidence of Mercy
Justifiable Means
Ulterior Motives
Presumption of Guilt

Second Chances
Never Again Good-bye
When Dreams Cross
Blind Trust
Broken Wings

With Beverly LaHaye
Seasons Under Heaven
Showers in Season
Times and Seasons

Novellas
Seaside

Presumption of Guilt

Terri Blackstock

SUN COAST ❹ CHRONICLES

ZONDERVAN™

GRAND RAPIDS, MICHIGAN 49530

We want to hear from you. Please send your comments about this
book to us in care of the address below. Thank you.

GRAND RAPIDS, MICHIGAN 49530

w w w . z o n d e r v a n . c o m

ZONDERVAN™

Presumption of Guilt
Copyright © 1997 by Terri Blackstock

Requests for information should be addressed to:
Zondervan, *Grand Rapids, Michigan 49530*

Library of Congress Cataloging-in-Publication Data

Blackstock, Terri, 1957–
    Presumption of guilt / Terri Blackstock.
        p.   cm. — (Sun coast chronicles ; [bk. 4])
    ISBN: 0-310-20018-0 (softcover)
    I. Title.   II. Series: Blackstock, Terri, 1957–   Sun coast chronicles ; bk. 4.
PS3552.L34285P74 1997
813'.54—dc21   97-254
                                                                  CIP

Published in association with the literary agency of Alive Communications, Inc., 7680
Goddard Street, Suite 200, Colorado Springs, CO 80920.

Interior design by Sue Vandenberg Koppenol

Printed in the United States of America

---

01 02 03 04 05 06/❖ DC / 22 21 20 19 18 17 16 15 14 13 12 11 10 9

This book is lovingly dedicated to the Nazarene

ACKNOWLEDGMENTS

I can't end this series without thanking the people who have shared my vision for it since the beginning. I'd like to thank my agent, Greg Johnson, for believing in what I was doing and sharing my enthusiasm. And I'd like to thank my Zondervan friends who have worked tirelessly beside me: Dave Lambert, the best editor I've ever worked with (and I've worked with plenty); Lori Walburg, the second best editor I've ever worked with; Sue Brower, who believed in the books enough to go to great lengths to get them into the hands of readers; and all of the others at Zondervan who have been such a pleasure to work with.

Thanks, also, to Bob Anderson from the attorney general's office in my state, for answering important law questions for me.

And thanks to you, all of the readers who have followed this series to the very end. You've been God's way of telling me over and over that this is where I'm supposed to be!

CHAPTER ONE

The Buick had been tailing Beth Wright for miles. She had first noticed it weaving in and out of traffic too closely behind her on the Courtney-Campbell Causeway, the driver making no attempt to hide the fact that he was after her. Now, nearing St. Clair, they had left most of the traffic behind, but he was still there. She pressed the accelerator harder, checking her rearview mirror.

It didn't take a genius to figure out who it was. She had known that, if word got out that she was doing the story on the St. Clair Children's Home, Bill Brandon would come after her. What he would do once he caught her was open to speculation, but she didn't want to find out.

The Buick sped up and switched lanes, cutting in front of a motorcycle, forcing it to swerve, and then pulled up beside her, as if trying to run her off the road. He must have found out somehow that she had interviewed his sister, and he didn't like it. Marlene had warned her that he wouldn't take it well, but Beth hadn't needed warning.

The Buick swerved sharply to the right, almost hitting Beth's car, and she caught her breath and rammed her right foot to the floor. Her car burst forward, leaving the Buick behind. If he ran her off the road, he would kill her. If he was desperate enough to chase her down on a state highway with other drivers watching, then he was desperate enough to commit murder.

Her hand trembled as she reached for her cellular phone. It had fallen to the floor, so she bent forward, groping for it. The Buick jolted her rear bumper, and she swerved onto the shoulder.

Grabbing the wheel, she pulled it quickly back into the right lane. The few other cars on the highway had begun pulling off the roadway to let her car and the Buick go by, probably alarmed by the Buick's erratic driving. Maybe someone had already called this in to the police.

She reached again into the darkness in front of the passenger seat for the phone, and this time her hand touched it. She picked it up and dialed 911 with her thumb.

"911, may I help you?"

"There's someone after me!" she cried. "He's trying to kill me!"

"What's your address?"

"No! I'm in my car! He's following me. We're on Highway 19 between St. Petersburg and St. Clair. I just passed the Ship's End restaurant. Please hurry!"

"What is he driving, ma'am?"

"A dark Buick—I'm not sure of the color."

He bumped the rear corner of her bumper again, and she screamed as her car veered to the shoulder. "He's ramming my car! Please, have you sent someone?"

"Yes," the dispatcher said. "We have a car on its way—"

But while the woman was still talking, Beth punched the "end" button, cutting her off, so she could pay attention to Bill Brandon's Buick. The stretch of road between St. Petersburg and St. Clair wasn't as busy as the others they'd been on. If there was a patrol car in the area, he'd spot them immediately—but if not, she might be dead before they showed up. To her right, she could see the beach, the turbulent waves smashing against the sand. If he stopped her, he could easily make her disappear in the Gulf Coast—and he wouldn't think twice about it. She looked in her rearview mirror. There was a car's distance between them now, but he was gaining. No other cars were in sight behind them. Where were the police?

Nick, she thought. *I have to call Nick.* He was expecting her to come straight to his house, to let him know what she'd found out from Marlene. But with this maniac following her, she might never get there. She'd better tell him what she'd learned—just in case.

She punched out his number and waited as it rang. "Come on, Nick," she whispered.

The answering machine picked up. "Hello, you have reached the home of Nick Hutchins . . ."

The Buick bumped her again, and tears sprang to her eyes. She punched off the phone and tried to think. *Where are you, Nick? You're supposed to be waiting for me!*

A message, she thought. *He must have left a message.* Maybe he'd called to tell her to meet him somewhere else instead. Her hand trembled, making it difficult, but she managed to punch out her own number, then waited for her machine to answer so that she could punch in her code and get her messages.

"Hello?"

It was the voice of a boy.

Startled, she asked, "Who is this?"

There was a long pause. "Who do you want?"

She turned on her bright lights, looking for a road, any road, that she could turn down in hopes of losing him. "I thought I was calling my own house," she said.

"You must have the wrong number."

Confused, she punched the "end" button, and followed the road's curve along the edge of the beach. The Buick did the same, right on her bumper. *Where were the police?* And what number had she just dialed? She punched "recall" and saw the digital readout. It was her number. So who had answered the phone at her house?

Her car jolted again, and she saw the Buick in the lane next to her. He was trying to force her off the road now. She had to get help—he would kill her if she didn't lose him.

She pressed "redial" and checked the number on her readout. She had dialed right the first time. She pressed "send" and waited as her own number rang again. This time, it rang on and on. The machine, which normally picked up on the fourth ring, never answered.

What's going on?

The car edged over, pushing her toward a drop-off. She looked in her rearview mirror and saw that no one was behind her. No witnesses, no one to notice if he sent her tumbling over a seawall.

She saw a road sign up ahead, and quickly breathed a prayer. Then, waiting for just the right moment, she slammed on her brakes until she was behind the Buick and screeched into a left turn, skidding around the corner onto a side street. She stomped on the accelerator and made another turn, and another, until she was completely out of his reach, hidden by trees.

She eased up on the accelerator only slightly, checking her rearview mirror every few seconds. It was more than fifteen minutes before she was certain that she had lost him; only then did she feel that she could safely try to make it home—hoping he hadn't figured out where that was yet. She had intentionally rented the little house out in the woods because it would be hard for unwelcome guests to find. So far, she'd kept herself insulated from him, but now she knew that interviewing Marlene had been a mistake. Bill Brandon was too smart and too suspicious not to keep close tabs on the sister who had once worked with him. He must have found out about the interview somehow, and followed Beth from Marlene's house.

So maybe he still didn't know where she lived. Maybe her little house in the woods was still a safe haven.

CHAPTER TWO

The car phone in the Buick rang, and Bill Brandon snatched it up. "Yeah, what is it?"

"Bill, it's me." The boy's voice was shaky and frightened.

"What are you doing?" the man asked. "Where are you?"

"Still in her house," the boy said in a half-whisper. "But I can't find any of the papers or any tapes. I've looked everywhere."

Bill cursed. "Does she have a desk? A file cabinet? Did you check her computer?"

"Yes. I looked in all those places, and I couldn't find anything on the computer. She has millions of directories, and I don't know what to look for."

"Well, keep trying. And hurry. You don't have much more time."

"Are you still following her?"

"No, I lost her."

There was a pause again. "She just called here."

"She *what?* What do you mean she called?" Bill's face darkened as he held the phone to his ear, taking it in. He heard the sirens, and quickly pulled off the road, cut his lights, and stopped behind a rickety-looking body shop.

"She called. I picked up the phone 'cause you told me you were gonna call and warn me when she was coming home. I thought it was you."

"You idiot! What did she say?"

"I made like she called the wrong number. She called back, and I just let it ring."

"Well, you'd better get out of there, you fool! She's on her way home!"

"I thought you were gonna stop her!"

"I didn't," he snapped. He saw the reflections of blue lights flashing against the trees and junk cars surrounding the body shop. He wiped his sweating temple as the lights continued on up the road. "You blew it already, kid. Next time I'll find someone else who can do the job without botching it up."

"But Bill, I tried—"

"That's not good enough!" Bill shouted. "I'll deal with you when we get home! Now, get out of there!"

"Where will I go?" the boy asked in a voice on the verge of tears.

"Go to the Fraser Gas Station on Banton Street. I'll pick you up."

"But that's five miles away, Bill! Will you wait for me?"

"I told you I'd pick you up, didn't I? Now don't let anyone see you. If anybody does, you don't say a word, you understand me? You don't know anything."

"Okay, Bill."

Bill slammed the phone down and cursed again as he pulled out of his hiding place and headed for the gas station.

CHAPTER THREE

A s he hung up the phone, ten-year-old Jimmy Westin heard tires on the gravel outside the house. Headlights swept through the windows of the darkened house, and the small red-haired boy froze, wondering which of the side doors she would come in, which door he could safely leave through. The little cocker spaniel at his feet yelped up at him, wanting to play. He shouldn't have given it so much attention when he'd first come in, but he'd never had a dog of his own, and he hadn't expected to find it here. Bill hadn't said anything about it.

"Shhh," he whispered, trying to quiet it. "I have to go."

He heard the car door slam in front of the house. Her keys rattled in the door.

Now it was too late to go out *any* of the doors. He would have to hide. He looked around frantically, then dashed up the stairs, leaving the fat, young puppy yelping after him. Halfway up, he looked back and saw it struggling to climb the first step. He left it behind, and hurried up to the woman's loft office, where he'd searched for the papers and tapes Bill wanted. There was a door there, next to a closet. He opened it.

It was a floored walk-in attic. He slipped in and closed the door quietly, just as he heard the door downstairs closing behind her. Instantly, he was surrounded by darkness, thicker darkness than that downstairs. Downstairs, there had been a night-light over the stove, and a small lamp she had left on. In here, the darkness was opaque, smothering . . .

He trembled as he shrugged off the black backpack he wore, unzipped it, and pulled out his flashlight. The beam revealed boxes against the walls—tall ones, short ones, empty ones, packed ones. Across the floor was a window. Perfect. He could get out that way. He walked softly, trying to make it to the window, but the floor creaked beneath him. He froze, afraid to take another step. What if she heard? What if he got caught? What would they do with him?

He was sweating, and his breath came harder. All of the heat of Florida seemed contained in this attic, locked in with no escape, just like him.

He stood there, motionless, listening. He could hear her downstairs, doors closing, footsteps moving across the floor. Was she looking for him? Had she figured out that the voice on the phone wasn't a wrong number? What if the puppy somehow led her to him?

He shone the beam around him again, looking for a hiding place, and he saw lots of them. Places where mice, too, could hide. Spiders. Snakes, even. There was no telling what could be in an attic in such an old house.

He eyed the window again, and tried taking another step. It didn't creak. Taking a deep breath, he tiptoed across the floor, walking as lightly, as quietly as he could, until he reached the window. He unlocked it and tried to slide it up, but it was stuck. With all his might he tugged, but it didn't budge.

For a panicked moment, he thought of breaking the glass and making a run for it, but it was a long way down. By the time he figured out a way to get to the ground without breaking both legs, she would have the whole police force surrounding the place.

He was stuck here. Stuck until she went to sleep. Then, if he was very careful, and the floor didn't creak, and the dog didn't bark, maybe he could get out. Bill would be furious that he hadn't made it to the gas station on time, and Jimmy would probably have to make it all the way back to the children's home on foot—unless he could get to a phone and call for someone to come get him. He reached into his empty pocket, wishing he had a quarter. Maybe the lady who lived here had one lying around somewhere. Maybe he could find it before he left.

Maybe.

He wondered what Bill would do to him for messing this up. Quickly, he shifted his thoughts. He couldn't dwell on that. He had to go back, and that was that. Lisa would bear the brunt of his punishment if he didn't. He couldn't let that happen.

He heard footsteps coming up the stairs, and quickly dove behind a box in the corner. He held his breath and listened. Her footsteps moved across the office floor; she was going to her desk. He realized that he had forgotten to turn the answering machine back on. How could he be so stupid?

He should have worn gloves. Could they trace the fingerprints of ten-year-old boys? And once they found him, would they put him in jail or send him to the detention center? Did they really have that room with the black walls and only a slit that they slid bread through—the room Bill had warned him about? Is that where they would keep him locked up until he was old enough for prison?

He closed his eyes and leaned back against the wall. He could hear her out there, doing something in her office, moving around. He heard her saying something to the puppy, heard the little animal yelp and scratch on the floor. Would the dog lead her to him?

"Please don't let her find me," he whispered. "Please . . ."

CHAPTER FOUR

Nick Hutchins stuffed the duffel bag full of the clothes the two frightened little boys—six and eight years old—would need, and wished they didn't have to listen to the string of expletives flying from the foul mouth of their drug-dealer father, who stood handcuffed in the corner of the living room. His wife, also involved in the family business, screamed over his curses that they couldn't take her children away. Tony Danks and Larry Millsaps, the cops who had called Nick to come take the children into state custody, ignored her pleas and continued recording the evidence they'd compiled. There was enough crack cocaine in the house to ruin the lives of everyone in St. Clair.

It wasn't an unusual event, but Nick had never gotten used to it. He zipped up the bag and went back into the living room where the two boys sat huddled together.

"My daddy didn't do anything!" the older child cried. "Neither did my mom. Why don't you just leave us alone?"

"Please don't take my kids!" their mother cried. "I didn't know nothing about what he was doing. He did it behind my back! Please!"

Nick glanced hopefully at Larry. If there was some way they could avoid arresting the mother tonight, then he could spare the children the trauma of being taken from their home, at least temporarily. But Larry shook his head.

"We caught her dealing on videotape," Larry said. "And with all the stuff we found in the back room, there's no way she didn't know what was going on."

Nick looked at the distraught woman. "Do you have any relatives we can call? Someone who can take the kids tonight?"

"No, my parents are dead," she cried. "And we don't even know where his parents are."

"Any cousins or aunts or uncles? Sisters or brothers? Anyone?"

"No!" she cried, struggling to make him understand. "So you *have* to let me stay with them. They don't have anybody to take care of them."

Wearily, Nick slid the strap of the duffel bag over his shoulder, then took the children's hands. "We'll see that they're cared for."

"But *I* can take care of them! Please don't take them."

"Come on, kids," Nick said. "Let's go."

The woman screamed and fought to get to her children, but the officers restrained her. "You're making this harder on them!" Tony shouted over her cries. "If you love them, help them through this."

"You're not—taking—my kids!" she screamed, fighting to break free.

The children pulled out of Nick's hands and ran to their mother, but with her hands cuffed, she couldn't hold them. As they screamed, Nick wrenched them away and hurried them out to his car and into the front seat. He positioned one wailing child in the middle of the bench seat, hooked his seat belt, then hooked the other one in on the passenger side. Agency policy was to put kids in the backseat, but Nick could imagine how lonely the backseat could be when you didn't know where you were going.

For a few moments after he got in, he could hardly speak. He cranked the car and pulled out of the driveway to get them away from the house as quickly as possible. Then he looked down at the kids, who were still sobbing quietly.

"My name's Nick," he said, patting the leg of the boy next to him. "And I promise you, this isn't going to be so bad, okay? We'll just find you a place to stay tonight, and you're going to be all right."

"But I want to stay at home tonight," the younger one cried. "I want my mom!"

"Are you taking them to jail?" the older child asked in a shaky voice. "For a long time?"

"I can't answer that, because I don't know," Nick said. "But you don't have to worry, because you'll be taken care of."

The children cried quietly now, tears glistening on their faces. His heart ached for them, but that voice that played like a tape in his mind reminded him not to get involved. His job was to find a place to put them tonight; tomorrow, he would try to find a more permanent temporary home. There was no rational reason for the guilt and grief that he felt; it wasn't his fault that these two boys were becoming wards of the state of Florida. He just wished their parents had thought about their kids before they'd started dealing drugs.

A few minutes later, Nick parked in front of his office. The building, a branch of the Department of Health and Rehabilitative Services, or HRS, was small, dirty, and structurally unsound, but it was all they could afford on their small budget. He dreamed of the day they could get a nicer place, with a playroom to cheer up broken-hearted kids as they waited to be processed. He unhooked the apprehensive boys and slid them across the seat and out of the car.

"Please, mister. Take us back to our mom. She's really nice." The eight-year-old wiped his face and hiccuped a sob. "She won't do anything bad or nothing."

Nick stooped in front of them and wiped the tears on both their faces. "The police have your parents," he said softly. "I can't do anything about that, and I can't make any promises about what's going to happen. But I can promise that we'll take good care of you and find you someplace nice to stay."

The boys clung together, weeping, and Nick stroked both of their heads. He couldn't mend their broken hearts or erase the trauma their parents' arrest had caused. But he could help with some of the uncertainty. "This is just my office, okay? Let's go in and see if I can find you a coke or something, maybe a couple of candy bars."

"We're not allowed to take candy from strangers."

The irony. Drug dealers for parents, and they'd managed to teach these kids not to take candy from strangers. "Then I'll give you each fifty cents and let you get it out of the vending machine yourself. And while you eat it, I'll make some phone calls and find a nice family who'll let you spend the night with them tonight. Sound fair?"

The boys shrugged.

No, you're right, Nick thought. *None of it is fair.* "Call me Nick," he said. "And I'll call you Matthew and Christopher, okay?"

"Matt and Chris," the little one corrected through his tears.

"Okay, Matt and Chris. Let's go on in. Nothing in there for you to be afraid of—just an ugly office and me." He glanced up at the other car parked next to his. "And it looks like my boss is here, too. But that's all. No big bad wolves."

He led them in and saw Sheila Axelrod, his supervisor, sitting at her desk, talking on the telephone. In a car seat on her desktop lay a screaming baby that couldn't have been more than three months old. She hung up the phone as Nick came in. "There's got to be a better way to make a living," she said listlessly.

Nick fished some quarters out of his pockets for the vending machine. "Who've you got there?"

"Abused baby," she said. "Police intervened in a domestic fight and saw her. Cigarette burns on her little legs prove the abuse. But it'll take a miracle to find anyone to take her tonight." She nodded toward the two still-crying boys beside him. "You're lucky. At least they're old enough for SCCH. I've got to go down the list until I find a taker."

SCCH—the St. Clair Children's Home—was the only private children's home in town. It had once been Nick's first choice in cases like this, but not anymore.

"I'm not calling SCCH," he said, going to the car seat and lifting the crying baby out. Instantly, the child grew quiet and lay her head on Nick's shoulder. He felt a wave of gratification—and concern—flood through him.

"What do you mean you're not calling them? Who will you call?"

Still holding the baby, Nick ushered the two little boys to the vending machine and handed them some quarters. They took them grudgingly and chose their candy. The baby on his shoulder whimpered softly as her eyes slowly closed.

"Did that baby's mom get arrested, too?" the younger boy, Matt, asked.

"I don't know," Nick evaded. "But it looks like she's in the same boat you're in. Tell you what, guys. You're older than she is. If you'll calm down and not look like we're sending you to the dungeon,

21

maybe she'll quit feeling like something bad is about to happen. What do you say?"

Chris shrugged. "What's SCCH? Is that where we're going?"

"No."

Sheila had the phone to her ear, but she put her hand over the receiver and asked, "Why not, Nick? They have a whole cottage just for temporaries. It's the easiest thing, and if this is long term, that's probably where they'll end up anyway."

"I told you, I have too many suspicions about some things going on at the home. Until I can give the place a clean bill of health, I'm not going to send any more kids to them."

Her face hardened, and her voice changed. "Nick, those two kids have to be placed tonight. You'll send them where I tell you to!"

He touched the baby's head again, trying to keep it calm in spite of Sheila's ranting. "Sheila, if I can find a home to take them tonight, what difference does it make to you?"

"Because I'm trying to find someone to take the baby. It's not likely that we can find more than one family this late to take them, and nobody's gonna take all three!"

"Let me try," he said. "That's all I ask, Sheila. Just give me a while to try."

She moaned. "If you don't send them to the home, you might have to split them up."

One of the boys gasped, and the other burst into tears again. "No! Please don't do that."

"We won't," Nick assured quietly. He pulled a tissue out and wiped the little boy's nose as he shot Sheila a look. "Sheila, why don't you let me take care of this, and you go on home? I can handle it."

"Really?" She looked at him as if he'd just offered her a week's vacation. Then she seemed to deflate. "I can't. Not until they're placed. I'll give you an hour to try to find a family to take them. If you don't, I'm taking them to SCCH myself. I'll work on the paperwork, and you work on the phone calling. Here, give me the baby."

"No, she's fine," he said softly. The baby was relaxing on his shoulder, and he could feel that she was close to falling asleep. "I can call while I hold her. And if I need a hand, my buddies here can help me, can't you, guys?"

The boys nodded quietly.

22

"All right," she said. "I'll be in here. Buzz if you need me."

He ushered them down the hall to the corner of the building he sometimes shared with two other caseworkers—except that they had both quit in the last month and hadn't yet been replaced. He looked over the baby's head to the boys. "You gonna eat that candy, or just let it melt in your hands?"

Matt put it into his mouth, but Chris just sat there. "Do we have to go anywhere with her?"

Most of the kids didn't like Sheila, which didn't surprise Nick. She could be cold sometimes, but he knew her coldness was stress-induced. She'd been at it longer than he had, and it was a job that got to you over the years. He sat down and leaned back in his chair, still stroking the baby's head. "I'll try to find a place for you myself, guys. And if I can, then I'll take you there."

"Why can't we stay with you?" the little one asked.

Nick smiled and messed up the boy's hair. "Because I'm not home much, kiddo. I couldn't watch you."

"We can watch ourselves. We'd be okay. We do it all the time."

"No can do. But trust me with this." He picked up the phone, breathed a silent prayer for help, and dialed the number of his first choice—a family he'd saddled with four new kids just this past week.

When they turned him down, he tried the next one on the list, and then the next, until he had almost given up. Little Matt had lain down on the small, garage-sale sofa against the wall, and had gone to sleep with his head in his brother's lap. The baby slept soundly, too. Chris just stared back at him with red, dismal eyes.

Not the St. Clair Children's Home, Nick prayed. *There's got to be somebody else.*

Holding the phone between ear and shoulder, he dialed the next number—a new family on their list. A retired couple who had volunteered to be foster parents, they had just today completed all the requirements to be accepted into the program. This would be their first placement call. He wondered if dumping three children on them this late at night their first time might frighten them away. He had no choice but to try.

"Hello?" The woman sounded kind—a good sign. He hadn't been the caseworker assigned to her—Sheila had done it—so he hadn't met her before. He hoped her voice wasn't deceiving.

"Mrs. Miller? This is Nick Hutchins with HRS. I have three children I need to place temporarily tonight. They're from two different families, so if you can't take all of them, we can give you one or two of them. But I'd at least like to keep the brothers together—"

"We'd be delighted to have them!" the woman said, then put her hand on the receiver and shouted, "Honey, they're bringing some children tonight." She came back to Nick. "Please, bring all three of them. What ages are they?"

Nick couldn't believe his ears. "The baby girl is probably three months, and then I have two brothers, six and eight. The baby's an abuse case, and the boys' parents are in police custody."

"Oh, the poor little things. Please, bring them right over. We'll have their beds all ready when you get here. I'll tell Vernon to get the crib out of the attic. We'll get it all dusted."

Nick mouthed "thank you" to the ceiling as he hung up the phone. He hurried to Sheila's door. "I found someone to take all three, Sheila. Grace and Vernon Miller. She's even excited about it."

Sheila didn't look impressed. "I wasn't planning to give them a trial by fire. I was going to ease them in. But I guess it can't be helped. Remind her not to get emotionally involved with them, Nick. They're new at this."

"I will," he said. But in his heart, he hoped they'd get a little involved. These kids were going to need someone who cared about them.

CHAPTER FIVE

Beth ignored her puppy as he whimpered and scratched at the attic door. Instead, she stared down at the answering machine. Why was it turned off? She had left it on; she was sure of it. Maybe the power had flickered, and the machine hadn't come back on.

Maybe. But that didn't explain the person who had answered the phone when she'd called.

Maybe the cellular phone company had mixed the signals. She'd heard of it happening. The fact that she was being followed at the time had made it all seem suspicious, but that didn't mean that the two events had anything to do with each other. She was probably being paranoid.

She started to turn the machine back on, but the yelping puppy distracted her. She scooped him up and stroked his head. "What's the matter, boy? You want to play?" He wiggled in her hands and reached up to lick her face. "We'll go down and play in a minute," she said, walking to the window near the apex of her roof. She peered out into the night, looking for headlights, any sign that Bill Brandon was out there, waiting, watching, ready to pounce.

No, of course he wasn't out there. She'd chosen this house very carefully. No one could just accidentally find it, and no one would be able to look her up, either. Her address was a post office box. It wasn't listed in the phone book, and it wasn't even in her files at school or the paper. Since she rented, there was no public record of where she lived. The only way to find her house would be to follow her here.

But a nagging voice in the back of her mind reminded her: *Bill Brandon has ways of finding out anything he wants. Everyone who knows him discovers that.*

Shivering, she carried the puppy back down the stairs, set him down, and went back to the phone to try Nick's office. Just as she picked up the phone, she heard a car on the gravel outside. She froze. Keeping her eyes on the door, she dropped the phone back in its cradle, pulled open a drawer in the end table, and grabbed the pistol she kept there. The doorbell rang, and the puppy erupted into a round of high-pitched barks.

He's here, she thought, holding the pistol aimed at the door. Her heart flipped into a triple-time cadence, and adrenaline pulsed through her.

The bell rang again, and a knock followed. "Beth? It's me, Nick!"

Nick. Not Bill.

She let out a huge breath of relief and lowered the gun. Feeling dizzy from the sheer terror that had gripped her, she headed for the door and opened it. "Nick, you scared me. I didn't know it was you. Where have you been? I tried to call."

Nick came in, his brown, slightly wavy hair tousled by the warm wind. His face looked tired, and the stubble on his jaw added to the picture of fatigue. "Didn't you get my message?"

"What message?"

"On your machine. Telling you I had an emergency and couldn't meet you at my house, that I would just come over here." He frowned as he saw the gun. "What's wrong?"

"I just got a little spooked, that's all." Embarrassed, she put the gun back into the drawer and closed it.

"Did something happen? Did the interview turn out badly?"

"No, no. It was fine." She shoved her hand through her short honey-colored hair and looked up the stairs toward the answering machine that had been off when she'd checked it. "It's just . . . a little weird."

"What is?"

"That you left a message. My machine was off when I got home. Are you sure it was on when you called?"

"Positive," he said. "I left a message that the police had just done a drug bust, and there were these two boys—their parents were dealing cocaine. I had to go get the children and place them in foster care tonight until we could find some relatives."

Her face whitened. "You didn't put them at SCCH, did you?"

"No," he said. "My supervisor would have, but I put them with a retired couple new to the foster-care program. They'll be okay." He paused and studied her for a moment. "Beth, you're pale. What is it?"

She breathed a self-conscious laugh and tried to calm herself. "Nothing, really. The interview went great. Better than I could have dreamed." She sank down on her couch and covered her face, and Nick sat down next to her.

She didn't really know Nick all that well, having met him just a few days ago when she'd called to interview him about his take on the children's home. Her questions had immediately piqued his interest because he'd also had suspicions about the home. So he'd spent a lot of time with Beth since that first meeting, trying to help her put the pieces together.

Although Beth tried to deny it or, better yet, ignore it, there was something about Nick Hutchins that made her feel safe. Her life up to this point had been anything but secure—ironically, that meant she distrusted nothing more than feelings of safety and security.

Still, something about Nick invited her trust. Maybe it was that he seemed to genuinely care about the children he watched over. It had been her experience that most social workers were so overburdened that they had little time to care about the people whose lives they affected. Nick seemed different.

She drew her mind back to the conversation. "Marlene was ready to talk," she said. "I taped our conversation. It was fascinating. She confirmed everything. Bill Brandon uses some of the kids in his care in a crime ring that breaks into people's homes and businesses and steals things. He has a central warehouse where he stores things until he can sell them—or until his people can sell them. Apparently, there are more people than just Bill and the kids involved. In fact, she said he has someone big running interference for him. Like someone on the police force or in government.

That's how he's gotten away with it. She didn't know any names or where the stuff is stored, but she said that he uses horrible tactics to force the kids into cooperating. Besides the abuse that you've suspected, he threatens them with harm to their sisters and brothers, their parents if they're living, or he makes them believe that they're as guilty as he is—that they're the ones breaking in, that his hands are clean, so if anyone goes down for the crime, it'll be the kids. And they have no way of knowing otherwise, so they cooperate."

Angered, Nick bolted up and paced across the floor, his fatigue evident. He needed to shave, and his light brown hair was tousled as though he hadn't given it a thought all day. Looking at his reddened eyes, she wondered if he ever got much sleep.

"We've got to put him away, Beth. We've got to get those kids out of there. Sheila, my supervisor, says I don't have enough evidence to start relocating the children. She thinks I'm nuts and Bill Brandon is a saint. I think she just can't face all the work it would take to relocate the kids. But it *has* to be done, and I don't care about the work."

Beth tried to think clearly. "First, we have to have enough evidence to convince the court. Maybe if you got some of the kids alone and told them you already knew what was going on, some of them would talk."

"I've tried. They all get this terrible look on their faces—fear, that's all I know to call it—and insist that they've never been happier and they've never been treated better."

"It's fear, all right. But we need more evidence. Marlene's statements are good, but she's just one person."

Nick frowned. "Why did she talk to you, anyway?"

Beth hesitated. "Well, I already knew she wasn't part of his organization anymore. She said that her life has changed in the past year. She seemed to genuinely care about the kids now, and she didn't want to sit by and let Bill do what he was doing."

"Are you sure you can trust her? What if she's just baiting you to see what you know?"

"She told me things I didn't know. It was real, Nick."

Nick sat slowly down and leaned forward. "Does Bill Brandon know that she talked?"

She was unsure how much to tell him. "Yes. I mean, I'm pretty sure he does. He—or someone in a dark Buick—was following me most of the way home."

"*What?*"

"Chasing me is more like it," she said, standing up again and setting her fists defiantly on her hips, as if the stance could erase the image of helpless victim. "It's okay. I made sure I lost him, so he couldn't follow me home. My car's got a few dents, though."

"He *hit* you? What was he trying to do?"

"Run me off the road," she said. "Near the seawalls."

"Beth, this is getting out of hand. He could have killed you!"

She went to the window, peered out through the blinds. "He almost did. I called the police, but it took them forever. By the time they came, I had lost him."

Nick went to stand behind her, and she turned around and looked up at him. "Beth, how do you know it wasn't a setup? The whole Marlene thing—all her deep confessions, and then her brother chasing you down and trying to kill you? What if they planned this together—"

"I don't think so," Beth said. "Marlene seemed scared herself. And she was sincere. She really was."

He blew out a frustrated breath. "No wonder you had a gun when you answered the door."

"It was stupid, really," she said. "He doesn't know where I live."

"Are you sure?"

"Positive," she said weakly.

"Then why do you keep looking out the window?"

"Just being careful. I mean, really, I can't even be sure it was him. I'm just assuming it was. Who else would come after me right after that interview? It had to be either him or someone who works for him."

"Beth, this is getting dangerous. You have to call the police again. Tell them who you think was following you."

She shook her head and plopped down on the couch. The puppy put its paws up on her shin, panting happily. She leaned over and picked him up. "I don't want to call them again. I did it before because I was desperate. But now that it's over, I don't think I want to bring them into this yet."

"Why not?" he asked. "Why would you wait?"

Determination tightened her features. "Because this is *my* story," she said, "and I don't want every paper in the state getting it before I can get the *whole* story out. If I call the police, it'll be public knowledge by morning. There'll be a barrage of articles, none with much meat, and Bill Brandon will clean up his act for a while and walk straight, and they won't catch him at anything, and everyone will write it off as hearsay and rumor, and go back to thinking he's the clean-cut, unsung hero who molds broken young kids into model citizens. I want to get him, Nick. And I'm not going to depend on the cops to do it."

He shook his head. "And how long will all this take?"

"I'm going to stay up late tonight transcribing the tapes of my conversation with Marlene. I'll start writing the story. Maybe tomorrow I can track down some other witnesses. If I could just find out where that warehouse is—and who he has in government working with him—"

"Beth, if you take too long, he's going to catch up with you. Then what?"

"I won't take too long," she said. "I'm as anxious to get this story out as you are. You have a list of kids in the home, don't you?"

"Yeah."

"Then start making plans to move them. I promise you, the story will be out within a week."

"I hope that's not too late. Especially now that he knows something's up."

She thought that over. "Maybe I can get it finished by tomorrow. If so, we could print it the day after—if I can convince my editor. Remember, I'm still just a grunt around there. The college kid, always looking for a front-page story. If he's going to print it, it has to be great."

Nick wasn't reassured. "What if he comes after you again? What if he *does* find where you live?"

"I can protect myself, Nick. I've done it for a long time."

He breathed a laugh. "Right. You're a junior in college. How old? Twenty?"

"Twenty-one."

"How long could you possibly have done it?"

"I'll be all right, Nick." She couldn't help the slight edge in her voice. "Now, why don't you go on home? You look really tired."

"I am tired," he said, "but I could sack out here. Make sure he doesn't show up. I'm really afraid to leave you."

She smiled slightly. "Spend the night, huh? I don't think so."

He shook his head again. "Not like that, Beth. That's not my style."

"Mine either."

"You have any objection to a guy wanting to watch out for you?"

"You have enough people to watch out for, Nick. Don't worry about me. If I can't take a little heat, I have no business being a reporter."

"That's what I figured," he said. "You're a hundred-ten-pound tough guy. What do you have for protection? Karate? Brass knuckles?"

"I have my wits," she said with a half-smile. "And the .22 in that drawer. Oh, and I have my dog." She set the puppy down, and he wagged over to Nick.

"Yeah, right." He bent down and petted the puppy, who instantly made a puddle on the floor. "Uh-oh. You're not walking him enough."

"We're working on the house-breaking thing," she said with a soft laugh as she ran to the kitchen to grab a towel. "I don't know if he's training me or if I'm training him. But he's only six weeks old. What can you expect, huh, Dodger?"

"Dodger?"

"Yeah. Like the Artful Dodger in *Oliver*."

"Any chance that name came from the story you're working on?"

She stood back up. "Yeah, I guess so. That and the fact that he loves stealing socks out of my laundry hamper. He chewed a hole in the side of it so he could get to them."

He chuckled and went to the door, opened it, and peered out into the woods surrounding the house. "It's kind of creepy out here. Are you sure you're not afraid?"

"One person's creepy is another person's refuge," she said. "He won't find me here, and very few people have the address. Reporters have to take certain precautions."

He turned back. "I guess I should feel honored that you gave it to me."

She smiled a little self-consciously, and looked down at the puppy. "Actually, you should. I don't even know why I did."

"I like to think it was my trustworthy eyes."

"They are pretty trustworthy," she said, bringing hers back to them again. For a moment, their eyes locked, and finally, she looked away, realizing her face was getting warm. "Look, I'll call you tomorrow and let you know what's happening. If you find out anything, let me know, too, okay?"

"All right."

He looked at her for a second, as if considering something else to say. "See you later."

"Yeah. Later."

She watched as he walked across the gravel, examined the dents in her car, then, shaking his head, went to his own vehicle. She checked the shadows of the trees on both sides of the house with a growing sense of unease, then shuddered and closed the door. She bolted it shut, then turned back to the puppy, who was curled up on a rug. "Yeah, that's right," she told him. "Go to sleep, just when the hard work is about to start. Never mind, I'll do it myself. Your spelling's pretty lousy, anyway."

CHAPTER SIX

Nick tried to shake the uneasy feeling taking hold of him as he pulled off the dirt road leading to her property and back onto the paved street where occasional cars drove by. She was tough, that was certain, but it didn't make him feel any better. A man like Bill Brandon had ways of breaking down toughness.

On the other hand, Bill was used to dealing with children. Maybe he'd not yet met the likes of Beth Wright.

Nick knew *he* hadn't. She had blown into his life like an answered prayer, one that he was still reeling from. Just when he'd felt so helpless and frustrated that he wanted to quit his job, she had come along with some answers and the encouragement he had sorely needed.

It hadn't even been two weeks ago that he'd gotten the phone call from the distraught mother who'd had visitation with her son at the children's home that afternoon and had found him bruised from a beating that the child told her had come from Bill Brandon. Since the mother was a drug addict going through rehab, Nick hadn't taken what she said at face value. Instead, he had ordered a medical exam of the child. The doctors confirmed that he *had* suffered a beating.

Finally, Nick had confronted Bill Brandon about it. Brandon told him that the child had been fine when he'd left for visitation, but that the mother herself must have beaten him. Bill had launched from there into an impassioned argument that parental visitations were detrimental to the healthy environment he tried to provide for "his" kids.

There were obvious problems with Bill's story. Why would the mother have called attention to abuse she'd inflicted herself? Besides, Nick had heard the despair in her voice, the urgency, the worry. Yes, her child had been taken from her due to neglect and drug addiction—but now she was clean. The sound of maternal worry in her voice had been authentic. Much more authentic than Bill Brandon's arguments.

Sheila, Nick's supervisor, had blown the whole thing off, convinced that Bill Brandon was right and that the mother was just trying to cover up for something she knew would be discovered eventually. She suggested they file to revoke the mother's visitation privileges.

Nick had allowed her to believe he would take care of it, but he hadn't. Something about Bill's and Sheila's rationales didn't ring true. Something about the mother's pleas did.

He had begun to look deeper into problems at the home. He had gone to the public school where Bill Brandon's children were sent, and had studied the records of the SCCH kids. He saw a repeating pattern of children falling asleep in class, over and over and over. When he spoke to their teachers—no small feat since it was summer and some of them had been difficult to locate—he was told that they had contacted Brandon about the problem, only to be told that he would "take care of it" when the kids got home from school. Fearing what Brandon's punishment might be, and sensing the terror on the kids' faces when they thought they were being reported to him, most of the teachers had fallen into a routine of letting it slide without calling the home. They, too, suspected that things might not be all they seemed at the home, but they had little evidence to back it up. There had also been a few reports of some SCCH kids being caught committing crimes, but everyone had written those incidents off to bad parenting or to the typical rebellion of low-status, high-risk kids. None of his suspicions, none of the facts he'd compiled, added up to enough evidence to close down the home, or even to start an official investigation.

He'd been at a dead end—and then he'd gotten a phone call from a young woman who had identified herself as a reporter with the *St. Clair News* and said she was working on a story about some alleged abuses in the St. Clair Children's Home. It had been just the encouragement he'd needed to convince him he was on the right track. But when Beth had told him that she suspected Brandon was using the children in a crime ring that worked in areas within a two-hour radius of St. Clair, Nick had been stunned. Was that why the children were so sleep-deprived?

The idea had been so far-fetched that it was almost unbelievable—yet some part of him believed it. First, he had beaten himself up about placing so many children in the home. Then, he'd determined to get them all out. But first he had to get enough proof.

He'd met with Beth, told her everything he knew, and promised to help her in any way he could. Since then, she'd been busy putting together the story that would outline all of Brandon's alleged crimes. Now they could add to it his attempt to run her off the road—if they could somehow prove that he was the driver.

Nick thought back over the things she'd said tonight, the look on her face when he'd frightened her, the shakiness with which she'd revealed, little by little, how she had been followed from the interview. She hadn't looked so tough then. She was scared.

I might regret this, he told himself as he made a U-turn. But the fear in Beth's eyes haunted him.

He pulled his car into a metered space in front of the St. Clair Police Department. Larry Millsaps and Tony Danks were probably still there processing the parents of the boys Nick had placed earlier. Maybe they'd have time to give him a minute.

The station was noisy, as usual, and smelled of sweat and booze from some of those who waited in handcuffs to be booked. He scanned the desks where cops answered phones and did paperwork. Tony Danks sat tapping at his computer keys, probably getting a history on the couple who sold dope for a living. Nick ambled over.

"Man, don't you ever go home?"

Tony looked up and grinned. "Don't *you*? You look tireder than I do, Nick. How are those kids? Get them placed okay?"

"Yeah, no problem. They were a little scared, but I think they'll be all right. That's not why I'm here." He took the chair across from Tony's desk, crossed his legs and slumped back until his neck almost rested on the top back of the chair. "You got a minute?"

"Sure," Tony said, turning away from his computer and leaning on his desk. "You want Larry in on this?"

Nick glanced over at Larry's desk, saw that he was filling out reports. "Yeah, if he can spare a minute. I just need some police advice."

"You came to the right place." He half stood and yelled, "Larry!" over the din, and Larry looked up. He saw Nick sitting there and got up to head over.

"You get those kids placed?" Larry asked as he approached the desk.

"Yeah," Nick said. "But there's something else I need to ask you. Off the record."

Larry's eyebrows lifted, and he sat down on the edge of Tony's desk. "Okay, shoot."

Nick dropped his foot and leaned forward, bracing his elbows on his knees. "I have this friend. A woman. She's a reporter, and was doing an important interview tonight, and she got followed most of the way home until she lost him. She thinks she knows who it was, and she thinks it has to do with the story she's working on. Basically, he wants to shut her up, so I don't know what he might do to her. But she's convinced he doesn't know where she lives."

"You're not convinced?" Tony asked.

"Well, I can't be sure. This guy's shrewd, and he has a lot to lose. And I'm not entirely convinced that the whole interview wasn't a setup. Anyway, she didn't want to involve the police for fear of having the story come out before she breaks it—you know, the competition might get it—but I'm not sure waiting is a good idea."

"It's not illegal to follow someone," Tony said. "And it could have been a coincidence. Did he do anything to her? Ram her fender? Try to force her off the road? Anything to indicate ill intent?"

"Absolutely. She has at least two dents on her car where he tried to run her off the road."

"Then he did break a law. Would she be willing to file a complaint?"

"No, she won't. Not yet."

Larry shook his head dolefully. "Sorry, Nick. Nothing we can do."

"Officially, no," Nick said. "But what about unofficially? Could you kind of keep an eye on her tonight? Watch over her so that nothing happens?"

Larry and Tony exchanged looks. Tony rubbed his eyes. "Truth is, we're a little busy here tonight, Nick. We could send a squad car to patrol her house every hour or so, but we can't leave anyone there all night."

"Well, maybe that would be enough. Anything you could do would help. And I'd prefer that you told the cop who does it not to pull all the way down the dirt road leading to her house. Just far enough to get a look at the house and make sure no other cars are there. Seeing headlights would scare her to death. Besides, I don't want her to know I came to you. She wouldn't like it."

Larry stared at him for a moment, then broke into a sly grin. "Who is this girl, Nick? She sounds important. Something you haven't told us?"

Nick rubbed his stubbled jaw. "Actually, I just met her a few days ago. But yeah, I like her. She's a little young. Only twenty-one—"

"And you're an old man at . . . what? Thirty?"

Nick grinned. "Not quite."

Tony had to laugh. "Nick Hutchins, the guy who's too busy for a woman. Looks like he's clearing some time."

"Don't get carried away," Nick said. "I've just been trying to help her out some. She's nice. Smart. Savvy. Different than the other women I know."

"Uh-oh. Famous last words," Tony teased.

Nick got to his feet, fighting his own grin. "All right, guys. I'm just worried about the lady, that's all." He grabbed a pen off Tony's desk and jotted her address on a pad. "If you could get someone to patrol around there, just watching for anything suspicious—a dark Buick in particular—I'd really appreciate it."

Larry looked down at the pad. "All right. No guarantees, though."

"Didn't expect any."

He gave them both friendly handshakes, then walked out of the police station, wishing he could rest easy now. But he knew he wouldn't—it would be a long night for him.

And it wouldn't be any better for Beth.

CHAPTER SEVEN

Beth loaded her tape recorder and began to play back the tapes of her conversation with Marlene, quickly typing the words into her laptop computer. Beside her, Dodger slept, his little rhythmic snore making her wish she could lie down herself. But she had to get this done—and she was too tense to sleep anyway.

She heard something creak over her head. Lifting her hands from the keyboard, she looked at the ceiling. Was it her imagination, or had the floor squeaked upstairs? She cut off the tape recorder and listened.

There it was again. Quickly, she grabbed for the gun she kept in the table beside the couch. She went to the stairs and stared up at the top. Nothing there. She started to go up, then thought better of it. Still aiming at the stairs, she backed up and groped for the telephone. She snatched it up and dialed 911.

Her voice trembled as she tried to get the words out quietly. "There's someone in my house. Please—send someone right away. It's on Kramer Road, the number 343 is on the mailbox at the beginning of a long dirt road. Turn in there, and you'll see my house about a quarter of a mile in. Please hurry."

She hung up, but kept the gun aimed at the stairs. If he came down, she would shoot him. She had no choice. If Bill Brandon had found her, if he had broken into her home, then he was planning to kill her. Her only hope was to kill him first.

A t the police station, one of the sergeants grabbed Tony on his way out. "Hey, Danks. That address you gave us to patrol? We just got a call from the lady who lives there. Says someone's in her house."

Surprised, Tony glanced over his shoulder at Larry, then back at the sergeant. "Have you sent a car out?"

"Yeah, there was one real close. In fact, he'd just made a swing by there and didn't see anything. Jane sent him back."

"We'll head over there, too," Larry said.

"Should we call Nick?" Tony asked as they hurried out to their car.

Larry shook his head grimly. "Let's see what's up first."

CHAPTER EIGHT

The Fraser Gas Station was closed this time of night, and Bill Brandon sat in the shadows of the pumps with his headlights off, waiting for the kid to get there. It shouldn't have taken Jimmy this long to make it the five miles from her house to the gas pumps. What if he'd gotten caught? What if he'd made an even bigger mess of this?

He should have expected it. Jimmy was too soft, too young. Bill knew he should have used one of the more experienced kids. But this should have been an easy job, and Jimmy was so small for his age that slipping him in through the small bathroom window they'd found unlocked had been a snap. Besides, Jimmy was a whiz when it came to computers, and he knew that if anyone could handle the computer end of the job, it would be him.

Yeah, that was the way it was *supposed* to have gone. That was the plan. Send Jimmy in through a window, then the kid gets all the tapes and papers he can find, copies her files onto a disk, then erases her hard drive. Then everything went wrong. Bill had planned to stop her from getting home, but she'd gotten away from him. And then the stupid kid had picked up the phone. He'd pay for that.

Bill cranked his car, turned on the lights, and started back toward her house, hoping he'd see Jimmy on the road somewhere. He drove slowly, scanning the trees, watching, waiting. The kid had been trained too well to be seen easily, but Bill hoped he'd recognize the Buick and show himself.

Nothing.

He pulled over to the side of the road and thought for a moment, trying to build a strategy. Maybe he needed to go back to the house, look into the windows, see if she was home.

He pulled back onto the street and headed for her dirt road.

But before he reached it, he heard a siren, then saw a police car's lights flickering through the trees. The squad car turned onto her dirt road.

She called the police, he thought, driving quickly past. *Which means the kid got caught. Now what?*

He wiped the sweat from his brow with his sleeve and decided to return to the home. The cops would probably call him to report that they had one of his kids in custody, and he'd better be there to take the call. He'd pretend that the kid had escaped through a window when Bill thought he was sleeping, that he always had trouble with this one.

Jimmy wouldn't dare tell them differently. Bill had done too good a job preparing him for a time like this.

Upstairs in Beth's house, the boy heard the sound of a siren approaching outside, and he strained to see through the window without moving. He saw blue lights flashing against the glass, a pale flicker illuminating the shadows of the attic. Did she know he was here? Had she called the police?

He heard the front door open, the dog yelping, and the lady's voice outside. With no one downstairs to hear him, he ran across the floor to the biggest box he could find, pulled out a four-foot Christmas tree, climbed into the box, then pulled the tree in on top of him. Trying to settle his breathing, he curled into as tight a ball as he could and waited.

It didn't take long. The door opened and a light came on, a light that seemed to flood through the attic, lighting every crack, every shadow, every particle of dust. He was sure it exposed him, too. Could they see him? Could they tell where he was hiding?

He heard voices—several of them—as they filed through the attic, searching. He squeezed his eyes shut and chanted in his mind, *Don't let them find me . . . don't let them find me . . .*

"There's nobody here," one of the men said. "Maybe she heard a mouse or something."

Someone else's feet creaked as he came closer to the Christmas tree box. Jimmy braced himself. "Yeah, this house is pretty old. Probably wouldn't take more than a mouse to make the floor squeak."

"But what about the guy following her, Tony? You don't think this is a coincidence?"

"Didn't seem like it at first. But there's nobody here. Are you sure you checked thoroughly downstairs?"

"Positive."

"Well, she's probably jumpy because of what happened in the car. Maybe she just needs a little reassurance. We can tell her we'll step up our patrols of her house. Maybe that'll put her mind to rest."

"Let's look again, just in case."

He heard them shuffling boxes near him, and suddenly panicked: he had left his backpack out, lying on top of a box. They would see it and know, and then they'd empty out all of the boxes until he came tumbling out . . .

"I give up," one of the cops said, finally. "Cut the light, will you?"

The light went out, and Jimmy sat paralyzed as the door closed. He was soaked with sweat, trembling, and the tree was cutting into his arm and the back of his neck, but he didn't dare move. What if they heard him? What if they came back? Even after they left, *she* could still hear him and call them back.

A tear rolled out of his eye, a tear that Bill would not have tolerated. He managed to wipe his wet face on his shoulder. This was hopeless. He was never going to get out of here.

Downstairs, Beth tried to find comfort in Larry and Tony's assurances that no one was in her house. "I'm really sorry to bother you guys. I guess I'm just getting paranoid."

"I can understand that," Larry said. "And don't apologize. It's our job to check things like this out."

"Yeah, but I didn't expect two detectives when I called."

Larry and Tony looked at each other, and finally, Larry decided to come clean. "The truth is that Nick Hutchins was worried about you and asked us to keep an eye on you."

Her eyebrows rose. "Nick? What did he tell you?"

Tony looked apologetic. "He said you were followed home tonight—and when we drove up, we saw the dents on your car. It's no wonder you would be nervous after that."

Her face tightened, and she looked down at the puppy. "I told him I could protect myself."

"That's what he said, but since we're here—why don't you file a complaint? Give us an idea who followed you so we can arrest him."

"He'd be out by morning. Besides, I can't prove it. I can only guess who it was."

"If you give us a name and he has complementary dents in his car, that'll be proof enough."

She thought it over for a moment as she peered off into the trees surrounding her yard. There were risks either way. If they could keep him in jail for a day or two, that might help her finish her investigation. "It's Bill Brandon. He runs the St. Clair Children's Home."

Tony wrote down the name. "I've heard of him."

"Yeah. Probably as a hero and protector of children. All lies."

"Why do you say that?"

She thought of telling them everything, but she just didn't have enough evidence yet. Alerting them to part of the problem might do more harm than good. "It'll all come out in the paper in the next couple of days, detectives. Then you'll see."

"So that's why you think it was him? Because you're doing some kind of story on him?"

"You got it."

"Would you be willing to file a complaint against him tonight?"

She considered that, then shook her head. "No, I'd rather hit him with the big guns in a couple of days. There's a lot at stake."

She walked them to the door, and the little dog bounded out into the night, its tail wagging. She grabbed his leash and hurried after him, clipped it to his collar, and watched as he found a bush to do his business. "Thanks for coming," she told the cops.

Larry held back. "I'd feel better if you were locked in before we left."

"Yeah, I guess I would, too." She waited for the puppy to finish, then hustled him back inside. "Thanks again."

She locked and bolted the door, then watched out the window as the car drove out of sight. She was losing it, she told herself. Calling the police just because the house creaked. Of course it creaked. It was old. It had probably creaked every day since she'd moved in. But that was before she'd taken on Bill Brandon. Now, everything was suspect.

But she was okay, she reminded herself. He couldn't find her here.

CHAPTER NINE

Marlene Brandon lay awake in bed, her mind reeling with the confessions she'd made to Beth tonight. She'd had to do it. It was the only way to set things right. Her newfound faith required it of her. It wasn't enough to simply believe; she had to put feet to that belief. Even if those feet led her into danger.

She looked at the clock and realized she had been lying here for two hours without closing her eyes. That uneasy feeling that had gripped her all day was almost strangling her now.

She turned over, fluffed her pillow, adjusted the covers, and tried to push her conversation with Beth out of her mind. Marlene had told her things that, most likely, would land her in jail, unless the prosecutor granted her immunity for testifying against her brother. The thought covered her in cold sweat.

I do not give to you as the world gives. Let not your heart be troubled, and do not be afraid. The remembered words brought her comfort, wrapping themselves around her heart. A strange, unexpected peace washed over her, and she began to think that she might sleep tonight, after all.

Her mind shifted back to Beth, so young and bright, so ambitious, so alone. She was proud of the way Beth was supporting herself through college by working at the small-town newspaper. Only twenty-one, but she'd come so far. And she was living a clean life with a pure heart, going to church faithfully and trying to follow the letter of God's law. Marlene only hoped that Beth would learn about his grace, as well. Maybe she should have made sure. Maybe she would call her tomorrow and do just that.

Her eyes began to drift shut, and her mind released its hold on her troubles as sleep pulled her under.

"Hello, Marlene."

She sat bolt upright in bed at the voice, and saw the silhouette of her brother standing in the doorway of her bedroom. "Bill!"

"Surprised?" he asked with that sinister amusement she'd heard so often when he spoke to the children. She had learned it from him, and had gotten good at using it herself over the years.

"How did you get in here?" she asked, pulling her covers up over her as though they could shield her from his wrath.

He laughed then, that condescending laugh that had crushed the spirits of young and old alike. "Marlene, Marlene. You know there isn't a lock anywhere that can keep me out." He came in and sat on the foot of her bed, gazing at her. "I'm hurt, you know. I always thought that, of all people, I could trust my sister."

"You don't trust anyone," she said, sliding back against her headboard.

His face was half lit by the hall night-light, half shadowed by the darkness in her room. "That's true, I guess. Sad, but true. It's hard to trust, Marlene, when people betray you left and right."

She swallowed, and her mind searched for the comfort of Scripture she'd recalled moments ago. *Let not your heart be troubled . . .*

"You want to talk betrayal, Bill, let's talk about what you're doing to those children."

He leaned back against the post at the foot of her bed. "I'm teaching them a trade, Marlene. One they can use all their lives."

"One that can ruin their lives and land them in prison when they're older. You're warping their minds, Bill; you're dragging them into hell. You'll pay for it. You'll be accountable for it someday."

"Is that what they tell you down at that church you've been going to? That some invisible force out there is going to swoop down and strike me dead?"

The fear seemed to have fled, and in its place was a boldness she had rarely felt around her brother. "You'll pay, Bill."

"And so will you."

"Yes, I was a part of it. I'm prepared to suffer the consequences. But I've been forgiven."

"What did you tell her, Marlene?"

His voice sliced like a knife through her words. She swallowed. "Very little that she didn't already know. She's going to expose you, Bill. She's not afraid of you."

"She should be. And so should you."

He pulled his hand out of his pocket, and she saw the shiny metal of the pistol as the hall light fell upon it. He got up and came closer; he aimed the gun at her forehead. Even so, that peace hung on, and so did the boldness. She wasn't afraid to die. "What are you going to do, Bill? Kill all of us? One by one? Me? Beth? Her editors? All the adults who grew up in your home, the ones who know the real story? The children who are working as your little slaves now?"

"Maybe," he said. "But I think for now I'll just settle for you."

CHAPTER TEN

I n Cottage B on the back side of the St. Clair Children's Home campus, seven-year-old Lisa Westin lay still in her bed, clutching her threadbare teddy bear with one arm. She stared up at the ceiling and forced her ears to listen hard, so hard that she'd hear her brother when he finally came home. But some long-held fear told her that he wasn't coming home.

She squeezed her eyes shut, trying to hold in the tears and block out the memories of three years ago. She had been only four, and Jimmy told her often that she was too young to remember, that she had gotten it all wrong, but she knew he was just trying to make the memories seem like a misty dream that hadn't really happened. But she knew better. They weren't her first memories—there were others, but they came more in sensations and scents, feelings that seemed warm and sad, tiny glimpses of happiness that she knew she'd felt then. The memory she had of what happened that day—the day their mother hadn't come home—was more vivid, more distinct. She remembered harsh faces of policemen, words that she didn't understand: neglect, abandonment, addiction. She remembered the realization, after two whole days of going without food, that their mother had forgotten them. And she remembered the inescapable panic, the what's-going-to-happen-to-us terror. Jimmy had seemed so much older than seven at the time; he had been the rock she had clung to, her big brother. But he had been the age then that she was now. He had promised her, as the policemen had carted them off to become wards of the state, that he wouldn't allow them to be separated—that, even though no one else in their lives had stuck around, he would never leave her.

She wiped her tears, held back the sob pulling at her throat, and slid out of bed, careful not to wake the other little girls sleeping in the beds around her. The home was supposed to look and feel like a real home, with ruffly bedspreads donated by local church groups, and frilly little dolls that no one was allowed to play with. But Lisa suspected that real homes weren't filled with fear, as this place was. Her long white gown dragged the floor as she padded barefoot across the carpet and peered out the window. Maybe Jimmy was out with Bill, doing that job he had said was so important. But she had heard Bill's car a few minutes ago, and had gotten up then to see if Jimmy was with him. When she saw under the streetlight in front of Bill's cottage that he was alone, she had known something was wrong.

Still clinging to one last fragment of hope, she padded out of the room and into the hall, past Stella, their house mother, whose loud snores reassured Lisa that Stella was asleep, and to the big room where all the boys in this cottage stayed. She tiptoed close to Jimmy's bed. Maybe he had come in quietly, not wanting to wake anyone. Maybe he didn't know she had waited and waited . . .

But the bed was still neatly made. Jimmy wasn't there.

She looked around for some of his belongings, wondering if he'd packed them. Then she'd know if he had planned to leave her.

She got down on her knees and peered under his bed, and found the box in which he kept everything in the world he owned. As quietly as she could, she slid it out. In it, she saw his baseball glove, his ball, the Atlanta Braves cap he'd gotten somewhere . . .

And she saw the envelope with the snapshots of them taken a few years ago, snapshots he kept because he said he always wanted to remember that they were sister and brother.

Wouldn't he have taken those if he'd intended to leave? Or had he left them here for her, so she could remember even though he'd chosen to forget?

"What are you doing in here?"

The harsh whisper startled her, and she swung around and saw Brad, one of Jimmy's roommates, sitting up in bed.

She put her finger to her lips to quiet him, and quickly slid the box back under the bed. But she kept the envelope of snapshots.

"I'm telling," he whispered louder. "I'm telling Stella. And I'm gonna tell Jimmy when he comes back. You're not supposed to be in his stuff!"

Another of the boys stirred. "Will you shut up? This is the first night I've been able to sleep all week!"

"That little creep is going through Jimmy's stuff."

"I am not," she whispered back. "I was looking for something that's mine. He was keeping it for me."

"What is it?" Brad taunted. "A pacifier?"

"I don't suck a pacifier!" Lisa flung back, struggling to hold her tears back. She got to her feet and headed for the door.

"I'm still telling!" he whispered.

She ignored him and tiptoed out into the hallway and past Stella's room. Her snoring hadn't changed its rhythm, and Lisa breathed a grateful sigh of relief. Maybe Brad wouldn't tell. If he did, Stella would spank her, then send her to Bill for further punishment. She'd never been sent to Bill before, but Jimmy had. She had seen the bruises herself.

She got back into bed and lay down, staring at the ceiling as she clutched the pictures to her chest. What would she do if Jimmy didn't come back?

Now she let the tears come, heavily, deeply. She turned over and buried her face in her pillow, muffling her sobs.

A dusty ray of sunlight from the attic window woke Jimmy the next morning, and it took a moment for him to realize where he was. He was hiding at the bottom of an old Christmas tree box, and the prickly tree still covered him.

But he hadn't been found.

He reached above him to move the tree and tried to stand up. Quietly, he set it down beside the box and stretched to his full height. It felt so good to stretch after a whole night crammed into that box. He listened . . .

Was the lady home, or had she gone to work? If she had, he could escape. He could get back to the home, let Bill punish him, and get back to normal.

He heard a television downstairs, and his heart sank. She was still here.

He sank back into the box, afraid to move. He needed to go to the bathroom, and he was hungry, and his body ached, and it was getting hotter in here.

When would she ever leave?

CHAPTER ELEVEN

Beth sat at her kitchen table. Spread out in front of her were the documents she'd collected from Nick about the things the children's teachers had said, as well as the statistics on the rise of burglaries in St. Clair and surrounding cities, and the few citizens who'd mentioned seeing children breaking in. She had spent most of the night transcribing Marlene's interview from the tape, and now she sat with a highlighter pen, marking off quotes she'd use in her story and trying to decide what her lead would be.

The television in the living room was on, and the Tampa news anchor droned on about last night's city council meeting, a fire in Oldsmar, a murder . . .

She tuned it all out and sipped her coffee as she reviewed the transcript of her conversation with Marlene.

"The victim was identified as fifty-one-year-old Marlene Brandon . . ."

Beth looked up, stunned. Through the doorway of the living room, the television flickered, showing footage of the police cars surrounding the house where she'd been last night. Slowly, she got to her feet.

"The murder was a result of an apparent burglary. Ms. Brandon's body was discovered early this morning by a neighbor . . ."

Gasping, Beth dove for the telephone and punched out the number of the newspaper. When her editor answered, she cried, "She was murdered, Phil! The woman I interviewed last night was murdered! Marlene Brandon. What do you know so far?"

"That was the woman you interviewed?" he asked, astounded. "Wow, Beth, all we have is that it was a burglary. The house was ransacked, according to the police."

"She was murdered because she talked to me!" Beth shouted. "Her brother did it, Phil!"

"Now, wait, Beth—unless you have proof, something we can take to the police . . ."

The floor above her squeaked again, this time twice in a row, and Dodger started barking. Catching her breath, she turned toward the staircase, the phone still clutched to her ear. "Phil, I'll call you back. No! Better yet, you hang on. I keep thinking I hear someone in my house. I'm going upstairs to look, but if I don't come back to the phone in a few minutes—"

"Beth, you're going off the deep end. You're overreacting a little, don't you think?"

"I'm not overreacting, Phil. The woman is dead. If he killed his own sister, he'll come after me next. Now, hold on, and call the police if I don't come back."

She set the phone down—and heard the squeak again. She grabbed her gun out of the drawer and, hand trembling, aimed it toward the top of the stairs as she started up.

Dodger tried to follow her, his fat stomach making it nearly impossible for him to pull himself up from one step to the next. His yelping gave her some degree of comfort, though. As long as she could hear it, she felt grounded in reality.

She swallowed as she got to the top of the stairs, crossed her little office, and flung the attic door open.

"All right," she said, beginning to sweat and tremble as she clutched the gun. "I know you're in here. I've heard you, and you're not going to get away with it, so you might as well come out and show yourself now, or I'm going to start shooting. I mean it!"

She looked around. Everything looked undisturbed. There was no sign of anyone. Mentally, she tried to calculate exactly where she'd heard the squeak. She'd been standing at the telephone, near her kitchen table; directly over that would be that back corner, where the Christmas tree box sat. Was that tree sticking further out than it had been last night?

Her heart pounded in her ears as she stepped closer to the box, breathing so loud that whoever was hiding there would know how terrified she was. *Someone* was in that box. Bill Brandon? Was he in here playing with her, trying to frighten her to death? Was she going to be his next victim?

Terror overwhelmed her, and she cocked the pistol. "I'm giving you to the count of three to come out, and then I'm going to start shooting. One.... two ... three ..."

Nothing happened, so she slipped her finger over the trigger. "I warned you," she said through her teeth. "You're underestimating me, Bill."

She heard a noise behind her and swung around. The gun went off.

The puppy yelped and squirted a puddle onto the floor. He had made it up the stairs, but now he stood there trembling just inches from the bullet hole.

She had almost shot her dog.

For a moment, she thought of dropping the gun and comforting the puppy, but someone was still here. She turned back around, took a step closer to the box, grabbed a branch of the Christmas tree, and in one quick motion jerked the tree out.

The box was empty.

Drenched in sweat now, she backed away, so relieved that she wanted to cry. The puppy got between her feet, almost knocking her over. She picked him up and gave the attic one last look around. Maybe she was losing her mind. Maybe what she'd heard was an opossum on the roof, or a squirrel, or even a rat. Any of those things would be preferable to Bill Brandon.

She left the attic and closed the door behind her, then hurried down to get a towel to clean up the dog's puddle. On her way to the kitchen, she went back to the phone. "Phil? Are you there?"

"Yeah, Beth. What's going on there? Did I hear a gunshot?"

"It was me. I thought I heard someone, but it was a false alarm. Maybe I am a little paranoid. But Marlene Brandon is still dead. I have to go to the police. Who's covering her story, Phil?"

"I don't even know if we're going to print anything about it, Beth. It was all the way in Tampa, and our St. Clair readers wouldn't be that interested. Besides, they're saying it was just a routine burglary."

"It was *not* a routine burglary, Phil!" she shouted. "She was the sister of Bill Brandon, who's the subject of the story I'm working on. She got killed right after telling me everything. You really think that's a coincidence?"

"Well—okay, no. But what do you want to do? Do *you* want to cover it?"

She hesitated and tried to slow her thoughts. "I don't know . . . yes. I guess I should go and see what I can find out."

"If what you're saying is true, Beth, then don't you think your time would be better served by finishing the story? Then the murder of Marlene Brandon will tie in and make more sense."

Confused, she sat for a moment, eyes fixed on the ceiling. "Yeah, I guess you're right. But would you put someone else on it? It's important, Phil. We have to know everything about her murder."

"All right. I'll send Todd."

"Good. Let me know everything you find out. Even if it seems insignificant."

"And you finish that story."

"I'll have it there this afternoon."

She hung up and started for the kitchen to splash water on her face, but the doorbell rang, startling her again. She snatched up the gun and peeked through the curtain. It was two police officers. Breathing a sigh of relief, she shoved the gun back into its drawer and answered it.

"Can I help you?" she asked, wondering if they noticed how badly she was still shaking.

"Yes," one of them said. "Are you Beth Wright?"

"Yes."

He introduced himself and showed her his badge. They were not from St. Clair, but from Tampa. "We'd like to come in and ask you a few questions about the murder of Marlene Brandon."

CHAPTER TWELVE

T he two police officers looked around her house as she ushered them in. She wondered if they had been there when she'd fired her gun. "I just heard about the murder," she said. "On the news." Her eyes welled with tears. "I couldn't believe it."

"We understand that you were the last one to see her alive."

She sat down and gestured for them to take the couch. "Obviously someone saw her after I did. How did you know I was there, anyway?"

"Her pastor."

"Her what?"

"Her pastor spoke to her after you left. Apparently she called him. He said she seemed exhilarated, because she had confessed some things to you. What we'd like to know from you is whether you saw anyone hanging around the house, a strange car, or someone walking up the street. Anything at all."

She closed her eyes and tried to think. "I didn't see anything, at least not at her house. But I was followed most of the way home."

"Followed?"

"Yeah. Someone was after me. I called 911, but I lost him before the police got there. And when I got home, I kept thinking someone was in my house. I even had the St. Clair police come out last night to check."

One of the cops began to jot that down. "Who were the officers?"

"Well, there were several, but I remember Larry Millsaps and Tony Danks."

They jotted the names down. "What time was that?"

"Around midnight, I think."

"Miss Wright, do you have any idea who could have followed you home?"

She hesitated, glancing at the table with so much evidence waiting to be printed. If she told them too much, and word got out, the rest of the media would jump on it before she had the chance to get her story into print. Because she was the last one to see Marlene alive, other reporters would piece it together, until they discovered more than she wanted them to know. Still, if she could get Bill Brandon off the streets . . .

"She mentioned that she wasn't getting along too well with her brother, Bill Brandon. And the things she confessed to me—they had a lot to do with him. Have you questioned him?"

"Yes. Ms. Brandon's pastor indicated that she and her brother were on the outs. But he was home last night. Several people, employees of his, confirmed it."

"I'll bet they did. Officers, if I were you, I'd check his story out with someone besides his employees."

"Why? Do you have reason to believe he wasn't at home?"

"I'm just saying that she told me she was afraid of her brother. He had warned her not to talk to me."

"About what, Miss Wright? What is the story you were interviewing her about?"

She glanced at the table again and swallowed. "I'm doing a story about children's homes. She used to work with her brother at the St. Clair Children's Home, but I learned that they had parted ways, and I wondered why. They'd had some philosophical differences, and her brother was still hot over her leaving." It was part of the truth, she thought, even if it wasn't all of it.

"Hot enough to kill over?" the officer asked.

"Maybe. I'm just telling you what I think."

The two cops exchanged looks, and finally, one asked, "Miss Wright, where were you around eleven last night?"

"Right here," she said. "I got home at about ten."

"Did you talk to anyone? See anyone?"

"I told you, I saw the police around midnight."

"Before that, was there anyone?"

She couldn't believe they were asking for her alibi, but she took it seriously. "Yes, as a matter of fact. Right after I got home, Nick Hutchins stopped by. Call him and ask him. He was here about half an hour."

They didn't write the name down. "Nick Hutchins. Could you give us a number where we can reach him, please?"

"Yes," she said, anxious to clear this up. "You can call him from my phone if you want. Check me out. Then maybe you can get out of here and arrest the real murderer."

CHAPTER THIRTEEN

immy hadn't moved a muscle since the lady had left. He'd been sure she was going to shoot him. He had walked over to the window and had been trying desperately to open it when he'd heard her coming up the stairs. So he had jumped behind a stack of old newspapers and balled himself up as small as he could get himself, and luckily she hadn't seen him. He had heard her say that she would shoot, and then he'd heard her pull out the Christmas tree—and even though he'd braced himself, expecting the gunshot, he had still wet himself when the gun went off. He'd been sure she was about to find him, but she hadn't.

Now he wondered who was downstairs with her. He had heard the doorbell, and there were voices down there. He half expected it to be Bill—but when he got up enough courage to creep a little closer to the window and look out, he saw a Tampa police car instead. Tampa? Were *they* looking for him? Had they tied him to any of the Tampa burglaries?

He had to get out of here. Somehow, he had to make a break for it.

If only he could use her bathroom and get a drink of water.

He heard the door close downstairs, and looked out the window to see the two cops going back to their car. She was out there, too, walking the dog, and he wished she'd walk up the dirt road, far enough that he could escape. But she hung around the front door, as if afraid to get too far from it.

He slid back down the wall, hopeless, helpless.

What was Bill doing about all this? Would he try to come after him and get him out? Or would he just leave him here to rot?

And what was Lisa thinking?

He closed his eyes and tried to come up with a plan, but there wasn't one. Until she left, he was stuck here.

Outside, Beth watched the police car drive away as the puppy tugged at the leash and sprinkled every leaf and bush he could find. She didn't want to get too far from the house, for fear that Bill Brandon would jump out of nowhere.

Her eyes drifted up to the window in her attic, and she tried to tell herself that no one was there. She had searched it, and the police had searched last night. Anyone would be paranoid after the events of the last few days.

But what was that? Something moving in the darkness beyond the dusty window. She stepped further back from the house and tried to focus better. Was it a reflection from the sun through the trees, or had she seen movement?

She stepped to the side, trying to see it without the glare of sunlight on it, and stared at the glass.

Then she saw it again. The slightest, slowest movement of something rising up, then jerking back down.

Someone's in there! They're watching me!

She jerked the puppy back into the house by its leash and grabbed her gun again. This time, with bold, renewed anger, she ran up the steps and burst into the attic. She kicked at the box beside the window, knocked over the four-foot stack of newspapers in the corner, clutching the gun in front of her.

"I saw you, you sleazeball! I know you're in here!"

She was shaking so hard she could hardly hold the gun, but she swung around, knocked over more boxes, kicked at others, shoved things aside.

Then she saw, on the far wall, the shadow cast by the light coming in from the window.

She took one step cautiously closer, then another, and cocked the pistol. He was behind that box in the corner, she told herself. Crouching like a coward, waiting to pounce on her or run like the wind . . .

"Don't move!" she screamed as she trained the gun on him and kicked the box away.

A little boy with red hair looked up at her with frightened green eyes, frozen like a doe in the glare of headlights. "Don't shoot, lady," he whimpered.

She caught her breath and stepped back, lowering the gun instantly. "You're—you're a kid! Just a kid! I almost shot you!"

"I know."

"What are you doing here?" she asked, breathless. "How did you get in?"

He slowly rose to his full height, no more than four-feet-four. The front of his black jeans were wet, and he was soaked with perspiration. "I was . . . uh . . . I was lost, and I saw your house . . . I knocked, but no one was home. I came in through a window downstairs just so I could call my mom . . . that's all I wanted to do . . . but then you came home and I got scared . . ."

"You've been here since last night?"

"Yeah."

"Why didn't you let me know you were here? I would have helped you."

"I was too scared."

She tried to stop trembling. She reached for his hand—it was dirty and rough—and pulled him around the box. "Come on, we'll call her now. She must be worried sick about you."

He grabbed up his backpack as she led him out of the attic, into the full light of her loft. "How did you get lost, anyway? What's a kid your age doing out alone at night?"

"It's a long story," he evaded. "Can I use your bathroom?"

"Of course." She glanced at the wet spot on his jeans. "If you'd like to change, you could probably wear a pair of my shorts. They'd be baggy, but—"

"That's okay," he said, embarrassed. "I don't need 'em." She led him downstairs and showed him the bathroom. He went in quickly and tried to bolt the door behind him.

"The lock's broken," she said through the door. "Tell me your number, and I'll call your mother."

There was no answer. In a moment, she heard a scraping sound, and realized he was raising the window—probably the same one he'd come through last night.

She burst through the door and caught him halfway out.

And suddenly it dawned on her. Black jeans. Black shirt. Black backpack. This child had been put here deliberately, planted in her house to rob her or spy on her or maybe even hurt her—

She grabbed him and wrestled him back in, her face reddening with escalating anger. "You lied to me," she said through her teeth. "You're not some lost kid. You're from SCCH. You're one of Bill Brandon's kids, aren't you?"

The kid looked stunned, and she knew instantly that she was right.

"Answer me," she demanded. "Did he make you break in here? What was he looking for? Papers? Tapes?"

He lowered his worried eyes to the floor, and she turned him around and yanked off his backpack.

"Answer me!" she bit out as she unzipped it and examined the contents.

"I didn't get anything!" he said. "You came home—"

"What *would* you have gotten?" she asked, jerking up his chin. "What did he tell you to get?"

The fear in his eyes was real. Instantly, she let him go, but she didn't break that lock she had on his eyes.

"He's gonna kill me," the boy whispered.

Her anger crashed. She knew that fear, understood that certainty.

"What's your name?"

"Jimmy," he muttered.

"How long have you been there, Jimmy? At the home?"

"Three years," he said. "Me and my sister. Lady, if you report me, they're gonna put me in the juvenile center, and there won't be anybody left to take care of my sister. She's only seven."

But the words weren't penetrating. She was too caught up in the realization that if this kid had gotten into her house, it was because Bill Brandon knew where she lived and how to get in. The fact that she wasn't already dead was a miracle.

"How did he know where I live?"

Jimmy shrugged. "How does he know where anybody lives? I don't know. He doesn't tell me stuff like that."

"So what *did* he tell you?"

He looked miserable as he struggled with the truth, and she knew that he wondered if any of his mission was salvageable now. He was probably hoping to get out, go back to the home, and act as though he'd never been caught.

"Come on, Jimmy. I'm not going to let that man hurt you."

"You can't stop him."

"I sure can. And he knows it. That's why he made you come here. He wants to stop me from telling what I know."

His eyes were raging as tears filled them. "He *will* stop you. He's mean, and he doesn't give up. He woulda stopped you last night if you hadn't lost him."

She caught her breath. "How do you know that?" Then her face changed as she remembered the phone call, the boy's voice . . . "That was you on the phone, wasn't it?"

He swiped at the tears spilling down his face. "He told me he'd call to warn me you were coming home. I thought it was him. It was stupid. I shouldn't have answered. Man, he's gonna kill me."

"No, he's not. Because you're not going back there."

His face began to redden now, and he looked up at her with pleading eyes. "I *gotta* go back. You don't understand. Lisa's still there. He told me the sins of the brothers are visited on the siblings. It's in the Bible."

"That's not in the Bible, Jimmy. That's something he made up."

"He'll still hurt Lisa if he thinks I ratted on him. He swore he would, and I know it's true."

"Jimmy, even if you did go back, don't you know Bill's going to go ballistic when he sees you after this botched-up break-in?"

"He hates mistakes," he whispered, leaning back against the wall and clutching his head. "But at least he'll go off on me and not Lisa. She didn't do anything. She doesn't even know about all the stuff Bill makes us do. I don't want her to know."

"But don't you want Bill stopped? Wouldn't it be great if he could get caught and arrested for what he's done?"

"No!" he shouted. "*I'll* get arrested, too. Bill didn't break into anybody's house. *I* did. I'll be the one they put in prison. Not him."

"Jimmy, that's all just a lie. He tells you that to keep you doing what he wants. He wants you to be afraid. But the truth is that they don't put little kids in prison. How old are you, anyway? Eight, nine?"

"I'm ten," he said, insulted. "I'm just . . . short for my age."

"Probably why he chose you. You can fit into small places. But Jimmy, they don't put ten-year-olds in prison. And if they stop Bill, they'll put you and Lisa and all the other kids into a decent place—"

"That *is* a decent place," he screamed. "Don't you get it?"

"Just because something is familiar, Jimmy, it doesn't mean it's good."

"It doesn't *have* to be good."

She rubbed her face, wondering what she should do. Call the police? Or Nick Hutchins? Go against this kid's will and turn him in, or let him go back?

He was afraid that he would go to prison, and she couldn't blame him. Bill had probably pounded that threat into his brain.

She took his arm and led him to the kitchen, picked up the phone, and started dialing.

"Who are you calling?" he asked.

"My friend, Nick Hutchins. He's a social worker. He'll know what to do."

"No!" The kid jerked away from her. "Are you crazy? No social workers! I'm tellin' you, he'll beat the daylights out of Lisa, just to get back at me."

"Maybe Nick can get your sister out of there."

"Nick? The one who *put* us in there? No way! Lady, you're gonna ruin everything!"

"Jimmy, I want you to call me Beth," she said. "I'm going to help you."

Tears came to his eyes, and he swatted them away. Under his breath, Jimmy muttered, "I ain't calling you nothing."

Beth heard what he said but ignored him. Of course he was angry. Of course he was afraid. So was she.

She breathed a sigh of relief when Nick answered the phone. "Nick, I was wondering if you could come over. I need to see you."

At the other end of the line, Nick hesitated. "I could get there in a couple of hours or so. I'm kind of tied up right now."

"It's really important." She glanced at the boy. "There's something I need for you to see."

"What is it? You're not going to keep me in suspense until I can get there, are you?"

65

"I have to," she said. "Nick, come as soon as you can."

"Is it the article? Have you finished it?"

"No," she said. "I got a little sidetracked. I'm still working on it, though."

"Are you all right?"

"Yes. For now, yes."

She could almost hear the wheels turning in Nick's head. "Beth, just hold tight. I'll be there as soon as I can tie up some loose ends here."

"All right, I'll see you then." She hung up the phone and gave Jimmy a look.

"I thought you were gonna tell him," he said, wiping his face.

"Not over the phone. I want him to see you in person. He's a nice guy, Jimmy. He cares about you."

"He doesn't care about me! None of them do! I *hate* social workers. They don't care if they separate sisters and brothers, or if they take you out of one place to put you in a worse place. They don't care about nothing."

Her heart ached for this jaded child. "Jimmy, you've obviously had some bad breaks. But Nick is going to change your opinion of social workers. I promise you."

"Yeah, I've heard promises before, too," he said. "Let's face it, lady. I'm sunk. The sooner we get this whole thing over with, the better."

CHAPTER FOURTEEN

While they waited for Nick, Beth made breakfast for the boy, who attacked the food as if he'd been starving to death. She sat with him as he ate, sipping on her coffee and studying him.

"What did Bill tell you about me?" she asked.

He hesitated, then shrugged. "Nothing. Just told me to come in here and get the papers and tapes. And dump the files about us on your computer."

She frowned. "He didn't say why?"

"Said you were gonna write a story about us. That we'd all go to jail if you did."

"I'm writing a story about *him*. He's the only one going to jail—he and the other adults working with him. But not the kids, Jimmy. I'm not out to get the kids." She wiped the wet ring from his glass off her table, then looked up at him again. "Did you find anything?"

"No, nothing."

"That's because I had most of it with me, and I hadn't put anything on the computer yet. I imagine he was planning to kill me before I got home, and then he would have destroyed any evidence I had with me." She thought about that for a moment. "Why do you think he *didn't* come out here last night? If he knew where I was, and that you were still here, why didn't he come?"

"I don't know. I kept thinking he would. Maybe he thought I got away, and that you called the police after he followed you. Maybe he was too scared to come."

"Bill Brandon, scared? I don't think so."

The boy looked up and stared at her for a moment. "You know him, don't you?"

She met his eyes, then looked away. The doorbell rang, and she got up, grateful for the chance to evade the question. "Maybe that's Nick," she said.

"Or maybe it's Bill."

She stopped halfway to the door, reached into her table drawer, and pulled out her pistol. *It's not as if Jimmy doesn't know I have one*, she thought, *I almost shot him with it an hour ago.*

Peeking through the curtain, she saw Nick, and quickly put the gun away before opening the door. "Nick, you got here sooner than I thought."

"Had to. You had me so curious." He stepped into the house and saw the little freckle-faced boy with a milk mustache, his red hair tousled and unkempt. "Who's this?"

Beth drew in a deep breath. "Nick, this is Jimmy. A very interesting kid, with a very interesting story. Why don't you sit down? This could take a while."

When he'd heard Jimmy's story, Nick seemed ready to burst with excitement. "He's just what we need! A witness, from the inside."

"They're not gonna listen to me. I'm just a kid," Jimmy said. "And none of the others will talk. They're too scared."

"They *will* listen to you," Nick said. "Once we get your story into the paper, the police will be banging down the doors of that home."

"And the kids will be scattered all over the state," Jimmy added, "and brothers and sisters will be separated, and some of us will be in awful places . . ."

Nick hesitated, giving Jimmy a long look. "Jimmy, don't you want out of that home? Don't you realize what he's done to you? He's not only risking your life, he's using you to commit crimes, training you and the others to be crooks. That's child abuse."

"Can you get Lisa out? Can you keep us together? If you can't, I'm not telling anything. Nothing. You can find another witness."

"Jimmy, I can try my best to keep the two of you together. But Lisa's going to be better off no matter where we put her."

"Bull!" Jimmy shouted, his eyes filling with angry tears. "She depends on me. She's probably worried to death right now. She thinks I left her, just like—" The word fell off, and he turned away. "When can you get her out?"

"As soon as I relate all this to the police." Nick paused and shot Beth an eloquent look. "I know you want to get the story done first, but do you think you can finish it in the next couple of hours? If Brandon thinks you're ready to go public, we don't have a lot of time. I want to get those kids out of there."

She looked at all her evidence scattered across the table. "I think I might be able to pull something together by then. But then my editor—"

"Great. Beth, do you realize that this is the break I've been looking for? That we might really be able to shut down that home?"

"Yes," she said softly, touching Jimmy's shoulder, though he shook her hand away. "I realize it. It's a dream of mine, too."

"Oh, man. Jimmy," Nick said, "you could be a hero because of this. A regular celebrity. And your life of crime is over. Nobody's going to make you break into people's homes ever again."

But Jimmy didn't look so sure.

"Hey, why don't you come with me, Jimmy? We could hang out while Beth finishes the story."

"I don't want to go anywhere with you."

"He can stay here," Beth said. "He can just watch TV or something while I work. It'll be all right. He's quiet as a mouse. Proved that last night. My only fear is that Brandon will show up."

"Don't worry about that. I think I'll pay him a visit right now."

"What for?"

"I'm allowed to make impromptu inspections whenever I want. I'll just hang around there, inspecting the cottages and all. That way we can be sure he stays where he is."

"Okay," Beth said. "I'll do the best I can. But are you going to mention Jimmy? Should we call the police about finding him?"

Nick considered that. "No, I don't think so. They'd just report it to Sheila or me. Let's keep this just between us for now. I could lose my job, but I'll risk it. And I can't wait to see how Bill handles Jimmy's disappearance."

He patted Jimmy's shoulder. "Jimmy, you just relax, all right? I'll try to check on Lisa while I'm there."

"Will you tell her I'm okay? That I haven't left her?"

Nick hesitated. "I don't think that's a good idea, Jimmy. It might put her in danger. If she tells anyone, Bill could hear about it."

"She keeps secrets," he said. "She won't tell."

"She might do it without meaning to. But relax. In a little while, we can go in there and get her out for good."

That wasn't good enough for Jimmy. Brooding, he slumped on the couch.

"I'll call you in a couple of hours, Beth," Nick said, rising.

Beth walked him to the door and bolted it behind him.

CHAPTER FIFTEEN

ock the door, Brad."

Bill's order was clipped and direct. The eleven-year-old boy could tell from Bill's voice and from the look on his face that this was going to be one of those meetings Brad would wish he hadn't attended. Not that he had a choice. He locked the door when the last of the dozen kids in Bill's group of "favorites" filed in, then took his seat beside his best friend, Keith.

The faces of the children were solemn—even frightened. Bill didn't often call them together in broad daylight. It drew too much attention from the other kids. But this morning he had made them all get up early, even though it was summer and they didn't have school, and file into the meeting room next to Bill's office for what he called a "briefing."

Something had happened, Brad thought, and he was sure it had something to do with Jimmy Westin.

Bill's face was angry as he paced in front of the dead-silent children, tapping a metal ruler against his palm and examining their faces one by one. "We've had a development, people," he said. "A rather upsetting development. I thought I should prepare you so you'd know what to expect." Suddenly he slammed the ruler down on a table, making all of them jump. "Jimmy Westin was arrested last night."

A collective gasp sounded in the room, and the children gaped up at him for more details.

"He got sloppy," he went on. "Let himself get caught during a mission. Now he's paying for it."

Brad whispered a curse, and anger surged inside him that his friend could be so stupid. He had always thought that Jimmy wasn't careful enough. He hadn't worked at it, like Brad had.

The boy looked up at Bill and struggled with the question weighing on his mind. "Was it adult jail, or the detention center?" Either way, it was bad, but in their room late at night, the boys sometimes speculated about what would happen if they got caught.

"I hate to say it," Bill said, "but they're holding him in the adult facility. A year ago, he may have gone to juvenile hall, but after the last election, Florida passed the Adult Crime-Adult Time Law. You do a grown-up crime—and they do include burglary—and you serve with the meanest, toughest criminals in the state.

"I wish I could tell you that I could get him out. But I'm afraid it doesn't work that way. Because he's a ward of the state, he's considered high risk, which means that—according to HRS—if I can't make something out of him, he's probably a lost cause. So they're processing him into the justice system, where he's likely to stay for at least ten or twenty years."

Brad wasn't sure he followed all of this. He often had a hard time understanding much of what Bill said. But the ten-to-twenty-years part didn't escape him. That was practically Jimmy's whole life.

"I think you all know what this means," Bill said, slapping his palm with the ruler again. "It means that every one of you is in trouble. If Jimmy Westin talks, you might go down with him."

Brad tried to imagine what Jimmy might say if he was tortured or threatened. Would he drag them all down with him? Or would he hang tough and keep his mouth shut?

"I don't think he'll talk," Bill went on, as if he'd read Brad's mind. "We have Lisa. As long as Jimmy knows that his sins will be visited on his sister, we'll be all right. And just to make sure *she* doesn't talk, I'm going to get her to replace Jimmy, and put a little fear into her myself."

Silence hung in the air as everyone imagined what he might mean by that.

"Okay, listen up. People are going to be coming around here, asking questions about Jimmy. Those people are *not* our friends;

they'll be out to get us. Until I tell you differently, I want you to pretend Jimmy's still here. If HRS comes snooping around, act like he just left the cottage, or the playground, or wherever you are. You just saw him a minute ago. Got it?"

One of the girls frowned. "Won't they *know* where he is?"

Bill shook his head. "Not necessarily. 'The right hand knows not what the left hand doeth.'" None of them knew what that meant, but it sounded biblical, and thus, scary. "HRS is not in touch that much with the police. And I don't want them to know that one of *my* kids is a jailbird. Besides, they might start looking at each of you, one at a time. I don't want you to wind up where Jimmy is."

He paced the room again, this time walking between their perches on arms of sofas, tabletops, or on the floor. "But we can overcome this obstacle, if we try. Are you people up for it?"

A weak chorus of yeses sounded around the room.

"I can't hear you!"

"Yes!" they shouted.

"You're not ordinary kids! You're gifted with special skills. As the Good Book says, 'Many are called, but few are chosen.' You are the chosen. *My* chosen. You're called to a higher purpose—a mission that isn't for the faint of heart. You're called to excellence, people. And you *are* excellent. That's why I chose you. That's why you are my hands and my feet. That's why you are favored among God and men!"

It didn't matter that his words made little sense to Brad or the others. It sounded good and hopeful, and it elevated them to something more than orphaned children. It made them special.

When the children had gone back to their cottages, Bill went through his office into the room where closed-circuit television screens showed him what was happening around the campus. He watched the children going back to their cottages. Some whispered among themselves, but he knew those conversations would be harmless, so he let it go. Seeing no cause for concern, he went back into his office, sat down behind his desk, and thought over the things he'd told them. They'd believed everything. It was so easy to manipulate them. "Adult Crime-Adult Time Law"—what a laugh. There was no such thing.

He just hoped that dirty-faced brat didn't turn on him. And why had no one called him about the boy yet? If he was in police custody, wouldn't they have reported it to him?

He looked at the phone and wondered if *he* should call *them* and act like a concerned guardian worried about a missing child. But then he would have to explain why it had taken him so long to report the disappearance. He could say that he'd put the boy to bed himself—but that Jimmy had sneaked away during the night, so that he hadn't known Jimmy was missing until this morning.

It might work. And it would certainly cover him in the event that Jimmy *did* talk.

But maybe he was jumping to conclusions here. What if the kid wasn't in custody? Calling could open a whole can of worms that Bill didn't want to open. Investigations, news reports, posters all over town . . .

No, he couldn't chance it. He'd have to wait. If the police did have the boy and if they showed up to ask him about Jimmy, he could say that he'd been duped. After all, the police were always quick to assume the worst about these parentless, high-risk kids, who'd been products of alcohol, drugs, selfishness. The police, like everyone else, expected the children to continue the pattern set by their parents. As Bill himself was often quick to remind the police and others, you could take the kid out of the trash, but you couldn't take the trash out of the kid. And no one ever argued with him about it.

Yes, his best bet was to do nothing, then plead ignorance if the police called. It was the safest course.

CHAPTER SIXTEEN

T he old Western on TV didn't hold Jimmy's attention, nor did the puppy who kept wanting to play tug-of-war with him. He could hear Beth's fingers on the keyboard upstairs as she wrote the story that would bring the walls of the St. Clair Children's Home tumbling down—exactly what Bill had sent him here to prevent.

He let the puppy win the tug-of-war with the sock, then watched him curl up on the floor to chew on it. Jimmy's eyes strayed up the open stairway. With just a slight lean, she could see him, and she'd kept a close watch on him all morning. He had kept an eye on her, too. Up there, disks were lying around. Papers. All the things that Bill wanted. If he took those things back to Bill, maybe Bill would go easy on him. Maybe Lisa wouldn't have to suffer.

But Beth wouldn't let that stop her; she would write the story anyway. Besides, she had been nice to him, and he didn't want to rip her off now. She could have reported him to the police, but she hadn't. It was like she believed he was a good person when she hardly even knew him—like she thought the bad things he had done weren't his fault. Anyone else would have hung a guilty sign on him and handed him over to the cops.

No, he couldn't turn on her now. But he still worried about Lisa. If there was just some way that he could talk to her, tell her to hold on, that he hadn't just left her.

His eyes strayed to the telephone. Could he get away with just calling her? Clicking the remote control, he turned up the television as the shoot-out raged louder. He picked up the phone, then took it to a part of the living room where he was just out of her sight. Quickly he dialed the direct number to his and Lisa's cottage. It rang, and Stella, the housemother, answered.

He tried to disguise his voice. "Can I speak to Lisa, please?"

"Who is this?" Stella asked. "Jimmy, is that you? Where in blue blazes are you?"

As if it had stung his hand, he hung up the phone quickly and backed away from it. Oh, great. Now Stella would tell Bill that he had called, and Bill would be madder than ever that he'd been near a phone and hadn't tried to reach him. When he found out Jimmy had tried to reach Lisa, Bill would fly into a rage—and when he finally found Jimmy, as he would eventually, he would get even.

The worst part was that Lisa still wouldn't know that her brother hadn't abandoned her just like every other person she'd ever loved had done.

CHAPTER SEVENTEEN

B
ill didn't like Nick Hutchins. The social worker seemed to have it in for him. Nick had been giving him too much grief lately. His monthly inspections of the home had stepped up to twice monthly, and he seemed too curious about the children, especially those who'd been caught in petty crimes. Bill had tried to explain to him that he wasn't responsible for the value systems of these kids before they came to his home, but that he did the best he could with what he got. If one of them occasionally got himself into trouble, it wasn't Bill's fault.

Now, as Bill followed the man from cottage to cottage, as if Nick expected to find some horrible violation that would warrant a severe reprimand from the state, he wondered what Nick was looking for. Did this impromptu inspection have anything to do with Jimmy's disappearance?

"Are all the kids on the premises right now?" Nick asked casually, walking into a playroom and scanning the children playing games.

So, he does know that Jimmy's missing. Bill struggled with the idea of candidly admitting to the kid's disappearance. But he couldn't understand why Nick was being so secretive. Why didn't Nick just come out and ask him where Jimmy was, and how long the boy had been missing? No, maybe he was just being paranoid. He decided not to mention it yet. "No, actually," he said. "We took a vanload to the library this morning. Some of the others had swimming lessons at the Y."

Nick peered at him skeptically.

They had just turned up the hall so that Nick could snoop in the bedrooms when Stella, the housemother of Cottage B, burst in. "Uh, Bill, could I have a word with you, please?"

"Certainly," Bill said. "Nick, you'll excuse me for a moment, won't you?"

Nick nodded but didn't say anything, and Bill felt the man's eyes on the back of his neck as he followed Stella out of earshot.

"What is it?"

"It's Jimmy. He called just now, trying to disguise his voice. He wanted to speak to Lisa."

His eyebrows shot up. "Where is he?"

"I don't know. He hung up before I could—"

"I'll find out. Go back in there and keep that jerk from doing us any harm. I have to go to my office for a minute."

He rushed out of the cottage and across the lawn to his office and bolted inside. He unlocked a closet and checked the Caller ID he kept so that he could monitor the origin of calls coming into each of the cottages. When he'd opened the home, he had had an extension to each line installed right here in his office. He also taped all of the calls made on any campus telephone, either incoming or outgoing. It was what he called quality control. You never really knew whom you could trust. And of course no one, not even his "inner circle" of staff, knew what was in this closet.

He checked the Caller ID for Cottage B—and saw the name *E. J. Wright*. Bill's heart jumped. Elizabeth Wright. Beth. Jimmy was still in her house? Was he nuts? Hadn't he told that kid to get out of there? But Jimmy hadn't asked to speak to Bill, who could come and get him, but he'd asked instead for Lisa—and in a disguised voice.

Something was wrong. Jimmy had turned on him.

What was he telling Beth? Bill rubbed his forehead and found it cool and wet with sweat. Was Jimmy giving her more fodder for her story? That little twerp knew enough to bring down his whole operation.

Bill hadn't had a lot of time to think this morning—first the cops had come to tell him about Marlene's death and ask a ton of questions, and then Nick Hutchins had shown up. But this situation didn't require a lot of thought.

He was going to have to kill both Beth and Jimmy, before she could turn that story in.

His face hardened with violent determination as he cut back across the lawn to the playground behind Cottage B. He saw Lisa, Jimmy's little sister, sitting alone on a swing, drawing figures in the dirt with the tip of her toe. Her strawberry-blonde hair strung down in her eyes, and he could see from her red eyes that she'd been crying.

He approached her, and she looked up fearfully. "Come here, darlin'," he said, taking her hand. "Come with me."

Her innocent eyes widened. "Where?"

"We got some trainin' to do. I'm about to promote you from orphan to executive. What do you think about that?"

He could see that she didn't have a clue what he was talking about. "I don't know."

"See, since Jimmy's gone and got himself in trouble, I'm giving you his job. It was a real important job. You think you're smart enough for it?"

Tears filled her eyes, but she nodded bravely. "When is Jimmy coming back?" she managed to ask through trembling lips.

"Good question," he said. "Probably never."

CHAPTER EIGHTEEN

Bill didn't like to get his hands dirty. That was why he always used the children. It kept him nice and distant, and if the children were ever caught breaking and entering, he could throw up his hands and insist that he'd tried as hard as he could to keep tabs on them, but children would be children, and there wasn't a lot he could do about kids who'd been born among criminals—except love them and show them compassion and hope that some good would rub off on them.

Sure, Bill had compassion. So much compassion that he really wished he could see the look on Beth and Jimmy's faces as they opened the cigar box he was "doctoring" for them.

"Know what this is, darlin'?" he asked Lisa, gesturing toward the cigar box open on the desk before him.

"No, sir."

"It's a little package we're sending to a friend," he said. "A friend who's been real good to me. And I'm gonna let you deliver it for me."

She didn't say anything, just sat in the corner, trying hard not to move.

He set the explosives in carefully, then rigged up the detonator caps so that the bomb would go off the moment the box was opened. He'd never done this before, actually, but he'd read all about it in articles on the Internet about the Unabomber. It was no secret, and he and some of his partners had discussed the precise methods more than once. He couldn't believe how perfectly this would work out—except that those two traitors wouldn't get this little present until tomorrow, which could be a problem if Beth finished her story and turned it in to her editor before that. In that case, he'd have to make sure the newspaper didn't get his story out by then. In any event, if there were any questions about Bill's involvement in the explosion, he would be able to prove that he was miles away when the explosion occurred.

He closed the box carefully and wrapped it, then addressed it to Beth Wright and affixed an Express Mail waybill.

"You ready to deliver this for me, darlin'?"

Lisa hesitated. "Where?"

"The post office. You're big enough to take something in by yourself, aren't you? You don't even have to talk to anybody. Just drop it in the slot, and my friend will have it by tomorrow."

She nodded.

"If you do a good job, Lisa, honey, I'll give you a more important job, like the kind I gave Jimmy. And if you do a bad job . . . well . . ." He propped his chin on his hand and smiled. "Remember that time Jimmy had to stay in bed for two days because he couldn't walk so good? Remember those bruises?"

She seemed frozen.

"Well, just don't do a bad job, darlin'." He took the package and her hand and led her out to his pickup. He'd parked his Buick in a toolshed at the back of the property; even a stupid cop would be able to match the dents and paint scratches on it to the marks on Beth's car, so he didn't plan to drive it until some of his staff had painted it.

Across the lawn, he saw Nick coming out of one of the cottages—and heading toward him.

He cursed. "Get in, Lisa, and put the package under the seat."

She did as she was told, and Bill closed the door and walked around to the driver's side. "You about finished snooping, Nick?" he asked in a pseudo-jovial voice.

"Maybe," Nick said. "I just wondered where you're taking her."

"To a birthday party," he said. "One of her little friends at school. Don't think a kid should miss all the fun just because they're wards of the state, do you?"

Nick looked down at the little girl, and Bill wondered if he knew who she was. He wished she didn't look quite so fragile.

"She's a little worried 'cause she's late. I clean forgot about it, but no harm done. She'll get there before they blow out the candles if we hurry."

Nick backed away from the truck. Bill could see that he was trying to think of a way to detain him. What was Nick up to?

"When will you be back, Bill? I want to talk to you."

"Won't be long. Haven't we talked enough? Don't you have something constructive to do? The state isn't paying you to hang around here all day, are they?"

Nick wasn't intimidated. "Get somebody else to take her, Bill. I'm not finished with you."

Bill groaned and got out of the truck. "All right, hold on. I'll get Stella, but I'll have to make sure somebody's watching the kids before she comes." He looked at Lisa with an apologetic face. "Sugar, you're gonna be a little bit late, but we'll get you there somehow."

Lisa looked perplexed.

He helped Lisa out of the truck and took her into his office to make sure that Nick didn't speak privately with her. He called over to Cottage B. "Stella, I need you to come run an errand for me. If you run into Nick, tell him that you're taking Lisa to a birthday party, but don't mention her name. Call her Susan. He might know about Jimmy, and her name might ring a bell."

"Doesn't he already know her?"

"It's been three years since he's dealt with either of them. He won't remember."

"Where am I really going?" she asked.

"To the post office. Drop Lisa off at the corner and let her put the package in the 'express' slot."

"Is Lisa going to be one of your regulars now?" she asked. "Isn't she a little young?"

"She's perfect. Just get over here. And don't botch this up. I've had enough problems lately, and I'm not in a good mood. If you mess this up, everything could blow up in our faces."

He hung up and took in a deep breath. "If that man asks your name, you tell him it's Susan. Do you hear me?"

Lisa nodded, her eyes big.

"You put the package in the Express Mail slot, and if anyone asks you what it is, you say it's a book for your grandma. Got it?"

She nodded.

"Just do as I say, and when you get back, I'll have a surprise for you."

Her eyebrows shot up. "Will Jimmy be home then?"

He decided he might need that leverage. "He might just be, darlin'."

He led her back outside as Stella hurried across the lawn. "Come on, sugar. Let's get you to that party."

CHAPTER NINETEEN

B eth sat back in her squeaky desk chair and sighed. Her article was finished—complete with the quotes by Marlene and Jimmy, along with the sad and suggestive news that Marlene had been murdered immediately after giving the interview. She wished she had another hour to tweak it, but she sensed that time was tight. Sitting forward again, she sent it by modem into the paper, then e-mailed her editor to look for it and call her back. As an afterthought, she electronically transferred the transcribed conversation with Marlene so that it would be on file at the newspaper office.

She went downstairs. Jimmy and the puppy were lying on the area rug in front of the television, curled up together as if they were old friends. She stepped around them and saw that they were both sound asleep.

She smiled. How exhausted Jimmy must be, after spending the night in terror in the attic.

The telephone rang, and she snapped it up. "Hello?"

"Beth, I got your article." It was Phil, her editor.

"Read it yet?"

"Yep. Interesting. Very interesting. Sure is going to cause a big stir."

"Phil, this is headline material. You'll print it in the Saturday edition tomorrow, won't you?"

He hesitated. "I don't know, Beth. I'm a little reluctant."

"Why?" she asked. "What's wrong with it?"

"I'd like a few more quotes. The only two people quoted are a dead woman and a little kid who might just have a vivid imagination."

"Was it my imagination that the kid broke into my house last night, Phil? I didn't make that up. He's here now."

"Still, I'd feel better if you could get another quote or two. Somebody who's not dead or a juvenile delinquent."

"Juvenile delinquent? How do you figure that?"

"Hey, don't get defensive. I'm just pointing out how it's going to look to a skeptical public. He did break into your house."

"Didn't you read the article? He was *forced* to. And Marlene's dead *because* of the article."

"The kid's story is suspect, Beth. Sorry, but that's the truth. And you *say* the woman died because of your interview; the police haven't concluded that yet. We need more. Maybe you can find someone who grew up in Brandon's home, someone who's not under his thumb anymore. Maybe they'd be willing to talk. That would be just what we need. And call the police stations in all of the towns within a two-hour radius. Find out how often there was evidence that kids had done it. You know, fingerprints, footprints, maybe they saw them but didn't catch them, that sort of thing."

She closed her eyes and started to feel sick. "If I compiled all that today, Phil, would you print it tomorrow? It's crucial. This whole thing is taking on a life of its own. Something has to be done with Jimmy, and he's worried about his little sister—with good reason—but we can't get the kids out of there until there's enough evidence. But if I turn him over to the police, *he* may suffer instead of Bill Brandon—"

"Yes, Beth," Phil cut in. "Get me what I asked for and I'll run it. You have my word."

She let out a heavy breath and dropped the phone in its cradle. What was she going to do?

She closed her eyes and asked herself if she had the guts to do what was necessary. The right thing never seemed that easy, and it had an awful lot of conditions attached.

But she had spent the last three years trying to make something of herself. She had found a church, and now she went every Sunday. She tried hard to live by the Ten Commandments—don't lie, don't covet, don't commit adultery. In fact, some people thought she followed God's laws to a fault, but she figured she had enough sin in her life that it would take fifty years of walking the straight and narrow to get to the point where she'd come close to making herself worthy of God.

But this was hard. Writing this story Phil's way meant digging deeper than she'd wanted to dig, exposing things she hadn't wanted exposed . . .

And it meant that she would need advice about the law.

She picked up the phone and dialed the number of Lynda Barrett's law office. Lynda, a devoted Christian and respected lawyer, was one of the teachers in Beth's Sunday school class. Maybe she could help.

Paige, Lynda's secretary and another friend from church, put Beth right through to Lynda.

"Hi, Beth. What's up?"

"Hi, Lynda. Uh . . . I'm sorry to bother you. I just . . . I wondered if you could come by and see me today. It's pretty important. I need some advice, and I need it quickly."

"Legal advice?"

"Yes. It has to do with a story I'm working on. It involves a little boy. I'd rather tell you about it in person, if you have time, and I'd rather not come there."

"I could come right now. I was supposed to be in court this afternoon, but it was postponed, so I'm free."

"Great. Oh, and bring Jake if you want. My little friend might like to meet him. Kids love pilots."

CHAPTER TWENTY

Stella let the truck idle at the corner near the post office. "All right, Lisa. Take the package and go. Put it in the Express Mail slot. Then hurry back to the truck. Try not to talk to anybody."

Lisa got the package from under the seat. It was heavier than it looked, but she dared not complain. She got out of the pickup, clutching the package against her chest, and backed into the door to close it.

Walking rapidly, she hurried toward the post office door. Shifting the package to one arm, she tried to open the door, but it was heavy and she almost dropped it.

A man came to the door and opened it for her. "There you go, honey."

"Thank you," she said almost inaudibly. She stood inside the post office, looking around at the boxes and stamp vending machines and slots. Through some glass doors were the postal workers, and a dozen people waited in line.

The package was getting heavier, so she shifted it again, trying to get a more comfortable hold on it. Stella had said to put it in a slot. She saw the slots marked "local" and "stamped" and "metered." He'd said to put it in Express Mail, but she didn't see that one.

It was too heavy for her to hold any longer, so she went to the "metered" slot and tried to fit it through the small opening. It wouldn't fit.

"That's not where you want to put that, pumpkin," one of the postal workers walking through told her. "That'll have to go in Express Mail over there."

"Oh." She headed across the room to where he pointed, and looked up at the lever, which was too high for her.

"Here, sweetheart, I'll get it," the postman said. He opened the small door and took the package from her. The weight surprised him. "Boy, this is heavy. Whatcha got in here, anyway?"

She tried to speak, but her voice wouldn't come. Clearing her throat, she tried again. "A book for my grandma," she said just under her breath.

He smiled and let the door close. "I'll just take it on back, pumpkin."

She only stood staring at him for a moment, not sure what to do. Finally, she decided she'd better get back to the car before Stella left her. "Thank you," she said again, and walked quickly to the door.

Stella was still waiting at the corner. Lisa ran up the sidewalk and climbed into the pickup.

"What took you so long?" Stella demanded.

"I don't know."

"Well, did you put the package in the Express Mail slot?"

Lisa thought of telling her about the man, but a dread came over her that she might be punished for giving the package to him. "Yes," she said.

"Did you talk to anyone?"

"No."

Stella breathed out a sigh of relief as she turned the corner and headed back to the home. After a moment, she muttered, "I oughta get hazard pay for this."

Lisa turned around and looked out the back window, wondering if the man had really mailed the package, or if he'd opened it and looked inside. She hoped it wasn't anything too awful.

She sat back down and tried to console herself with the thought that Jimmy might be back when she returned to the home. Wouldn't he be proud that she was smart enough to work for Bill now, too?

CHAPTER TWENTY-ONE

Beth poured two cups of coffee and brought them to the table where Lynda sat, filling in the notes she had made as Beth told her of the allegations she was about to make concerning the home, and what Jimmy's part had been in it. As Jimmy and Jake sat on the floor playing with the puppy, Beth quietly popped the question she had been waiting to ask.

"I wondered, Lynda, what kind of responsibility Jimmy and the other kids who've worked in Bill Brandon's crime ring will have. In other words, are they accountable for something they were forced to do?"

"You mean, can they be prosecuted?" Lynda asked.

Jimmy looked up, and she knew he'd overheard. She wished she hadn't asked.

"Well, breaking and entering is definitely a crime," Lynda said, "and under ordinary circumstances, a child Jimmy's age who committed a crime like that would be sent to the detention center, depending on the judge's disposition and the number of offenses against the child. But these are extenuating circumstances, and I find it hard to believe that any judge or jury would blame Jimmy or the other kids for being victims of Brandon's control."

Beth looked down at the coffee cup in her hand. "There's someone I know, who I might try to interview. She's someone who was in Brandon's home a few years ago. She's an adult now, and I'm hoping she'll corroborate what I've already uncovered. But she might be worried that she'll be prosecuted if she confesses. Would she?"

"Well, that depends. How old was she when she stopped committing the crimes?"

"Eighteen. She stopped when she left the home."

Lynda blew out a breath, and shook her head. "That's a tough one. A jury might say that she was old enough to know right from wrong."

"But if she'd been doing it since she was ten, and she was scared to death of him, and she knew that she had no choice but to do everything he said . . ."

"It would depend on her lawyer, Beth, and what kind of case he laid out."

"But you think she would *need* a lawyer? That there would be charges against her? Isn't the statute of limitations in Florida three years?"

"Well, yes. Has it been longer than that?"

"Just barely," Beth said. "Does that means she'd be clear?"

"Yes, she would. But any of those legal adults who stole for Bill within that three-year period would be at the judge's mercy."

"What about loopholes? Is there any way they could ignore the statute of limitations and prosecute her anyway?"

"It's possible that they could get her for something else. Something like withholding evidence or aiding and abetting."

"But she hasn't aided or abetted. Not since she left the home."

"Still, just by keeping her mouth shut she was allowing the crimes to go on."

"But that isn't fair! How much can someone be accountable when they've never had free will? When their every thought has been controlled by that man? When they're totally dependent on him for food and clothing and shelter, and they're afraid of his discipline if they don't do what he asks?"

"It may not be fair, Beth, but that's the justice system."

"Well, if that's the case, then it wouldn't be worth her while to talk, would it? Anyone would be better off keeping their mouth shut, even if they were outside the statute of limitations. And even then their reputation could be ruined—future job opportunities, credit, housing . . ."

"Technically, yes. But there's a moral issue that might outweigh all that," Lynda said. "There are children being abused and warped. Without *someone* stepping forward, it'll never end. Is it worth her reputation? I can't answer that. All I know is that God honors those who honor him by doing the right thing."

"When?" Beth asked, staring at the lines of her palm.

"When what?"

"When does God honor the person who honors him? How much of a sacrifice does he demand first?"

Lynda looked a little surprised by the question. "That depends on the person, Beth," Lynda said. "To one man Christ said to sell everything he owned. To another, he just said to go and sin no more. It all depends on what dark thing is in a person's heart, separating them from him. Mostly all he wants is confession and repentance."

"Yeah, that's the part I have trouble with," Beth said. "There are some buried things in life that you just don't want to dig up again."

Lynda's eyes lingered on her for a moment. "Confession is risky, all right. No question. But it's cleansing, Beth. Tell your source that the release that she feels afterward will overshadow anything the justice system can do to her. After repentance, she still might face consequences of some kind, but she won't be alone. God will walk with her and provide for her in all of that."

Beth tried to let it all soak in, but she wasn't sure she bought it.

"So when do you think the story will come out?" Jake asked from the floor.

"Tomorrow, if I can manage to get everything finished. It really has to be tomorrow. We can't wait any longer."

"My sister's there," Jimmy explained.

Lynda and Jake looked fully at Jimmy and saw the concern on his face. "Are you worried about your sister, Jimmy?" Lynda asked.

"Yes. He warned me. He said, 'The sins of the brothers are visited upon their siblings.' He knows the Bible real good."

"That's not in the Bible, kiddo," Jake said.

"I told him that," Beth said. "But Brandon always misquotes Scripture. He rewords verses and gives them a perverted, sinister meaning, and uses them like weapons against the children." She hesitated. "I've heard that from several people."

"Well, the more I hear, the more I think you need to get this story finished no matter what you have to do. Why don't Jake and I take Jimmy to stay with us while you work?"

Jimmy looked hopefully up at her.

"Sure," Jake said. "We could do some guy stuff."

"But we haven't reported finding him. I'm not sure what the police would do. We were just going to hide him until the arrests are made."

Jimmy sprang to his feet. "Please? It'll be all right. Nobody'll see me."

Beth gave Lynda a narrow look. "Are you sure you wouldn't feel compelled to report him?"

"Of course not," Lynda said. "I agree with you. It's best to hide him quietly for a while, as long as HRS knows."

"We could go out to the airport and take him up."

"In an airplane?" Jimmy asked, his eyes huge.

"Sure, in an airplane. Unless you know some other way to fly."

"Can I, Beth? That would be so great! None of the other kids would even believe it!"

Beth couldn't help laughing. "I guess that's all right, if Jake promises he won't crash."

"I beg your pardon," Jake said, insulted.

"It's not like you haven't done it before."

Jake gave a smirk. "It'll never happen again. Jimmy's not scared, are you, Jimmy?"

Jimmy looked a little less exuberant now. "You crashed?"

They all laughed. "It's a long story. We'll tell you about it on the way."

Beth walked them all to the door, said her good-byes to Jimmy, and watched them drive away.

For a moment, she contemplated what Lynda had said, trying to draw it into the core of her heart, her faith. It was too great a risk—yet all those children had no one fighting for them, no one to make things right. *Somebody* had to talk.

She looked through her Rolodex and found her old friend's number. All of the "graduates" of Bill Brandon's home kept unlisted phone numbers and very private addresses, so he couldn't reach them. They all continued to live in fear, to one degree or another. But Maria had trustingly shared her number with Beth, who had never expected to use it for a favor like this.

She picked up the phone and dialed Maria's number at home. Maria had gotten pregnant shortly after leaving the home, and was now the mother of twin two-year-olds. She had a sweet, support-ive husband—ten years her senior. Beth hoped that Maria was happy; she hated to drag all this up now. But Maria was her best chance for getting cooperation.

"Hello?"

Beth smiled at the sound of her voice. "Maria, hi. It's Beth Wright. I mean . . . Beth Sullivan." It had been a long time since she'd used that name.

"Beth! It's good to hear from you. How are you?"

"I'm great," she said, but couldn't manage to work any enthu-siasm into her voice. "Listen, I was wondering if you'd have time to meet me for lunch today. I know you have the kids and all. I could pick up hamburgers and meet you at the park or something so they could play. I just need to talk to you about something."

"Sure. I'd love to see you. But what do you need to talk to me about?"

"It's about Bill Brandon."

Dead silence hung between them for an intense moment. Finally, Maria said, "What about him?"

"There's just some stuff I need to talk to you about, but I'd rather do it in person."

"All right. What time?"

Beth didn't know what to expect Maria to look like; it had been nearly three years since she'd seen her. But the girl looked much more beautiful now than she had at eighteen. They hugged, and Beth admired the twins.

"Two babies. Wow."

"We want at least five," Maria said with a laugh as the chil-dren went to play in the sandbox. "The family I never had." They took a bench just a few feet away, so Maria could rescue them if anything happened. "You dyed your hair! I might not have recog-nized you if I'd seen you on the street."

"That was the point," Beth said.

Maria touched Beth's honey-colored hair. "Don't you ever miss being a brunette?"

"Sometimes. But it's worth it. Staying in St. Clair had its risks, you know."

"Tell me about it. But I was so glad to hear from you. We should stay in touch more. I didn't know how to call. I didn't know you had changed your name."

"Yeah," Beth said, watching the little girls in the sandbox. "I didn't have a husband to give me his name, like you did, so I just made one up. It made me feel more secure to have a different name."

"Maybe if we'd kept in touch, we could have supported each other."

"It's hard," Beth said. "We're both so busy. I've been working myself to death."

"I know, Beth, but I'm real proud of you. How close are you to getting your degree?"

"One more year."

"You're really going to do it, aren't you?"

"Yeah, and I've got huge student loans to prove it," Beth said.

"You always were determined. And working at the paper. I didn't expect you to get a job this soon."

"Yeah, well, they hired me as an intern my freshman year. They don't usually give bylines to interns, but I've worked so hard and dug up such good stuff, that Phil, my editor, has started treating me like a regular staff writer. During the summers, he pays me like one, but believe me, I have to work for it."

"I'm so proud of you, I guess I can forgive you for never calling me."

Beth smiled and squeezed her hand.

"So what's up, Beth? Why did you want to talk to me about Bill?"

Every muscle in Beth's body tensed as she took in a deep breath. "Maria, I've decided to expose him."

Maria's face showed no expression. She merely stared at her. "Are you sure you want to do that? He'll come after you."

"He already has."

Her face grew pale. "You're braver than I am."

Beth almost laughed. She tried to push down her own self-loathing. "It's not bravery," she said. "Not on my part. But I can't stand the thought of Bill abusing those children, training them to be thieves, preparing them for prison. Or worse. But I know that the minute this story comes out, hopefully tomorrow, Bill will be arrested. I'm not worried about him hurting me after that."

Maria stiffened. "Why are you telling me all this?"

Beth shrugged. "Well, I thought you would want to know. And—I thought you might let me interview you. My editor says I need more sources, someone who was there, who's grown now. Someone besides a dead woman and a little kid."

"Dead woman? What are you talking about?"

"Marlene," Beth said. Her mouth trembled slightly, but she managed to add, "She talked to me, and Bill killed her."

Maria threw her hand over her mouth and sprang up. With terror in her eyes, she hurried to the sandbox and picked up one of the twins, then grabbed the other by the hand and started to her car.

"Maria, where are you going?"

"Home!" Maria shouted as tears came to her eyes. "Why didn't you tell me on the phone that Bill knows you're doing this? I never would have come! If he killed Marlene for talking to you, then he'll kill me, too!"

"No, he won't! He's not following me now."

"You don't know that!" Maria shouted. She spun, her face red and raging as she glared at Beth. "I thought better of you, Beth, than to risk my life and the lives of my children. I have a family now! It took me three years to stop being afraid all the time, and now, just when I have some peace, you have to drag me into something that Bill's already killed his sister over?"

"I'm not dragging you into it, Maria. I just want to stop him."

"Then stop him yourself!" she shouted. "You don't need me. We have the same story!"

Beth froze, unable to find an argument to counter Maria's. Her story *was* the same. As much as she tried to deny it, hide it, wipe it from her mind, it was almost identical. "I can't use myself as a source," she choked out. "It wouldn't be objective."

"Are you kidding?" Maria shouted. "You'd probably win a Pulitzer Prize, if you didn't wind up in jail. Is that what you're scared of, Beth? That you'll wind up in jail?"

Beth looked down at her feet. "No. I made sure that I waited long enough. Three years. They can't try us after three years have passed."

"Oh, that's noble." Maria said with a sarcastic laugh. "You were so worried about the kids that you waited three years to make sure your own crimes were covered!"

"So did you!" Beth returned.

"That's right," she said. "Because *my* kids are more important to me right now. But I'm not the one trying to make some noble cause out of the whole thing—all that compassion and concern for those kids, while you were waiting for time to pass so you wouldn't go down with them!"

"No one but Bill is going down, Maria!" Beth bit out through her teeth. "We're not guilty! We didn't do any of it of our own free will. We were just kids."

"I was old enough to be a mother, Beth!"

"But we didn't have a choice! We were wards of the state. They put us in his care. It's *their* fault, not ours."

"Right," Maria said. "Just don't say that to a jury. When you start blaming other people for your own sins, they lose sympathy real fast. We knew that what we were doing was wrong."

Tears came to Beth's eyes, and her face was crimson as she took a step toward her old roommate. "What could we have done?"

"We could have run away," she said. "Or we could have turned him in then."

"He had us brainwashed! He wanted us to think that we would all go to jail. He *still* has us brainwashed!"

"Maybe so," Maria said. "I heard it from the time I was eight years old—that I'd be the one to go to jail, not him. I'm still hearing it. And if it's true, if any part of it is true, Beth, I can't even think about it, statute of limitations or not. I have two babies who need their mother, and I don't want them to grow up knowing I was a thief."

Beth just watched as Maria headed back to her old car. As the car drove off, she sat back down on the bench and stared ahead of her.

Maria was right. It was cowardly to expect her friend to talk, when Beth wouldn't talk herself. What kind of friend was she, anyway?

The hot breeze feathered through her hair, making little wisps stick to her face. What did God think of her, looking down from his throne that seemed so far away? Did he give her any points at all for deciding to go after Bill? Or would some of the points be taken away because she'd waited three years? Would she be docked more points for hesitating to come forward herself?

He must understand that the mere admission that she had been one of Bill's kids would immediately make people presume her guilt—not just in those crimes, but in others. She had once been branded *abandoned, orphaned, trash*—she had outgrown those labels, had overcome them. She didn't want to be known as a thief now.

Maybe she should have left town when she'd left Bill's home—gone somewhere she'd have been free to start over without constant reminders of Bill's presence nearby. But she'd spent her senior year of high school filling out forms for financial aid at St. Clair University, and when the loans and grants had been approved, it had seemed silly to go elsewhere. Now she was bound to St. Clair until she graduated, no matter how she wished she could relocate to someplace where she'd never fear Bill Brandon or think of him again.

It was too late now. She had to think of the children.

And she had to give Phil something he couldn't deny.

She got up from the bench and squinted against the sun in the direction Maria had gone. She had a decision to make. A big one. She only hoped that she had the guts to make the right one.

CHAPTER TWENTY-TWO

So you were a real pilot? The kind that flies those big planes with hundreds of people on them?" Jimmy asked as he and Jake and Lynda strolled across the tarmac to the Cessna they had rented for the afternoon.

"That's right," Jake said. "A commercial pilot. I thought I was hot stuff."

"You were!" Jimmy cried. "Go to all those cool places, whenever you wanted, and all those people trusted you—"

"And the money," Jake said, winking at Lynda. "Don't forget the money. For a bachelor with no responsibilities, I made pretty good. I was real proud of myself."

Jimmy sighed. "I wish I could learn to fly. I'd fly me and Lisa to Brazil or somewhere far away. We'd have it made."

Lynda smiled as they reached the plane. "Look, Jimmy," she said. "See over there, on Runway 3?"

"Yeah," he said.

"That's where we crashed when our landing gear wouldn't drop."

"Right there?" Jimmy asked. "You really crashed?"

"We were trying to land."

Jimmy gazed out at the runway. "Wow," he said, awestruck. "You almost died right there."

"In a way, I did die," Jake said. "But you know what? That crash was the best thing that ever happened to me."

"Yeah, right."

"No, really. That was when I learned that God's in control of my life, not me. And once I knew that, I really started to live."

Jimmy breathed a laugh that sounded much too cynical for a boy his age. "God's not in control of *my* life. Bill is."

"Not anymore, he's not," Lynda said.

"You watch. He'll get me back, some way. And he'll make me and my sister pay."

Lynda bent down until her face was even with his. He was so small for his age, and his Opie-like expression belied the experiences he'd had. "Jimmy, I know this is easier said than done, but I want you to trust Beth and the others working on this."

But the expression that crossed his face was just the opposite of trust, and he turned away from her to peer out at Runway 3 again. "My mom said that to me once. To trust her." He didn't cry, but the tough look on his face had an amazingly fragile quality. "Are we gonna fly or what?"

Lynda looked at Jake, and silently they agreed to back off.

"All aboard," Jake said, and climbed onto the wing. Bending over, he pulled Jimmy up behind him. "Get ready, Jimmy Westin, to experience the ride of your life."

CHAPTER TWENTY-THREE

Nick sat over the books and files on his desk, trying to find a loophole in the law that would allow him to get Lisa out of the children's home immediately so that he could satisfy Jimmy's—and his own—fears. But there was nothing. Nick's suspicions were unproven, and today's inspection had been fine, even though he'd known that Bill was tap-dancing to cover the fact that all of the children weren't accounted for.

To all outward appearances, SCCH seemed to offer the children a loving, compassionate environment. Taking the kids swimming, to the library, to birthday parties—it was all very impressive, if one didn't know better.

He got up and pulled Jimmy and Lisa's files out of the file cabinet, hoping to find some forgotten aspect of their situation that would offer him some reason to pull her out. He flipped through the file and saw a picture of the two kids. Jimmy a couple of years ago, and his little sister—

It was her. The little girl in the picture was the same one Bill had put into the car to take to the birthday party. She had looked pale, almost afraid. She was shy, Bill had said.

But that was Lisa—and if Jimmy was right, Bill was already taking his anger out on her. No wonder she'd been frightened.

He rubbed his eyes with the heels of his hands. How could he have stood there and not realized that it was her? He had placed them in SCCH, after all. But she'd been three years younger then, and her hair had been short and sparse—she'd been malnourished.

No wonder he hadn't recognized her. They had driven her off right under his nose.

He grabbed his keys off the desk and rushed back out to the truck. He had to go back. He had to see if Lisa was back yet or if they were still claiming she was at the party. He had to make sure she was okay. If something had happened to her today, he would never forgive himself.

And Jimmy and Beth would never forgive him, either.

CHAPTER TWENTY-FOUR

Bill Brandon was getting angry with him, but Nick didn't care. Bill glared at him from across the lawn as Nick walked toward Cottage B, where he had learned Lisa was assigned. Some children were playing in a playground behind the cottage, and the required number of adults were on hand to supervise. He walked to the fence and scanned the faces.

Stella, the woman who had spirited Lisa off earlier, was sitting in a lawn chair watching the children. She looked up at him as he approached the fence. "Business sure must be slow at HRS, to warrant this much attention from you in one day."

"I thought I might have left something here," he said. "I can't find my favorite pen. It was a Mont Blanc that I got as a gift. You didn't happen to find it, did you?" Actually, he really *had* been given one as a college graduation gift, and it had been lost—for over two years.

"Nope. Sorry."

"So how was that birthday party?" he asked, his eyes still sweeping across the children, looking for Lisa.

"Fine," she said. Her tone was defensive, questioning.

He spotted Lisa now, sitting alone in a corner of the fenced area, leaning her head against one of the posts and peering out to the street, as if watching for someone. Was she looking for Jimmy?

"I was thinking I might have dropped my pen over there," he said, pointing to the area where Lisa was sitting. "Mind if I check?"

She got up then, and looked back over his shoulder. Bill was approaching him from behind.

"Nick, I know you're supposed to do surprise inspections," Bill Brandon said as he got closer, "but don't you think two in one day is a little ridiculous?"

"He left something," Stella said. "A pen."

"A Mont Blanc. I wanted to look around and see if I could find it." As he spoke, he started walking around the fence to where Lisa sat. "I was thinking that I might have dropped it when I came out here—"

Lisa looked up at him as he drew closer. He looked down at her legs and arms, searching for some sign of a bruise or scrape, any indication that she may have been beaten or abused.

Bill was right on his heels, trying to distract him from her. "If you'd dropped it, I'm sure we would have found it by now. If it turns up, we'll call."

Nick bent over the fence. "But I was right over here, and I may have bent over. It could have fallen out of my pocket." He pretended to look on the ground around the fence, then acted surprised as his eyes collided with Lisa's. "Hey, you're the little girl who went to the birthday party. What was your name again?"

She started to answer, but Bill interrupted. "Susan. Her name's Susan."

"Hi, Susan," Nick said. "How was that party?"

Lisa had the same pale, wide eyes as Jimmy. "Fine."

"Good. I love birthday parties. Did you have cake and ice cream?"

She glanced up at Bill, waiting for him to prompt her. Nick couldn't see him, since Bill stood behind him, but he must have signaled for her to say yes. She nodded.

There was no point in pushing it. He was obviously making Lisa uncomfortable. She was here, and she wasn't hurt—at least not that he could see.

Frustrated, he turned and started back toward his car. Bill followed. "Call if you find it, will you? It's a valuable pen. I hate to think I lost it."

"Sure. I'll call," Bill said suspiciously.

Nick headed back around the fence, his eyes scanning the other children, reading their expressions—

He froze as he saw Chris and Matt, the two little boys he'd placed in the Millers' home just last night. They sat huddled together in a corner of the yard, watching the other children with wan, miserable faces.

Nick swung back toward Bill. "Those two boys over there. When did you get them?"

Bill glanced over at them. "They're temporaries. Sheila Axelrod brought them this afternoon."

"Sheila?" Nick asked. "But I put them in a foster home last night."

"Take it up with her, Nick. She brought them to us, and we took them in."

He turned back toward the two boys, fighting the urge to leap over the fence and tell them that he hadn't meant for this to happen. The older boy, Chris, caught his gaze, and his face hardened. He muttered something to his little brother, and they both glared at him.

They think I betrayed them.

With an aching heart, Nick got back into his car and drove away.

But before he'd gone two miles, he pulled over and tried to decide what to do now. Bill and his employees were onto him. Maybe that was good. They wouldn't hurt Lisa as long as they knew he was watching. And maybe they wouldn't hurt Chris or Matt.

But that wasn't good enough. He had to get them all out.

He leaned back on the headrest and looked up at the ceiling. His eyes misted as angry sorrow rose within him. "Lord, you've got to help me. Right now I'm so mad at Sheila Axelrod I could strangle her. How could she have put those two boys there? And why? They were fine with the Millers."

He wrapped his arms around the steering wheel and rested his forehead on them. "This is too much for me," he said. "I can't handle it—without you."

A turbulent peace fell over him—peace that fighting for the kids was the right thing to do, but turbulent because he couldn't rest. God wasn't going to take that anger away from him, not yet. Maybe he was supposed to use it.

He pulled his car back out into traffic and headed to the HRS building. Sheila's car was there, and as he got out, his rage escalated.

She was at her desk, talking on the telephone. She looked up as he entered, and he strode toward her and bent over her desk. "Want to tell me what's going on with the kids I placed last night?"

She rolled her eyes. "Let me call you back, okay?" she said into the phone. She hung up and looked up at Nick, unintimidated. "You got a problem?"

"Yeah. Those kids were welcome in the Millers' home. Why did you take them out?"

"Because the Millers weren't ready for three kids. They still have the baby."

Nick's teeth came together. "I didn't want those kids in SCCH, and you know it."

"And I told you that we're not going to quit placing children there just because you don't like Bill Brandon. I am the supervisor of this office, and I have the final word. If you can't live with that, Nick, you know where the door is."

"And where would that leave you, Sheila? You can't handle this office alone."

"Watch me."

They stared each other down for a long moment. Nick thought of quitting, of insulting her, of reaching across the desk and throttling her. But if he resigned, he couldn't help Beth; he could do nothing for the kids. Working from the inside, he could help bring Bill Brandon down. When Beth's story hit the streets, Sheila would understand.

He straightened and massaged his temples. He was getting a headache. "Sheila, those kids were scared to death. The Millers were nurturing. They made them feel protected."

"It's not my job to make them feel protected, Nick. It's my job to make sure they have a secure place to stay for as long as they're wards of the state."

"It's not just about paperwork, Sheila!"

She laughed bitterly as she got up. "Don't tell me about paperwork, Nick. I've been at this longer than you've been an adult. I've seen cases that would curl your hair."

"You've seen too many," Nick said. "You've lost your compassion."

"Well, maybe it wouldn't hurt for you to do the same. That compassion will kill you, Nick. It'll turn your hair gray and keep you awake nights. And for what? For the peanuts the state pays us?"

"Then why are you still here?"

"Because this is what I was trained to do, and in case you haven't noticed, jobs aren't easy to come by in this state. After a while, you stop worrying. You stop losing sleep. Those things don't help the kids anyway—they just make you miserable. You find ways to stretch a dollar, or you supplement your income selling catalog makeup or magazine subscriptions. And you go on. You do the job, because you're the only one here to do it."

"There's got to be more to it than that, Sheila," Nick said. "I came into this because I believed it was a calling from God."

"Right," she said on a laugh. "Let me tell you something, Nick. If there were a God, there wouldn't be a need for social workers."

Nick's anger faded as he realized how little Sheila understood. "Maybe we *are* the way God's solving the problem. Maybe you and I are like angels to these miserable, abused children."

She snorted. "Yeah, well, I lost my halo a long time ago." She dropped back into her chair and picked up the phone. "This conversation is wearing me out, Nick. And I have about a million phone calls to return."

He watched as she dialed a number and began talking, ignoring him. His anger was gone, but in its place was a sad frustration, so deep that he didn't know how to combat it. Breathing out a defeated sigh, he headed out of the building and got back into his car.

There was nothing he could do for Matt and Chris right now. But there had to be something he could do for Lisa.

He pulled her file out of his briefcase. He hadn't finished studying it earlier. Now he flipped through the many forms that had been filled out to make Lisa and Jimmy wards of the state. Someone else—one of his coworkers who had long ago quit for a less stressful job—had removed them from the home. Then Nick had taken over the case, moving them from temporary foster care into SCCH, so he had never really studied their past.

They were not orphans. The forms revealed that the original social worker had been unable to locate their father. But they still had a mother.

He read intently about the woman who had voluntarily abandoned her children to the state.

Her name was Tracy, and she'd been twenty-five years old at the time. HRS had received reports of neglect, investigated, and found that she was a heavy drug abuser. Shortly after the investigation began, she had left the children, ages four and seven then, home alone for two days while she reveled in an ecstasy binge. The state had taken the children.

Nick ached for the pain those kids must have endured. He sat back in his seat. What would make a mother have such disregard for her children? That precocious little boy, that beautiful little girl—no wonder Jimmy distrusted adults. After a history of abandonment and neglect, Nick—who should have gotten things right—had dumped him from the frying pan into the fire. How many other times had he made the same mistake?

He closed his eyes and leaned his head back against his headrest. Where was that mother now? The papers said she was a resident of St. Clair, but she could have moved on since then. He wondered if her life was still controlled by drug abuse.

He closed his eyes and tried to think. He couldn't get any of the kids out of the home on his own, not until Bill was exposed tomorrow and charges filed. And plenty of things could go wrong. The state could get caught in a mire of bureaucracy and fail to act immediately. That could be a fatal mistake, because as soon as Bill Brandon read Jimmy's quotes in the article, he would be sure to take his vengeance out on Lisa.

Unless . . .

It was a long shot, but—he could at least *try* to track down their mother.

CHAPTER TWENTY-FIVE

Beth spent the afternoon writing the story of a little girl neglected and abused, then placed in what was considered the nicest, most stable home in the state. She wrote of how that child was forcefully recruited into a crime ring at the age of eight, how she was taught to pick locks, slip into small openings in windows, crawl into homes through crawl spaces with garage entrances. She told how the girl learned to unlock jewelry boxes, search for cash, unhook VCRs, TVs, computers. She explained how she had worked for hours each night in her young life of crime, only to fall asleep in class the next day and suffer punishment at the hands of teachers and principals—and then again from Bill Brandon on returning home. And she told of the "tapes" that still played in her mind, tapes of Brandon's voice telling her that *she* was the thief, not he, that she had the dirty hands, that if she ever told this story, she would have to fear not only prison, but death at his vicious hands.

The sun was low in the sky behind the trees when she finished. Just writing this anonymous confession had exhausted her. And it might not even be enough. Phil would want substantiation. He would want a name, and she wasn't ready to give hers.

Drained and depressed, she called her editor. He sounded rushed as he answered. "Yeah, Beth. What's up?"

"Phil, it's about the article. I've finished it, but—"

"But what?"

"But the other source I got. It's anonymous. It's a woman who used to live in Brandon's home and worked in his crime ring . . . but she doesn't want me to use her name."

"You realize, don't you, that we're making some fierce allegations here? If we intend to accuse an upstanding citizen of charges this serious, we have to be prepared to defend them in court, Beth. I can't take the chance of getting the paper sued, because we made allegations that we can't back up."

"We *can* back them up, Phil. It's not my fault that Marlene was murdered, and that Jimmy is a little boy."

"I know that. But you're putting me between a rock and a hard place here."

She slammed her hand on the table, waking Dodger who slept at her feet. "Phil, someone's going to get hurt if we wait! Bill Brandon already knows I'm working on the story. He's going to do everything he can to stop me. The longer we put off printing this story, the more danger I'm in, and the more danger those kids are in."

"You're asking me to ignore my legal counsel."

"I'm asking you to have a little courage, Phil. Get some guts, for heaven's sake!"

He hesitated. "Beth, are you sure that you've gotten the facts right? Are you positive?"

"Phil, I'd stake my life on it. In fact, that's exactly what I'm doing."

She could tell from his sigh that she'd made her point. "All right. Send the story in, and I'll take a look."

She closed her eyes. "Do more than take a look, Phil. Please. This could be the biggest story of the year."

"Sure, it could. It could win you an award. We could also get our pants sued off."

"Forget the awards, Phil. Don't even give me a byline. I don't care. Just print it."

"I'll read it, Beth. We'll see."

"Call me as soon as you decide," she said.

"I will."

She hung up and rested her face in her hands. She'd done her part. Now, if Phil printed the story, her career—even her life—might be ruined. Or Bill might decide to go out in a blazing act of vengeance, and come after her.

She just hoped God hadn't forgotten to record this in her scorebook.

ick found the woman's apartment building, an old structure with peeling paint, busted-out windows, and trash and old furniture on the front lawn. He found it hard to believe that people lived here; it looked as if it should be torn down.

A toddler played at the bottom of a staircase, wearing nothing but a filthy diaper. As Nick walked from his car across the lawn, he looked for some sign of an adult nearby. Seeing none, he leaned down, hands on knees, and smiled at the child. The baby's face was dirty and sticky, and his nose was runny. He smiled back and reached up to hand Nick a cigarette butt that he'd, no doubt, picked up from the clutter at his feet. His fingers were crusted with filth.

"Hi there." Nick took the butt. "Where's your mommy?"

"Who wants to know?" a hoarse voice said from behind the broken staircase.

Taking a couple of steps, Nick peered around the staircase and saw a girl of no more than fifteen sitting on a cracked slab of concrete, smoking a cigarette. "Hi," Nick said. "I didn't see you there. I thought the baby was out here alone."

"What's it to you?"

He shrugged. "Just worried me, that's all. There are a lot of things around here that could hurt him."

"So what do you want, anyway?" the girl demanded.

"Uh . . ." He looked back down at the dirty toddler. His instinct was to scoop the baby up and take it away to a place where it would be cared for. But he reminded himself, as he had to several times a day, that not every child was his responsibility, and that things weren't always as bad as they seemed. "I was looking for a woman named Tracy Westin. I think she lives upstairs. Do you know her?"

"Yeah, I know her."

"Is she home?"

"I haven't seen her come out."

He looked up the broken staircase. "So she's in that apartment up there?"

"Give the man an award."

Annoyed, Nick started to respond in kind—and then realized that she was, herself, a child, unable to handle the weight of hopelessness that so obviously held her down.

He looked at the baby again, then back at the girl. Sister? Mother? One could never tell. He only hoped that she was a better caretaker than his first impression suggested. He could only hope that she *had* a better caretaker for herself.

He went up the staircase, stepping over the broken steps. A garbage bag with trash spilling out of a gnawed-out hole sat at the top of the steps, and a cat prowled in the refuse. He stepped over it, ignoring the stench, and knocked on the door.

For a moment, he heard nothing, and almost turned to go. Then he heard a voice.

He pressed his ear to the door and knocked again. He heard the voice again, but couldn't make out the words.

He checked the doorknob—unlocked. Slowly, he opened the door.

The apartment was dark and filthy. He stepped inside and looked around. There was little furniture except for an old torn-up card table in the kitchenette, covered, as was the kitchen counter, by dishes piled on dishes, old crud dried on them. There was a mattress in the far corner of the cluttered room.

On the mattress was a woman in shorts and a dirty tank top, curled up in a fetal position, shivering. Her hair was long and red, tangled and matted. He stepped toward her. "Tracy?"

She didn't answer.

"Tracy?" he tried again.

She still didn't respond, so he stepped over the clothes lying on the floor, the sandals, the wadded sheets that had been kicked off the mattress. She looked tiny, anorexic, no more than eighty pounds. And she was sick—that was clear. He knelt beside her and reached out to touch her forehead. It was alarmingly hot.

"Tracy, can you hear me?"

Her eyes, glassy from the fever, focused on him for a second, and she moaned, "Help me."

He wasn't sure if this was drug withdrawal or a real illness, but either way she needed to be in a hospital. He looked around. "Do you have a phone?"

"No," she whispered.

He thought of rushing off to find a pay phone and call an ambulance, but decided that she would get help more quickly if he took her himself. "Tracy, can you get up?"

She only closed her eyes.

"All right," he said. "I'll pick you up. I'm going to carry you out to my car and get you to the hospital, okay?"

No answer.

He scooped her up, surprised at how light she was in his arms. She probably hadn't eaten in days—maybe even weeks. He wondered how long she had been like this.

He carried her out, stepping back over the reeking garbage, and carefully made his way down the stairs. The girl with the baby was still sitting there. She watched him blankly as he carried Tracy out.

"Can you tell me how long Tracy's been sick?" he asked her.

"Do I look like her mother?" the girl responded.

"When's the last time you saw her?"

"I don't know," she said, putting her cigarette out on the concrete. "A week maybe."

"Was she sick then?"

"How should I know?"

Frustrated, he hurried her to his car and laid her in the back seat. She curled back up in a little ball as he jumped into the front, turned on his lights, and drove away.

CHAPTER TWENTY-SEVEN

Beth dove for the phone. "Hello?"

"Beth, it's Phil."

She closed her eyes, bracing herself. "Phil, tell me you're going to print the article. Please. I don't think I can handle it—"

"Relax, I'm printing it. It was great, Beth. Thank your anonymous source for me."

"Then it'll be in tomorrow's paper?"

"Absolutely."

"Yes!" she said, punching the air. "Thank you, Phil. You may have saved my life."

"I wish you didn't mean that literally, but I guess you do."

"You bet I do. Listen, Phil, I know you're not going to go for this, but I'd like to give a copy of the story to the police department tonight."

"No! That's too soon!" he said. "That's our story. I don't want every other newspaper in the area getting it before we do, and that's exactly what will happen if you give it to the police. You know better than that."

"I don't care about being scooped anymore, Phil. Jimmy's little sister is still in that home, and so are a lot of other innocent victims. Not to mention the fact that Bill Brandon is after me. I want him locked up. Now."

He moaned. "All right, Beth. Maybe the other papers still won't get the whole story. Or maybe the police won't act quickly."

"They will. They have to."

He hesitated, and Beth knew that all his editor's instincts told him not to risk losing the scoop. "All right. Do what you have to do."

"I will."

She hung up and immediately clicked her mouse on the "print" button. Watching as the article slid out of her printer, she picked up the phone to call Nick and tell him the good news, but she only got his machine.

She grabbed the printed article, folded it in half, and headed for the door. Dodger was right behind her, begging to go out. She picked him up, clipped on his leash, and put him back down. He scurried out the door the second she opened it and made a puddle on her doorstep.

"Good boy!" she said, petting him. "You're getting the hang of this, aren't you?" When he was finished, she hurried him back into the house.

The sun was setting as she headed to the police station, hoping those two detectives, Larry and Tony, would be there. She wanted to make sure this didn't fall through the cracks.

Larry was on his way out as she came in, and she grabbed his arm and stopped him. "Detective Millsaps?"

He looked down at her, and she could tell that he couldn't place her.

"Beth Wright. You were at my house last night, remember?"

"Oh, yeah," he said. "Nick Hutchins's friend."

"Right. Listen, I need to talk to you about something really important. Do you have a minute?"

He checked his watch. "Yeah, I can give you a few minutes."

He led her back through the maze of desks in the noisy room, and offered a chair in front of his desk. Plopping into his own chair, he asked, "So what's up? Did you hear something in your house again?"

"Yes, I did, as a matter of fact. And I found the culprit. It was a ten-year-old boy."

"A ten-year-old boy?"

"Yes. And Bill Brandon, the man who runs the home where this little boy lives, is the one who forced him to break into my house so that he could find and destroy any evidence I had against him."

"Oh, that's right," Larry said. "You were working on a story about him." He pulled a pen out of his drawer and began to take notes. "You're sure he was behind it?"

"Positive." She handed him the article. "The boy is still with us—Nick knows all about it. Don't you think it's odd that a child is missing from the St. Clair Children's Home and no one there has reported it?"

"Well, yeah . . ."

"Read the article," she said, sitting back and crossing her arms. "I'll wait."

She watched as he read the article, skimming at first, then settling in as a wrinkle of concentration and concern gradually deepened across his forehead. When he'd finished, he looked up at her and rubbed his hand across the stubble around his mouth. "That's some article."

"It's all true."

"So let me see if I got all this. Brandon has a crime ring that might explain dozens of break-ins in St. Clair over the last several years. He's abusing these kids. He probably murdered his sister to keep her quiet. And he ran you off the road—"

"Tried to," she cut in.

"Tried to run you off the road." He shook his head and looked up as he saw Tony hurrying through. "Hey, Tony. Come here."

Tony seemed a little distracted as he headed toward them.

"You got to read this," he said. "It's coming out tomorrow in the *St. Clair News.*"

They both watched as Tony read. As his interest in the article increased, he dropped the sport coat he'd been holding by one finger over his shoulder. "This is bad."

"Then you'll do something about it? Tonight?" Beth asked.

Tony glanced at Larry. "What do you think?"

"Well, we'll have to talk to the kid first . . ."

"Where is he now?" Tony asked.

"With some friends of mine," Beth said. "Lynda Barrett and Jake Stevens."

"Yeah, we know them. We'll head over there and interview him right now."

115

"He's scared to death that something will happen to his sister if an arrest isn't made soon. I think he has reason to be."

"I think *you* have reason to be, if what you're saying is true." She stared at them. "Why would I lie?"

"I'm not suggesting you are," Larry said. "But we have to have more substantial proof than a newspaper article and the word of a little boy who got caught breaking the law. Kids have been known to lie their way out of tight spots."

"He isn't lying! Check the dents on my car! Check out Bill Brandon's alibi the night his sister was murdered! You think it was a coincidence that Jimmy broke into *my* house when I was working on a story about Bill?"

"We're going to check it all out, Beth," Tony said. "We aren't doubting you. We're just doing our job. Now, do you think Nick is up to placing all those kids when we arrest Brandon and take the rest of his staff in for questioning?"

"He's been ready."

"None of us may get any sleep tonight," Larry said.

Tony reached for the phone. "I'll call Sharon and cancel our date tonight."

"Yeah, I'd better call Melissa, too. Beth, if I were you, I'd wait at Lynda's until you hear from us. It's safe there. We can follow you over right now."

"All right," she said. "But you'll call me when you've got him?"

"Sure thing. Come on, Tony, we've got to get all this done so we can catch Judge Wyatt to get a warrant before he leaves for the day."

Tony shrugged on his blazer to conceal his gun. "He's the presiding judge in town," he told her. "This is worth going straight to the top."

As they hurried out ahead of her, she felt a huge weight drop from her shoulders. At last, her case was in good hands.

CHAPTER TWENTY-EIGHT

Nick knew all of the emergency room doctors and nurses, because he was called here frequently when injuries to youngsters suggested the possibility of child abuse. As soon as he'd brought Tracy in and told them how he'd found her, they'd rushed her back, intent on finding the reason for her illness. She was in good hands.

While he waited, he went to the pay phone and tried to call Beth. Her machine answered, so he left a message, hung up, and dialed his own number. Beth had left a message that she had gotten approval from the paper, that the story would be out tomorrow, and that she was giving it to the police so they could arrest Bill Brandon tonight.

He grinned and hung up, then dropped into a chair. Part of him wanted to relax, but the other part knew that he needed to be at the office finding qualified foster parents to stay with the kids tonight. He had already thought this through and decided that, instead of scattering them all over the state in private homes, it would be better, at least for the next few days, to get couples to come replace SCCH's employees so the children could stay where they were. That would be less traumatic for the kids, and less work for Sheila and him.

The emergency room physician, a guy he'd played racquetball with a few times, came out and scanned the faces in the waiting room, spotted Nick, and came to take the chair at right angles to his.

"So what is it?" Nick asked. "Drugs?"

"Actually, no. No drugs in her bloodstream at all. What your friend has is probably the worst case of double pneumonia I've ever seen."

"Pneumonia? This time of year?"

"Yeah. She's in bad shape, Nick. She may not pull through. We're admitting her into intensive care right now. Can you fill out the paperwork? Give us her insurance company, that sort of thing?"

He shook his head. "I don't know anything about her other than her name. And I seriously doubt that she has insurance. Judging from the place she lives, I'd say she's indigent. That's why I brought her here."

It was a charity hospital, so he had known that they wouldn't turn her away.

"All right. We'll take care of things," the doctor said. "Do you know if she has any next of kin?"

He thought of Jimmy and Lisa. "She has two kids that were taken away from her. They're seven and ten."

"Any adults?"

"I couldn't tell you."

The doctor suddenly looked very tired. "I'll level with you, Nick. If you hadn't brought her in here when you did, that girl wouldn't have lasted through the night. I hate to see a person that near death, without a person in the world who cares about her."

Nick rubbed his weary eyes. "Yeah, me too."

The doctor slapped his knee and got up. "We've got her on an IV, and we're starting a round of serious antibiotics. ICU doesn't allow nonfamily members to visit, but I'll pull some strings if you want to come back and see her tonight."

He nodded. "Yeah, I'll do that."

"Thanks for bringing her in, man."

Nick checked his watch as he headed out of the emergency room. He wondered if Bill Brandon had been arrested yet—and if Beth was safe.

Walking out into the night, he looked up at the stars spread by the millions across the sky like a paint-spattered canopy. God had been with him today. "Thank you," he whispered, grateful that the Holy Spirit had prompted him to find Tracy, just in the nick of time. There must have been a reason.

It wasn't all hopeless. There was a plan. There were times when Nick *did* act as an angel to a dying world. That realization gave him the energy to keep going tonight.

And he knew he wasn't working alone.

CHAPTER TWENTY-NINE

I can't give you a warrant for Bill Brandon's arrest." Judge Wyatt said the words with such finality as he packed his briefcase that Tony and Larry only stared at him.

"Excuse me, Judge, but did you say you *can't?*" Tony asked.

"No, I can't! Not on such outlandish charges with absolutely nothing to support them."

Larry touched Tony's arm to quiet him, and tried again. "Judge, maybe we didn't make ourselves clear. There's the account given by the boy from the home who was caught breaking into this reporter's house. We just talked to him ourselves. The reporter has another source who used to live in Brandon's home, who corroborated that story. And Marlene Brandon, Bill Brandon's sister, was murdered right after she talked to the reporter. We've been in touch with the Tampa PD, and the only ones backing up Brandon's alibi are his employees, who could also be involved."

"I read the article, gentlemen," the elderly judge said. "But I'm not issuing a warrant for anybody's arrest based on some trumped-up charges by a newspaper that won't print anything unless it's painted yellow!"

"Your honor," Tony tried, hoping a little more respect might calm things a bit, "this isn't yellow journalism. This article matches the facts we do have. We have a lot of unexplained break-ins. Kids have been seen in some of the areas before or after a crime was committed. We have small unidentifiable fingerprints at the scene of some of these crimes. We didn't pursue that angle very hard in our previous investigations of the robberies because it seemed so farfetched. But if this is a professional crime ring—"

"Then where are they keeping the stolen goods?" the judge demanded. "Where are they selling it? Have you gotten down to that, yet?"

"Well, no, not yet. But—"

"Then how do you expect me to give you a warrant for this man's arrest? This is pretty shoddy police work, gentlemen. And I'm not going to wind up with egg on my face when it comes out that a decent, upstanding citizen who provides a good home to so many children was wrongly arrested because of some cockamamie story by an overzealous reporter trying to make a name for herself! Until you come up with something I can see, something other than a kid with a strong imagination who's trying to get himself out of trouble, don't waste my time with this again."

"Judge, you can't be serious—"

"Good-bye, detectives," he said, grabbing up his briefcase and ushering them out. "I have a meeting in twenty minutes, and I don't intend to be late."

"Judge Wyatt, you're acting irresponsibly here!" Tony cried.

The judge swung around. "What did you say?"

Tony's face was red. "I said, you're acting irresponsibly. Children's lives are at stake, for Pete's sake."

"If you don't get off these premises in the next three seconds, detectives, I'll call my bailiff and have you thrown into jail yourselves."

Tony and Larry stood there, stunned, as the judge headed out of the office without another word.

"Great going," Larry bit out. "He's right. We shouldn't have been in such a hurry. We should have gotten more evidence before we came here."

"Then let's go get it now," Tony said. "Time is running out for those kids."

CHAPTER THIRTY

B ill Brandon thanked his source for the tip, hung up his phone, and stared down at his desk for a moment. So the article was scheduled to come out in tomorrow's newspaper. Beth Sullivan—alias Beth Wright, he thought with amusement—actually thought she was going to expose him. But she was so wrong.

He picked up the phone again and dialed the extension for Cottage B. One of the children answered. "Put Stella on the phone," he ordered. He waited a few seconds, then the house-mother answered.

"Stella, send the team over for me, pronto. We have a job to do. Oh, and include Lisa Westin."

He went to the closet and pulled the rolled-up blueprints off the top shelf. There was one for City Hall, one for the Police Station, one for the courthouse, one for the St. Clair First National Bank . . . He pulled them out one by one, until he came to the one for the building housing the *St. Clair News*. He put the others back carefully, then went to his desk and opened the blueprint, spreading it out across his desk.

There it was: all of the rooms at the *St. Clair News*, carefully labeled with their purposes and the machinery housed there. His sources were nothing if not thorough.

A knock sounded on the door, and he called, "Come in."

Brad, an eleven-year-old he'd been grooming for the last four years, opened the door. "Bill, you called for us?"

"Yeah, guys, come on in."

Seven boys and four girls, ranging in age from eight to fifteen, filed in quietly and found places around the room. Tailing the group was little Lisa Westin, her big green eyes looking frightened and apprehensive as she stepped into his office.

"What's she doing here?" Brad asked with contempt. "She's too little."

"She's taking Jimmy's place," Bill explained.

"Any word on Jimmy?" Brad asked.

"No. And things don't look good for him."

Bill knew that would give them all images of the child rotting in a jail cell. Enough incentive to keep them from messing things up.

He glanced at Lisa and saw that those big eyes were full of tears. "Lisa's already done one job for me, and she did such a good job that I thought I'd reward her by giving her a little more responsibility."

She didn't look all that proud.

"And she knows that if she botches anything up, Jimmy will be in even worse shape than he is now. You all know I can get to him if I have a point to make. There's not a lock made, even in a jail cell, that I can't open. You know that if you mess up, Lisa, that Jimmy will pay for it, don't you? That's how it works."

She swallowed and nodded her head.

He turned his attention back to the others. "It's come to my attention, people, that there's supposed to be a newspaper article coming out about us in the paper tomorrow. It will point fingers at each of you, exposing you as thieves, and will probably result in the police arresting all of you before daylight."

There was a collective gasp all over the room.

"Bill, what are we gonna do?"

"I don't want to go to jail!"

"Can't you tell them we're not thieves?"

Bill sat back and shrugged. "Wouldn't do any good. They have proof. Some of you have been seen, but that's not the worst of it. Jimmy Westin has turned state's evidence."

"What's that?" Brad asked.

"He's told them everything he knows about our operation."

"No! He wouldn't."

"*Au contraire.*" He chuckled in his sinister way, and met the eyes of each individual kid around the room. Satisfied that he had put sufficient fear in them to manipulate them into doing anything, he smiled. "But don't worry. Bill is going to take care of you. Doesn't he always?"

A few of them nodded.

"I've got a plan. But it's going to require a lot of hard work and a few risks. Somebody might even have to get hurt. But sometimes sacrifices have to be made. As the Good Book says, 'Greater courage hath no man, than to lay down a life for his cause.'"

The children all gazed somberly at him. He had them right where he wanted them.

"Oh, don't worry. I'm not asking any of *you* to lay down your lives. I just want that kind of commitment to this project—that you would if it came to it, which it won't. No, it's not your lives that'll be in danger. But the people in the building . . . well, some things are just in God's hands."

He looked down at the blueprint. "This, my friends, is the blueprint for the newspaper offices. In this big room, here at the back, is the printing press that puts out every copy of the newspaper that will be distributed all over town the first thing in the morning. Your job, should you decide to accept it," he said, drawing on the *Mission Impossible* theme, even though he knew they didn't have the option of refusing it, "is to stop the presses. Literally. That way, the story won't come out, and you won't be arrested."

Some of the kids let out huge breaths of relief, and Bill smiled and said, "I told you I'd take care of things, didn't I? Now, come on over here and get around the desk, so I can show each of you what your job will be. We've still got a few hours before we need to go. That gives us plenty of time to plan every move."

CHAPTER THIRTY-ONE

The waiting room for the family members of those in the Intensive Care Unit was full of rumpled, tired people with lines on their faces and worry in their eyes. Beth followed Nick past the reception desk, where a woman stood consoling a family whose loved one had just been in a car accident. On the desk were two stacks of towels and a sign that said that toilet articles were available if anyone needed them.

"They take showers up here?" Beth asked quietly.

"Yeah. Many of these people are here twenty-four hours a day. They're afraid to leave."

"But I thought visiting hours were only thirty minutes every four hours."

"Right. They sit by the bedside for thirty minutes, then come back to the waiting room and worry for four hours until the next visit."

"Seems cruel."

"Maybe it is. But those short visiting times are usually in the best interest of the patients. They need quiet."

He led her into the huge room lined with vinyl recliners and chairs. Families had nested in certain areas of the room, surrounded by books and little bags with their belongings, Walkmans, and canned drinks. It was easy to distinguish the family members from occasional visitors. They looked more worn, more stressed, more near the breaking point. In one corner, a woman crocheted an afghan furiously, and already it was big enough to cover her legs. Beth wondered when she'd started it. Across the room, someone else worked on a laptop, and next to her, a red-eyed teenaged girl did cross-stitch as if her life depended on getting every stitch exactly in line.

The five telephones on the wall rang constantly, and they were always answered by one of those nearby. Then they would call out, "Smith family" or "Jackson family," and someone would rush to answer it.

"It's like a little community up here," Beth said.

"Yeah. My dad was in ICU for three weeks before he died. I didn't leave the unit except for meals. I ate those downstairs, and only if I had to. A lot of times, churches brought sandwiches and stuff right here to the waiting room."

"But what's the point in staying? I mean, if you can't visit them . . ."

"It's the fear that something will go wrong. That the doctor will need you to help make a decision. Even the irrational fear that if you leave, if you're not there hanging on, they'll slip away."

"I can't imagine being sick and having someone waiting out here that diligently for me."

"What about your mother?" he asked.

"She's dead." The words came so matter-of-factly that she feared Nick would think she was cold. The truth was, if Beth's mother were alive, she wouldn't have waited in the ICU waiting room for Beth anyway. The deep sadness of that fact washed over her. She was really no different than Tracy Westin, lying in there so sick with no one out here in this room, representing her and praying for her, refusing to leave because they had to stay and fight with her.

"I'm sorry."

She didn't say anything, but watched the dynamics of a family in the corner. "Poor Tracy."

Nick looked at her. "What do you mean?"

"She's all alone."

"We're here."

"Yeah, but she doesn't know us. We don't love her."

"Yes, we do. I love her because I'm a Christian. I'm ordered to love her."

Beth smiled grimly at the irony. She hadn't had much experience with love, but she knew *that* was wrong. "Love isn't something you can be ordered to do, Nick. You have to feel something."

"Love is first something you do, Beth," Nick said. "The feelings are important, yes, but love is a verb, not a noun. We're here to love her because no one else is."

Well, there was something in that. She sat quietly for a moment, looking around the room at all the people so steeped in the act of loving. She wondered what it would be like to have people like that caring for her, waiting hours to see her, not willing to leave for fear that she might need them. She couldn't even fathom it.

The crackle of the intercom quieted the room, and a voice said, "ICU visitation will begin now. The following families may go back: Anderson, Aldredge, Burton . . ." Eventually, they came to the name Westin, and Beth and Nick got up and followed the stream of visitors through the double doors into ICU. As he had promised, the doctor had bent the rules to allow Nick and Beth to visit Tracy.

There were no doorways in ICU, only three-sided rooms open to the nursing station so that the nurses could see and hear the patients at all times. Tracy lay on her bed, sitting up at a forty-five degree angle, with an IV in her hand and an oxygen mask on her face. Several cords ran out from under her sheet and hooked to monitors that kept close watch on her vital signs.

She looked so tiny, so emaciated. Beth hesitated at the foot of the bed, feeling like an intruder in this woman's private hell.

Nick went to her bedside and leaned over her. He looked carefully at her face to see if she was sleeping, but her eyes were half opened. "Tracy? Can you hear me?"

"Don't wake her up," Beth said softly.

"I don't think she's asleep," he said. "Tracy, I'm Nick. The one who found you and brought you here."

She looked up then, and met his eyes. "Thank you," she whispered.

"No problem. They're going to do everything they can for you here. Did they tell you you have double pneumonia? You're in ICU so they can watch you real closely."

She closed her eyes.

Nick looked at Beth, not sure what to do. "My friend here, Beth, knows your son. We thought—"

Her eyes fluttered back open, and she tried to rise up. "Jimmy?" she asked weakly.

"Yes," Beth said, stepping forward. "He's a great kid."

Weakly, she dropped back down. "Haven't seen him in three years. I have a little girl—"

"Lisa?" Nick asked.

Her eyes grew rounder. "You know Lisa?"

"Yes, Tracy. That's why I was coming to see you today. I'm a social worker, and I've taken an interest in your kids."

Tears began to roll down her face. "Are they all right?"

"They're good," he said. "Healthy, smart . . ."

Her face contorted in anguish, and she asked, "Do they hate me?"

Nick looked up at Beth, not sure how to answer that. Beth felt her own eyes filling, which rarely happened. She hated herself when she cried. "I don't think they hate you," she whispered.

"I left them, you know . . ." Her voice broke off, and she closed her eyes and covered her face with a scrawny hand that had the IV needle taped in place. "You should have just let me die."

Something about the heartfelt regret touched Beth in a deep place, a place of wounds that had never fully healed. She turned away, blinking back her tears, *ordering* back her tears. When she turned back to the woman on the bed, her eyes were dry. "We don't want you to die, Tracy."

Nick shook his head. "That's right. God might need you to get well so you can help your kids understand why you did it."

"*I* don't understand why," she said.

Nick leaned closer. "Tracy, are you still addicted?"

"No. Been through treatment . . . three times. Always fell back. But this last time . . . clean for two months."

"Do you work? Do you have a job?"

"No."

"Are you on welfare?"

"No. I was living with my husband . . ."

He looked up at Beth, surprised. "Husband? You're married?"

"Six months. Doomed."

"Where is your husband now?"

"Who knows? Gone. He's worse off than I was."

"Do you mean he was sick, too?"

"He's a junkie." She wiped her tear-streaked face with the hand her IV was taped to. "When I got sick, he took off. Couldn't stand to hear me hacking all the time."

"Why didn't you go to the doctor?"

"No money."

"But you could have gone to the health department."

"Too weak."

"You didn't have anyone to take you? No one?"

"No . . . no one."

The nurse came into the room and told them their visiting time was up, and Nick touched Tracy's hand. "Tracy, we have to go now, but we'll be back. You get better, okay? We're praying for you."

She nodded mutely, her face contorted with sorrow and regret.

As they stepped out into the night, Beth felt anguish gaining on her again, sneaking closer to her breaking point, pulling her under. Nick seemed to sense it. He put his arm across her shoulders and said, "Let's not go to the car just yet."

When she didn't protest, he led her down the cobblestone walkway that led through the hospital's courtyard and around the little pond. Moonlight flickered on the surface of the water, lending a sense of peace and beauty to the world that had so much ugly darkness.

"I think she's remorseful," he said. "I don't always see that."

Beth couldn't answer.

"I just hope she lives. Maybe through some miracle we could reunite the kids with her."

"Don't you think you're jumping the gun a little?" Beth asked quietly.

He shrugged. "Maybe. I guess I'm just a believer in miracles."

Beth reached a bench, sank down, and pulled her feet up to hug her knees. "I believe in miracles, too, Nick. But I've learned that you can't custom order them."

Quiet settled between them as he sat down next to her, watching her face. She couldn't look at him, for those tears were slipping up on her again, threatening her. She looked out over the water, trying to sort out the storm of emotions whirling through her mind. Anger, rage, sorrow, loneliness, rejection, frustration, fear . . .

"We sure have screwed things up, haven't we?"

"Who?" she asked.

"Us. The human race. God gave us families, such a wonderful gift, and we break them into tiny pieces, reject them, throw them away . . ."

"That's it," she whispered, still staring across the water. "Thrown away. That's how those kids feel. And no matter what happens to them, that feeling doesn't quite go away."

"And then there's Tracy."

"Yes. I wonder how Jimmy will feel when we tell him we found his mother."

Nick tried to imagine. "Well, he'll put on a tough-guy act. But deep down, kids love their mothers. Even kids who have been abused and rejected."

"Sometimes there are other things that cover that love so deeply that you can never get back down to it. I don't think we should let him see his mother like that. I don't think we should even tell him we've found her until she's better."

"That's true. Besides, she might die, and then he'd have to grieve for her all over again."

"Again?" she asked, finally looking at him. "I doubt he grieved for her at all. Being taken from her may have been a relief to some extent. And he was probably so hurt, so angry that she left him like that . . . So worried for Lisa . . ."

"He's still worried for Lisa. Like I said, this isn't the kind of thing God ever meant for a kid to have to worry about. Families are supposed to protect each other. Love each other. When I have kids, nothing in heaven or earth could force me to leave them. And the best thing I'll do for them is to love their mother."

A soft, gentle, wistful smile curved her lips. "I believe you could do that." She watched his face as he propped it on his hand and smiled at her. "Tell me about your family, Nick. Did you have a mother and father who loved you? Did you eat at the table at night, all together, talking about your day?"

He gave her a strange look that told her the question had been too revealing. "Yeah, I guess we did. I had four sisters and brothers, and my parents have been married forty-five years. It was a busy household. What about yours?"

Her smile faded and her eyes drifted back to the water. "My household was very busy, too," she said. "But not like yours. You might say I'm one of the pieces my family broke into."

He gazed at her for a moment, and she wondered if it was pity or disdain she saw on his face. Was he measuring her against himself, finding her flawed and scarred? Did he look at potential mates against a measuring stick of broken families and dysfunctional childhoods, as she sometimes did? She had broken a budding relationship recently when she'd discovered that the man had been raised fatherless. She had told herself that she desperately needed someone who had not suffered the battles she had as a child, someone who had more parts to him than she had to her.

Yet she knew it was a double standard, for if others measured her the same way, she would always be alone.

"I wondered where that tough edge came from," he whispered. "Is that where? From a broken family?"

She smiled. She liked that he'd seen a tough edge in her. She had cultivated it for years. "Maybe."

"I'm sorry if you had to go through pain as a child, Beth. But God works all things for good. And if you had to go through all you did to be who you are today, well, it turned out pretty good, didn't it?"

She sighed. "You don't really know who I am. Not really."

"Then show me."

It was a challenge, and she rarely backed down from challenges. Yet what he was asking was too intimate, too revealing, and she couldn't risk it. He couldn't know that she had once been one of those kids in the homes he monitored, one of the names in the files he kept stacked on his desk. He couldn't know that she had been a trained thief, a practiced liar . . .

"You don't have to show me," he said, finally, when he could see that she struggled with the challenge. "I've seen it. In the way you're fighting for these kids, risking your life, daring to make a change. Not many people would do that."

"Given the proper motivation," she said coolly, "people will do lots of things."

"Yeah, you're real tough," he said with a hint of amusement as he touched her soft, short hair. "But you know what I saw the first time you came to me to get information about the home?"

She looked reluctantly at him. "What?"

"I saw a woman who sent my heart stumbling in triple-time. A beautiful woman with those big, clear blue eyes, and that smile that made me want to sit and stare at it for hours . . . And then I heard you talk, heard how you cared for those kids, how passionate you were about this story . . ."

She smiled uneasily and looked down at her hands. Suddenly they were clammy. Suddenly, she was shaking.

"You cared the way I cared. I had cared about those kids for some time, had worried about them, and I felt a bond with you. I thought that maybe God had crossed our paths for a reason."

She looked at him curiously then. "You see God working in everything, don't you? Nothing's accidental. Nothing's left to chance."

"Absolutely nothing. Don't you believe that?"

"I don't know," she said honestly. "I don't think God's working in my life yet. I haven't done enough. Things are still too off balance."

"What do you mean 'off balance'?"

"You know. I'm sort of behind on this religion thing. I got a late start. I have a lot of work to do before I can expect anything from God. But I'm willing to do what it takes."

"It doesn't take work, Beth. It just takes surrender. Repentance. You just have to give all of yourself to Christ."

"I'm not sure he wants even *some* of me," she said with a self-deprecating smile.

"Trust me. He wants all of you. And you don't have to wait until your good deeds outweigh your bad ones. Look at the thief on the cross."

She looked up at him, stricken. Why had he chosen that example? Did he suspect her past? "What about him?" she asked.

"He told Jesus he believed in him. To remember him when he came into his kingdom. Did Jesus tell him to clean up his act and work hard?"

"No."

"What did he say?"

Her Bible knowledge was shaky, but she did remember that. "He said, 'Today you shall be with me in Paradise.'"

"That's right. He took him just like he was, hanging on a cross for crimes he *had* committed, while Jesus hung there for no crime at all. But that man's sins were transferred to Jesus, and when that thief got to heaven, he was clean. Not because of anything he had done, but because he believed in his heart."

Beth sighed. She had never compared herself to the thief on the cross, not until now. But she'd heard about this concept of *grace* before—they always sang and preached about it at church. Somehow, she doubted that Nick or any of them had it right. There had to be more. It had to be tied into behavior, or none of it made any sense. She couldn't believe that, after everything she'd done, God could just accept her, forgive her, welcome her into heaven—at least not without her first having to *do* something to make up for all of those sins, and that something should be substantial. Because if that was true, if God just accepted and forgave us no matter what we'd done, then . . .

Well, then, someone like Bill Brandon—who professed to believe in Christ but used Scripture for his own evils, and who had ruined the lives of hundreds of children just as he had tried to ruin hers—could be readily accepted into heaven if he made a deathbed conversion.

And that could *never* be true.

"Tell me something, Beth," Nick said. "Look ahead five years, ten years, whatever, and tell me, if you could be everything you think God wants you to be, what will you be doing? Who will you be?"

She shifted on the bench and propped her elbow on the back. "Maybe I'll be married to a wonderful man I don't deserve. And I'll have babies . . ." That smile grew across her face. "Lots of babies. And my husband will love them, and never hurt them, and I'll live my life the way a mother should, so that they'll always trust me and count on me, so that no one will ever be able to take them away."

His smile faded as she spoke, and she realized she had said too much. He was watching her with misty eyes now, hanging on every word.

But she couldn't help going on in a strange, wistful voice. "And that family will be so great. The whole world can fall apart around us, but we'll be so strong, so tightly knit, that nothing will ever break us."

"'What God has joined together let no man put asunder.'"

"Yes!" she said. "I know exactly what that means."

"Do you believe that family you described is the plan God has for you? In other words, that he has good plans for you instead of calamity?"

"Yes," she whispered. "But sometimes we bring calamity on ourselves. Sometimes other people bring it on us." She shrugged. "On the other hand, he may plan for me to be alone. Some people are supposed to be single. Some people never find the right mate."

"That thought has run through my mind a few times, too," he admitted. "But I'd prefer to think that there's a terrific family that's already a snapshot in God's mind, and that I'm standing at the head of it."

"That would be a beautiful snapshot," she said. "Send me a wallet size of it, will you?"

His smile was eloquent, but she couldn't decipher what it could mean. She was too busy wishing she could be in that snapshot.

He touched her face, feather stroking it with gentle fingertips, testing her, as if he thought she might pull away. She didn't. Their eyes met in a startling moment of awareness, and she unconsciously wet her lips.

Slowly, his face moved closer to hers, and those fingertips moved into her hair and pulled her toward him. His lips brushed hers, gently, sweetly, and she felt her heart bursting into a Fourth-of-July display as their kiss deepened.

For a moment, all time was suspended, all tragedy was held at bay, all calamity was delayed. For a moment, she saw herself in that snapshot, standing under his arm with a serene smile on her face, surrounded by children that looked like him.

The joy of that hope brought real tears to her eyes, tears that she didn't try to blink back.

He broke the kiss and pressed his forehead into hers. He wiped one of her tears away with his thumb. For a moment, neither of them could speak.

His mouth seemed engaged in the same emotional struggle as he finally tried to find words. "You're a beautiful woman, Beth. Do you know that?"

She swallowed.

"A very beautiful woman."

He pulled her into his arms then, and held her while her tough facade crumbled and she melted into tears. She didn't remember ever being held like that, not in her life, and as she reveled in that warmth, she feared the ending of it.

Finally, he let her go and stood up, taking her hand. "We'd better go. Tomorrow's going to be a big day."

"Yeah," she whispered. "I guess I do need to get home."

"I'm not taking you home," he said. "It's too dangerous. I'm taking you back to Lynda's."

"But I can't impose on her that way."

"She insisted when we left," he said. "She took me aside and made me promise not to let you go home tonight. She even invited your puppy. Besides, I want to say good night to Jimmy."

"All right, then," she whispered, leaning into him as he slid his arm around her shoulders. "If I can go by and get Dodger."

"Sure. No problem."

Smiling gently, she walked with him to his car.

CHAPTER THIRTY-TWO

The parking lot at the *St. Clair News* was never empty, and tonight was no exception. At least a dozen cars were parked in scattered spaces, testifying to the fact that people were in the building, working to get out the next morning's edition of the paper.

Bill Brandon had timed things just right. Earlier that day, he had phoned the paper and spoken to a building maintenance supervisor. He'd told him that he was teaching a summer class in journalism for the University of Florida—Clearwater Campus's "College for Kids" program, and that he would like to bring a group on a field trip to tour the paper. But he wanted them to see the paper actually being printed.

That was impossible, the supervisor had told him. The paper was printed after midnight, and he doubted that any children's parents would be willing to send their children on a field trip at that hour. Bill had sighed and agreed.

But by the time he got off the phone, he knew exactly where in the building the paper was printed, and what time would be best to strike. Then he'd called one of his associates, who had much to lose if the article was printed and who had agreed to help. Since his associate was a prominent member of St. Clair's government, he would show up at the paper to complain about a political editorial that had been done the week before. Before he left, he would unlock two or three windows, so that later, the kids could get in. He had called back shortly after that with the location of the windows.

The children were quiet as he drove them through the parking lot flanking the building. He pointed down a hill toward a basement door with a light on, and said, "There. You see? That's the area you want to get into. But the windows are unlocked on the other side of the building, second floor. You'll have to go through the building to the right place." He drove around until the other side was in view. Lights glowed on that side of the building, as well, but not in the area where they would break in.

"Take the ladder and go in. Remember, quiet as mice, like I taught you. Space far enough apart that if one of you is seen, everyone else won't be given away. Now, what did I tell you to say if anyone sees you?"

Brad was the first to speak up. "I'm John's boy. He brought me to work with him tonight."

"What if nobody named John works here?" one of them asked.

"Somebody named John works everywhere," Bill said. "There are people scattered all over the building, so they'll accept that without thinking about it. Now stay in the dark places, and follow the route that I gave you. Everybody got their backpacks loaded?"

The team that consisted of four rough-looking boys, and three girls, including Lisa, all clothed in black, was ready.

"Remember," Bill said as they filed out of the van. "If you botch this up, you'll go to jail tomorrow. When that article comes out—"

"We won't botch it up, Bill," one of the kids said.

"All right. Now once you've done what you came to do, you take off through that door and don't waste any time. I'll be waiting."

The kids filed out, one by one, adjusting their backpacks on their shoulders. Three of the boys unloaded the ladder that was tied to the top of the van, the ladder they would leave behind, and carried it quickly to the side of the building where the three windows on the second floor had been unlocked.

They set the ladder under the window, and two of the girls held it while Brad scurried up it and slid the window up. No one said a word as Brad stepped through. Lisa was next. She climbed the ladder carefully, not fast enough, she was sure, but she was terrified of falling, and the weight of the load on her back made it more difficult to keep her balance. She reached the window and slid under. Brad helped her down without a word. It was the quietest she'd ever seen him.

She watched as he took off through the building, exactly the direction Bill had drilled them on. She waited and helped Kevin in, then took off herself, leaving him behind to help the one behind him.

A sense of importance filled her as she took off through the dark hallway to the exit sign that was her first marker. She quietly went through the door, took the stairs down, and came out on the first floor. She saw Brad a little ahead of her, hurrying past lit offices with people working at computers, past a huge room with dozens of cluttered desks, but only two or three people working. She could hear something clicking in there, something like a fast typewriter or printer. Maybe the noise would keep the workers from hearing them.

She looked behind her and saw Kevin gaining on her. She ducked past the door and to the next exit door, and headed down to the basement.

She was big enough to do this, she thought with satisfaction. Wouldn't Bill be proud of her, that she'd taken directions so carefully and hadn't messed it up?

She heard the sound of machines running as she came out of the stairwell into the basement. It was so loud that no one was ever going to hear them. She saw Brad looking around for anyone nearby.

There were two men in one of the rooms, their skin shiny with sweat as they operated the machines. It was hot down here, even though there was air conditioning and the fans overhead hummed. The machines put out a lot of heat. But she knew that it was about to get hotter.

Brad motioned for her to follow him, and she looked behind her and gave the same gesture to the person following her. He pointed to the room where the men were. "Somebody has to go in there," he said, his voice muffled by the drone of the machinery.

"No! They'll see us. We'll get caught," one of the children protested.

"If we don't do it, we're only half doing the job, and the article will come out."

"Send Lisa. She's the littlest. They won't see her."

Lisa's eyes widened. "I'm not going."

"Yes, you are," Brad said. "If you don't, I'll tell Bill. Now go. Head under the machine, and douse it good."

She got tears in her eyes as one of the kids unzipped her backpack and pulled the hose with the trigger spray nozzle out. "We'll be in here. Now hurry."

Lisa wanted to burst into tears, but she knew that if she did, she would be punished. She had to get the job done. It's what Jimmy would have done.

Biting her lip, she went to the edge of the door and peered around the doorway. She could see the sweating men doing something with the gadgets on the machine as the pages of the paper were spat out one by one. The room smelled of sweat, mildew, ink, and paper.

She ducked out of their sight behind the machinery and began to spray the inner workings of the machine, the floor around it, and the paper behind her against the wall awaiting its turn on the printer.

She heard voices. The men were talking to each other, but she couldn't hear what they were saying. Did they smell the gas, or was the artificial wind created by the fan pushing the smell down? Would it blow the fire out as soon as it got started?

She emptied the container of gas on her back, concentrating only on that one side of the machine, since she couldn't get to the other side without the men seeing her. Then she scurried back out of the room.

The others had been busily emptying their own containers, and she smelled the acrid fumes of gasoline soaked into curtains, carpet, dripping on the machinery in every room along the darkened hallway. Brad motioned for them to follow him, and they all ran down the hall to the door through which they would escape, the last person trailing a line of gasoline behind him.

When they reached the outside door, the others sprinted toward the van. But Brad grabbed Lisa and stopped her. "You're not finished," he whispered.

"What?" she asked.

"You get to light the match," he said. "It's your initiation. Bill said."

She didn't know what an initiation was, but she didn't object to it. She took the match from his hand, struck it against the gritty side of the matchbox, and smiled at the flame dancing on the end of the matchstick.

"Throw it in, stupid!" he whispered harshly. "Don't just stand there with it."

She threw the match down in the puddle of gasoline and watched it billow into flames. She caught her breath and jumped back as the fire raced down the hall. Brad grabbed her hand and began to pull her away from the door as the rooms they had doused went up in a quiet conflagration.

Lisa felt a sudden rush of fear. Looking back at the building as Brad pulled her along, she cried, "Those men! Brad, those men were in there!"

"They'll get out," he said. "Everybody will get out as soon as the fire alarm goes off. Now hurry!"

The van was moving as they reached it, and Brad forced Lisa into it, then jumped into it himself and closed the door just as they heard the fire alarm ring out.

Lisa rolled on the van floor, unable to find her footing, as the van accelerated out of the parking lot. But she managed to claw her way up to a window and peer out in time to see people fleeing from the burning building.

CHAPTER THIRTY-THREE

T he trucks that delivered Express Mail for the St. Clair area were lined up against the back of the post office, their rear doors open as graveyard shift postal workers loaded the next day's deliveries. On top of one of the stacks was the package Lisa had delivered earlier that day. The one addressed to Beth Wright, with the return address of Marlene Brandon.

As the sky began to take on the rose tints of dawn, one of the postal workers stopped for a moment to rest. He wiped his sweating brow and opened his thermos for some lukewarm coffee. "Hey, Alice," he called to the woman sitting at the front desk, "has the paper come yet?"

"Nope. Sorry. Looks like the delivery boy slept late today."

The man brooded as he slurped his coffee. Oh, well. He could always read one of the magazines before it got loaded onto a truck for delivery. He grabbed one out of a stack of mail, propped his feet up, and began to flip through.

CHAPTER THIRTY-FOUR

A ll that night, Beth lay awake in Lynda's guest room, anticipating the arrival of the *St. Clair News* on the front steps of a hundred thousand readers.

She dressed as the first hints of morning began to peek through her window, put her leash on Dodger, and tiptoed past Lynda's room, then past the room where Jimmy slept, sprawled on top of his bedcovers. She went through the living room and kitchen and quietly slipped out the door into the early morning mist. She put Dodger down and walked him around to the front of the house. While he sniffed around in the bushes, she sat on the front porch steps, watching for the paperboy.

A tremendous sense of peace about what had happened with Nick last night enveloped her—only to be offset by a sense of dread about Bill Brandon.

She wondered if Bill had been arrested last night, if they'd found a way to make it stick so that he wouldn't be able to simply talk his way out of jail.

As the warm wind whipped through her hair, she pulled her feet up onto the top step of the porch. The sky was gray, but a faint pink hue crept up over the trees across the street. Maybe what happened today would wash away the sorrow and pain from the past.

Her eyes strayed up the street, where the paperboy should soon appear. She wished he would hurry.

At the end of the street she spotted a jogger dressed in black running shorts and a white tank top. She started to stand up and go inside, for she didn't trust strangers, especially not on this isolated street where no one ever came unless they were invited. And then she saw that the man was Jake.

He waved as he reached the halfway point on the block, then slowed his jog and walked the rest of the way, cooling down. When he reached the driveway, he picked up the towel he'd left on the trunk of his car, threw it around his neck, and came toward her.

"You're up awfully early," he said, his breath still coming hard. He bent down to pet Dodger, who wagged his tail stub and slobbered all over him.

"So are you. I was just waiting for the paperboy. I didn't know you jogged."

"Yeah, for about the last month or so. I'm trying to get in shape for my medical."

"Your what?"

"My medical. I have to get a medical release to get my pilot's license back. This afternoon is the moment of truth."

"Well, that shouldn't be a problem, should it?"

"No, ordinarily it wouldn't." He sat down on the steps next to her and rubbed the sweat from his face. "But this false eye could play against me, so I'm trying to overcompensate with the rest. If I can prove I'm more fit than most people, they might overlook the eye."

Beth narrowed her eyes and stared at him. "I didn't know you had a false eye, Jake. Which one?"

He chuckled. "If you can't tell, I'm not going to."

"Your eyes look just alike. And they move together. I didn't know false eyes could do that."

"They look just like ordinary eyes, but that's not what the licensing board cares about. They want to make sure that I can *see* like I'm supposed to. Half of my peripheral vision is gone now, so I can't fly for the commercial airline I used to fly for. They have pretty high standards. But if I can get my license back, I could buy a small plane and start a chartering service or something."

"That's great, Jake. They'll give it to you, won't they?"

"I think so. I'm just a little nervous. A lot is riding on this."

Thankful for the diversion, she asked, "Like what?"

He smiled and looked off in the direction from which he had just jogged. "Like . . . my relationship with Lynda."

"I thought that was pretty solid."

"It is. But I'd like for it to move forward. Have a little more permanency. I never thought I'd say this, but I don't want Lynda to just be my lady. I want her to be my wife."

Beth grinned. "Does she know this?"

"I'm sure she suspects it. But I haven't said it, straight out. Not when I have so little to offer her."

"Lynda doesn't need much."

"No, but she deserves everything." He sat down next to her on the steps. "I've been out of work and living on savings and odd jobs since the accident. I want to have an income, and be contributing something, before I ask her to marry me."

"That's admirable," Beth said. "I hope somebody will care about me like that one day."

"You're still young. No hurry."

"Yeah," she said. "And there's a lot of unfinished business I have to take care of before then." Her eyes strayed back to the end of the street. Still no paperboy.

"Unfinished business?"

"Yeah. This article is just part of it."

"Well, it should be here soon. But come to think of it, I usually see the paperboy when I'm jogging, and I didn't see him today. He must be running late. Tell you what. I'll go shower, then if it still hasn't come, I'll go pick up one at the closest newsstand. I'm anxious to see it, too." He got up and threw the towel back around his neck.

She smiled and watched him head back around the house and into the garage apartment. She wondered if Lynda had any idea how blessed she was to have a man like that in love with her.

After watching for the paperboy for a few more minutes, she decided not to wait any longer. She went back into the house and got her purse. Lynda was coming up the hall in her robe. "Beth, where are you going so early?"

"To try to find a newspaper," she said. "The paperboy is late. I'm just really anxious to see the article. There's a truck stop near my house that is always one of the earliest to get a paper. I'll go there and see if I can get one. I'll call you from home. Thanks for letting me stay here last night, okay? And tell Jimmy I'll be back to see him this afternoon."

"Okay. He'll be fine."

"Oh, and tell Jake that I'm sorry I couldn't wait."

Beth carried Dodger out to her car as that sense of uneasiness crept over her again. After she'd left Lynda's isolated street, she scanned the driveways for the rolled-up newspapers that always came with the morning. She saw none. She grabbed her car phone and dialed the number of the newspaper, planning to ask someone in circulation if there had been some delay in getting the papers out that morning.

A discordant tone came on instead of the ring, and an operator's recorded voice said that the number was temporarily out of order.

She cut the phone off, frowning, and wove her way through the neighborhood, neat little houses all lined up with no newspapers in the driveways.

Something is wrong.

She dialed the number of the police station and told the sergeant who answered the phone who she was. "I'm checking to see if Bill Brandon was arrested last night. Larry Millsaps and Tony Danks were on the case."

The sergeant checked his records, then came back to the phone. "No, I don't show an arrest made last night for a Brandon."

She closed her eyes. "All right, thanks."

She almost ran a red light, then slammed on her brakes and rubbed her forehead, trying to ease a rapidly escalating headache. What was going on? The telephone at the newspaper out of order, the arrest never carried out—

She whipped a quick U-turn at the intersection and headed back in the direction of the newspaper office.

It took her a few minutes to get to the street on which the *St. Clair News* was housed. And then she saw why the phone was out of order. The building was in shambles, half of it burned to the ground, and the other half, though still standing, only a monument of crumbling brick and slanted beams, with smoke-scalded ceilings and walls, and computer equipment and file cabinets smashed where the building had collapsed on one side.

She sat stunned, staring through her windshield at the smoldering ashes.

She hadn't realized anyone was coming toward her until a police officer knocked on her window.

"Ma'am, you'll have to move your car."

She rolled the window down. "I work here," she said. "What happened?"

"There was a fire last night," he said, as if that wasn't obvious.

"No, I mean, how did it start?"

"We suspect arson, but we're still investigating. Now, if you don't mind moving your car—"

"But the paper! The paper got out this morning, didn't it? The paper will still be delivered!"

"I don't think there's going to be an edition today, ma'am. Most of the machinery is toast."

She sat back hard on her seat and covered her mouth. The article wasn't coming out. Not today. A sense of injustice crashed over her. Familiar injustice. Predictable injustice.

"When did this happen? Did anyone see who started it?"

"No, no one saw anything. Two men who were right in the area where the fire was the most concentrated were killed."

"Killed? Oh, no! Who?"

He checked his clipboard, then asked her, "Are you asking as a member of the press, or a friend?"

"A friend!" she shouted. "Who died?"

"Off the record until we notify next of kin . . . Hank Morland and Stu Singer."

She didn't know them well, but she did know them, and now she closed her eyes and hugged herself as if she might split right down the middle and fall apart. Had her article caused someone's death? Did she have to bear that guilt now, too? She slammed her car into park, cut off the engine, and climbed out. "I need to get in touch with Larry Millsaps or Tony Danks. I need to talk to them now. Get me their home numbers, please!"

"I can't do that, ma'am. But if you have some information about who might have started this fire, you can tell me."

"Of course I know who started the fire!" she shouted. "It was Bill Brandon! You've got to tell them! Please, get in touch with them for me."

He didn't seem anxious to call in such an emotional revelation from a woman who seemed unstable, but he went to his squad car and asked the dispatcher for their home numbers.

Beth was with him when the answer was radioed back, and she bolted out of the squad car.

"Ma'am? Where are you going?"

"To call them," she said. "From my car phone."

He came to stand beside the open door as she punched out Tony's number.

He answered quickly. "Tony? This is Beth Wright."

"Yeah, Beth." His voice was gritty, as if she had awakened him. "I tried to call you last night, but you weren't home."

"What happened?" she demanded. "Why didn't you arrest him?"

"We couldn't get a warrant. Judge Wyatt was really hard-nosed about it. He said we didn't have enough evidence to arrest him."

"Not enough evidence? Are you kidding?" She looked at the building, still smoldering, and cried, "Did you show him my article?"

"I did. But he doesn't have a lot of faith in journalism. He's going to have to see more. We plan to make it our business to get him more so we can get Bill Brandon today. We're stuck with his decision because he's the presiding judge in St. Clair. There's no one higher up to go to."

"Well, if you're looking for evidence that Bill Brandon is too dangerous to be running loose, I've got it right in front of me."

"What do you mean, Beth?"

"I mean that the newspaper article is not going to come out today, Tony, because there's not going to *be* a newspaper today, because Bill Brandon burned the blasted place down last night. He killed two people in the process!"

"What?"

She was about to cry, and she fought it, hating herself for it. "He did it, Tony. You know he did. Somebody told him about the article—he's got lots of connections. So he took care of it."

"You're sure it was him?"

"He didn't sign his name, if that's what you want. He probably didn't even get within fifty feet of the building himself. He probably used his kids to do it, like he does everything. Think of that, Tony—such a dangerous thing, and the kids are so young ..."

His pause told her she was getting too emotional, giving herself away, so she tried to rein in her emotions. "Look, you've got to arrest him before he does anything else. He stopped the presses last night, kept the article from coming out today. Now he has to get to the source of that article, and that, we both know, is me."

"You're right," he said. "Beth, stay there. Larry and I will be there in twenty minutes. Maybe we can find something to prove definitively that Bill Brandon or his kids were behind this. Something we can show Judge Wyatt."

"All right," she said. She glanced at the police officer's name tag. Lt. J.T. Mills. "Tell your friend Lt. Mills, so he'll let me stay."

"Okay. Hand him the phone."

She did, then got out of her car and took a few steps toward the building. Flashes came back to her, flashes of those late-night planning sessions with Bill and the rest of his kids, memorizing of blueprints, the endless drilling on which way they were to turn when they broke in, what they were to take, how they were to escape. She remembered the feel of her heightened senses as he'd let them out of his dark van, the urgency and adrenaline rush as they'd climbed into windows or cut glass out to unlock back doors, the smothering fear as they'd stolen through dark hallways ...

Bill had never asked her to start a fire or take someone's life. But he was getting desperate now, and his crimes were more catastrophic. What guilt those children would live with! She hoped they didn't know they had killed someone last night.

She heard the officer close her car door and come toward her. "You can stay, ma'am, but please stay back. Danks and Millsaps will be here soon."

She nodded her head. Leaning against her car, she watched the smoke softly swirling above the rubble, like prayers that would never find their way to heaven.

CHAPTER THIRTY-FIVE

The television news woke Jimmy. He sat up in bed and looked around, trying to figure out where he was. Oh, yeah. Lynda Barrett's house. Today was the day that Beth's article would come out, and Bill would be arrested, and he'd see Lisa again.

He quickly got dressed, then walked barefoot into the den. Lynda and Jake were glued to the television, and neither of them saw him.

"... suspected arson. The building went up in flames at approximately one A.M. Fire crews were on the scene within five minutes of the alarm going off, but it was too late to save the millions of dollars worth of equipment ... or the lives of the two men who were trapped in the flames ..."

"What building is that?" Jimmy asked, startling them. They both turned around.

"Good morning, Jimmy," Lynda said. "Did you sleep well?"

"Sure, but what building is that?"

"It's the building for the *St. Clair News.*"

"The newspaper building," Jimmy said, staring at the footage of the building engulfed in flames. He felt as if a fist had just whopped him in the stomach, knocking the wind out of him.

Bill's fist. His face reddened, and he tightened his lips to keep them from trembling with the emotion gripping him. "So he did it."

"Who?" Lynda asked.

"Bill. I told you he'd never let it come out." He knew his expression belied his matter-of-fact tone, but he couldn't seem to control it.

Lynda stepped toward him, but he backed away.

"I told you he'd never let Lisa out, either. They're never gonna hang anything on him. He's just gonna keep doing what he does, and now I've blown it and I can't go back, and Lisa's trapped there—"

"Jimmy, we don't know for sure that he was behind this. Even if he was—"

"*I* know for sure," he cut in. "*I* know!"

He ran out of the room, back to the bedroom where he had slept last night, and slammed the door. He sat down on the bed, trying to think. Somehow, he had to reach Lisa.

He went to the phone extension that sat on his bed table and put his trembling hand on it, wondering if he should risk calling her again. Then he wondered if he could risk *not* calling her.

Lisa wasn't safe.

He picked up the phone, punched in the number of Cottage B at the St. Clair Children's Home, and waited, holding his breath.

In Cottage B, Stella stood like a sentry over the children, making sure they all finished every last bite of their cereal. Some of the children woke up more easily than others, but all were awakened at the same time. Those who'd gone out with Bill last night, and had come in smelling of gasoline fumes, could barely hold their heads up, but they could have no one sleeping because that Nick fellow might pop in for an inspection again, and it wouldn't do to have children sleeping in the daylight. To keep up appearances, everyone had to be out of bed at the same time. It was good for them. It would make them tough.

The telephone rang, and Stella picked it up. "Hello?"

Click.

Annoyed, she hung it back up just in time to see Lisa's little head bobbing toward her cereal bowl, as though she might fall asleep right in the milk. "Lisa!" she shouted, startling the child. "Get a grip, would ya?"

The child propped her chin and tried to make her eyes stay open.

Frustrated, Jimmy admitted to himself that he'd never get to talk to Lisa—at least, not by phone. He closed his eyes and tried to

150

think of a way to communicate with her. He wished she had a computer, that he could e-mail her as easily as he did the friends he corresponded with across the country on one of the computers that had been donated to the children's home. Bill had always encouraged Jimmy's interest in computers—after all, he'd been able to use the boy's knowledge on a number of occasions. That was why Jimmy'd been chosen to break into Beth's house; Bill had needed someone who could find Beth's files on SCCH.

No, Lisa didn't have access to the home's computers—but others did. Was there someone he could trust?

Brad. He was Jimmy's best friend, and there was nothing Brad liked more than keeping a secret. It made him feel important. That was why he seemed to thrive on the jobs Bill sent him to do. They were all secrets, and Brad went on all his missions like a miniature spy sent out into the night to risk his life to save his country.

Yes, Brad would keep Jimmy's secret. As loyal as Brad was to Bill, he'd been beaten enough to harbor the same smoldering hatred for him that Jimmy had.

Jimmy found Lynda in the kitchen. "Lynda, do you care if I play on your computer?"

She grinned. "Well, I don't mind, Jimmy, but I don't have any games on there."

"Do you have access to the Internet?"

Lynda couldn't help chuckling. "Yes, as a matter of fact. My modem is hooked to a second phone line, so you can use it all you want. You can probably find some good games on the network I subscribe to."

She told him the name of the network she used, and he smiled. It was the same one they used at the home.

"You're not an Internet addict, are you?" she asked.

"I just like to surf around and see what's there."

"Okay. Sure. I'll show you how to turn it on."

"No, I already know how," he said.

He went into the area of the great room where the computer sat, and turned it on. He found the icon for her network, registered himself as Lynda's guest, and entered his own screen name from the home's system. Quickly, he got on-line and clicked the "compose mail" button.

He sat there a moment, trying to remember what Brad's screen name was. It was something weird, some combination of letters from his name. Darb? Arbd? Drab? Yes, that was it. Drab and some numbers. His age. That was it. Drab11.

He addressed the letter, under "Subject" put "Secret," and then tabbed his cursor down to the body of the letter.

Brad,

It's me, Jimmy. Don't tell anybody you saw me here. I don't know what Bill told you, but I'm okay and I'm staying with a friend. I got caught on my mission the other night, but they were nice and didn't turn me in. If Bill finds me, he'll kill me. You know he will. Please don't tell.

Get a message to Lisa. Tell her I'm okay, and I'm trying to get her out of there. Tell her to be ready. I don't know how I'll do it yet, but I will. She can write me back if she wants. I think I can get my e-mail here.

Don't touch any of my stuff, and don't let anybody else get it. Especially my baseball cards. And if you tell, I'll tell the police everything you've ever done. If you keep my secret, maybe I'll try to get you out, too, and we can all find a boxcar to live in like the kids in that book and have fun from now on. Wouldn't that be cool?

Your friend,
Jimmy

He clicked the "send" button, and sat back. *Please let him see it. Please let him see it.*

"So how's it going?" Lynda asked.

"Good," he said, clicking the network off-line, and cutting the computer off.

"Hungry?"

"Sure."

She led him into the kitchen where a huge breakfast waited. He wished Lisa was here to share it with him.

CHAPTER THIRTY-SIX

B rad sat down at the computer, too tired to go outside where it was hot and muggy. Instead, he'd gotten permission to stay inside and play on the computer. It was one of the perks that the kids in Bill's "inner circle" got.

He turned on the network, got on-line, and checked his e-mail for a message from one of his pen pals in another part of the country, a pen pal who didn't know that he was an orphan, or that he lived in a children's home, or that he was a thief.

There was only one message from someone named JWMan. JWMan? It was familiar, but he couldn't remember who used that name. He clicked "read mail," and saw instantly that it was from Jimmy.

He sat up straighter as he read.

When he was finished, he looked out the window and saw Lisa sitting on a swing on the playground, leaning her head against the chains, as though she might fall asleep and come tumbling off. He went to the door and called out for her. "Lisa!"

She looked up.

"Come here. I have to show you something."

She looked like she didn't want to, but she got up and shuffled to the door. "What?" she asked belligerently.

"I've got a message for you from Jimmy," he whispered, taking her hand and pulling her to the computer.

Her eyebrows popped up. "Where?"

"Here. Look."

Lisa sat down in front of the screen and began to slowly read the letter. She had made A's in reading her first-grade year, but she still had to read slowly and concentrate very hard. Her finger followed the words, and she whispered them as she sounded them out, while Brad stood guard making sure no one came in.

Her eyes widened as she got to the part about him seeing her soon. "He's coming to get me!" she said. "We're gonna live in a boxcar! I want to write him back."

"All right," Brad said. "Hit 'reply' and type it in. It'll be under my screen name, but that's okay."

"Will you type it for me?" she asked.

He glanced toward both doors, then sat back down and put his fingers on the keyboard. "Okay. Tell me what to say."

"Say, 'Dear Jimmy, I miss you.'"

"I'm not typing that," Brad said. "That's gross."

"You said you would. It's my letter. I can say it if I want."

He moaned and typed the words. "What else?"

"Please hurry to get me. Bill gave me your job, and I don't like it."

"Not so fast," Brad said, still hunting and pecking on the word h-u-r-r-y. He made his way through the rest of the sentence.

"I guess that's all," she said, her lips beginning to quiver as tears filled her eyes. "I'm glad he's okay. I thought he wasn't coming back. I thought he left me here."

Brad didn't tell her that he had believed Bill's story about Jimmy being in jail. He might have known it was a lie. The boxcar thing sounded good—real good. They could get somewhere where Bill would never find them. They could get jobs—and until they did they could steal enough to get by. He hoped it would happen soon, before the police tried to arrest all of them.

"Tell me if he writes back," Lisa said.

Typing his own note now, Brad nodded. "Yeah, don't worry, I will."

In his secret room, Bill Brandon scanned the closed-circuit television monitors that kept him informed of everything that went on at SCCH. He watched with mild curiosity as Brad played in the computer room—then with suspicious puzzlement, watched as Brad called Lisa Westin in. They weren't good friends—in fact,

Brad could hardly tolerate the girl. So why the sudden camaraderie?

He saw Lisa sit down and read something on the computer; Brad shuffled around the door, seeming to stand guard. Whatever was going on here, Bill didn't like it.

He waited, stiff, until the boy had turned off the computer and left the room. Then Bill headed across the campus to the computer room. A couple of kids had drifted in since Brad had left. Bill said loudly, "Outside, kids. It's too pretty a day to be playing inside."

They quickly turned off the computers and headed outside, leaving him alone. He locked the doors, then sat down at the computer Brad had been using. He turned it on, opened the on-line network he allowed them to use, and typed in Brad's screen name. His list of recent mail came up, but there were only three letters. One from some kid who was under the impression that Brad was the son of a congressman and lived in a mansion with a pool. Bill chuckled with disdain.

He clicked the next message, saw that it was part of a stupid conversation that didn't interest him.

Then he clicked the third. It was from someone going by the name of JWMan. He read the first line and knew that JWMan was Jimmy Westin.

His face reddened, and he clicked open the "Read Mail You've Sent" area, where outgoing messages were held. When Brad's log of messages appeared, Bill clicked the most recent one.

Lisa's letter came up, along with Brad's addition.

After he'd read them, he sat staring at the screen, trying to decide what to do. There was no question that Lisa and Brad should be punished for communicating with Jimmy, but he had to do more. He had to put the fear in them, so that they wouldn't tell the other kids what they'd learned. He hoped it wasn't too late. He looked out the window, saw Brad and Lisa talking quietly together at the back of the playground. Lisa was more animated than he'd seen her in days.

He looked back at the screen. Besides punishing the two of them, he had to find a way to make Jimmy come to him, so that he could put him out of commission. Too much was going wrong;

there were too many people out there who knew too much. HRS people sniffing around, reporters trying to write exposes of his operation, cops trying to get warrants for his arrest . . . Bill's whole world was in danger unless he could do some quick damage control, and Jimmy, little Jimmy, was right in the middle of it all. He had to lure Jimmy in somehow.

He clicked "unsend" on the letter the two kids had sent Jimmy, and waited anxiously to see if it was too late. If Jimmy had already opened it, he couldn't get it back. But if he hadn't . . .

The computer said that the letter had been unsent, and he grinned. He clicked "edit," then made a few changes. He deleted Lisa's portion, then on Brad's typed in, "Lisa's hurt real bad from the beating Bill gave her. Jimmy, you need to come get her before he kills her. I'll leave Stella's window unlocked so you can get in. Please hurry!"

He grinned as he sent the letter across cyberspace. Now all he had to do was be ready when Jimmy came.

He cut off the computer, then went to the back door and called for Brad and Lisa. Reluctantly, apprehensively, they both came in.

He locked the door behind them, then turned around to Brad. His arm swung and he backhanded the boy with a fist across the chest, knocking him down. Then he kicked him twice, once in each side, until the child was balled up in fetal position, moaning and crying and begging Bill to stop.

When he was satisfied that he'd done enough damage, he turned to Lisa. She shrank back against the wall, tears in her eyes and her face as red as the shirt she wore. "I didn't do anything."

"You've been communicating with your brother, and so has Brad," he said in a surprisingly gentle voice. "And I can't have that."

He grabbed her shoulders, shook her violently, then flung her across the room. But he didn't kick her, like he had Brad. Nick or someone else might come around asking about her, and she'd better not have a mark on her. He left Brad lying on the floor, and grabbed Lisa up. Marching her out of the computer room, he dragged her across the campus to another specially built room near his office. This one had been designed for discipline. It had

no windows, no lights, and no furniture. Just a bare floor and darkness.

He flung her in there as she screamed in protest, and he locked the door behind her, blocking out the sound of her cries.

Then he sat down behind his desk and tried to catch his breath. No, there wouldn't be a mark on her—at least not on her body. Just on her mind. And if anyone came asking about either of the Westin kids . . . he could get her out of his "special room" quickly and no one would be the wiser.

As for Brad—no one cared about Brad anyway, so he didn't expect anyone to ask. He only hoped the beating had taught the kid a lesson.

He couldn't wait for Jimmy to get his message and show up at the home. With a grin, Bill jumped up and hurried across campus to Cottage B, where he unlocked Stella's window.

CHAPTER THIRTY-SEVEN

A few minutes after he got up that morning, Nick saw the news reports about the burning of the newspaper building, and quickly phoned Lynda's house to see if Beth had heard. When he didn't catch her there or at her own house, he decided to drive to the newspaper building itself. Just as he'd suspected, she stood there in the parking lot, leaning on the fender of her car, staring, stunned, at the smoldering ruins.

He pulled up beside her and got out of the car. "Beth, are you all right?"

She shrugged, then said in a dull monotone, "He stopped us. I knew he would."

"You really think Bill Brandon did this?"

She sighed. "They just found footprints of children's sneakers. They came in that window." She pointed to the part of the building that had not burned to the ground. "There was a ladder left behind, and children's fingerprints all over it."

"But I thought Brandon was arrested last night."

"The stupid judge refused to give them a warrant." Her voice was so flat, so calm, that he could hear the defeat there. "Now two people are dead, and those poor kids have this guilt on their heads."

He looked around. "Have Larry and Tony been out here?"

"Yeah, but they've gone back to try again to get a warrant." She looked up at him. "Nick, I'm worried about the kids. What if one of them was burned in the fire? What if they got too close?"

"I'll go back to SCCH today," he said.

"What good can you do there? They already know you're onto them."

"So I've got nothing to lose. If I'm there, he can't do anything to foil the police's arrest attempts."

"All right," she said. "Do it. Do whatever you have to."

"And you go back to Lynda's."

"No, I can't. I've still got the article on computer. I'm going to take it to the *St. Petersburg Times* today. Somehow, I'll convince them to print it."

"But you can't go to your house, now that Bill knows where it is. It's not safe."

"Nick, I have to. I have to get the disks that the story is on."

"Then I'll go with you."

She sighed. "All right. Follow me. It'll just take a minute."

She climbed into her car, took a moment to greet Dodger, who had been asleep on the front seat, and cranked her engine. Nick followed her closely all the way home.

"It's almost over, Dodger," she said to the puppy. "The article will still come out, regardless of the fire, and Bill will still get arrested, and Jimmy and Lisa and the other kids will be put in safe homes..." She tried to believe what she said as she reached the dirt road leading through the trees to her house—but the truth was, Bill had beaten them all. As, deep down, she had known he would.

The house looked undisturbed as she pulled up to it and parked. She got out, put Dodger on the ground, and waited as Nick pulled to a halt beside her car.

Nick insisted on going in first, but Dodger beat him to it. The puppy sniffed around, wagging his tail, and headed for the chew toy lying on the floor. As though he'd never ceased to work on it, he began to chew with his little tail stub wagging.

"It looks all right," Nick said. "Then again, somebody could be hiding in your attic and we'd never know. Is your computer upstairs?"

"Yeah," she said. "I'll just go up and get the disk..."

"I'll go first." He went up the stairs, checked around the corner, then motioned for her to follow. He stood with her as she found the disk and her briefcase, in which she had put a hard copy of the article. "Here it is."

"All right, let's go."

She followed him down. "I'll leave Dodger here, I guess. We can come back for him later." She checked the puppy's food supply and water, then locked the door and followed Nick back to her car.

He leaned over and dropped a kiss on her lips. "I'll head over to the home, and you call me when you get back from St. Pete. Go to Lynda's first—not home, okay?"

"All right. Be careful, Nick."

"You too."

With Beth's car in the lead, they headed down the dirt road leading to the street. They were almost to the end of the road when a postal truck turned in. Since the mailman always left Beth's mail in her box out by the street, she assumed he must have a package for her, so she did a quick U-turn and rolled her window down as she came next to Nick. "It's a package. I'd better get it."

He turned his car around and followed her back.

She got out just as the postman began to knock on her door. "Hi," she called up to the house. "Is that for me?"

"Beth Wright?" he asked.

"Yes."

"It's an overnight delivery." He stepped down the porch steps and handed her his clipboard. "Sign here."

She could hear Dodger inside, whimpering and scratching to get out. He didn't like being left any more than she did. She signed the clipboard, then took the package, surprised at the weight of it.

"Thanks," the postman said. "You have a nice day."

"You too."

Dodger began to howl and whine, and rolling her eyes, she shoved the package under one arm. Nick had rolled his window down so he could hear the exchange, and she called back to him, "I have to get Dodger, Nick. He's having a fit in there."

Before he could respond, she stuck the key back into the door and opened it. Dodger panted and jumped up on her calves, as if he hadn't seen her in weeks. "I was coming back, you silly little thing," she said, bending down to pet him. "I wasn't leaving you forever. Come on, let's put your leash back on and you can go with me."

She headed for the kitchen to get the leash. Dodger took the opportunity to dash outside, and she heard Nick's car door slam. "I'll get him!" After a second, he brought the squirming puppy back to the door. "Throw me the leash and I'll walk him. Who's the package from?"

"I'm trying to see." In the kitchen, she took the leash off its hanger and tossed it to Nick. Nick stooped in the doorway and tried to clip it to Dodger's collar, but he slipped free and bolted into the kitchen, his feet sliding on the hardwood floor.

She knelt down to make him quit jumping on her, still looking for the return address. She froze as her eyes located the "From" square. "It can't be."

"What?" Nick asked, leaning against the doorjamb to block it if the dog decided to make a break for it again.

"It's from Marlene Brandon. The woman who was murdered after she talked to me. But it's postmarked in St. Clair." Quickly, she got a knife and began to tear open the wrapping paper as she walked back into the living room. She tore off a strip of it, but the package was heavily taped. The dog frolicked beside her, trying to reach the torn strip hanging down.

"But this was an overnight package," Beth said, puzzled. "How could Marlene have mailed it yesterday? She was dead the night before."

"Maybe she mailed it before you talked. Maybe the post office just took longer than they should have."

She sat down on the couch, and Dodger tried to jump up onto it. She helped him, then slid the box halfway out of the envelope. Had Marlene sent her more documents? Photographs? Tapes?

Before she had the chance to slide it all the way out, Dodger rammed his nose against it, sniffing, and it slipped out of her hands. Dodger slipped off the couch with it as it hit the floor and, playfully, he grabbed a corner of the thick wrapping, the cigar box still held half inside, and dragged it across the room, inviting a game of hide-and-seek or tug-of-war.

Beth stood up as he scurried away from her, his tail wagging. "Dodger, stop that!"

The box slid all the way out of the express envelope, landing on its side, and the top fell open.

The explosion sounded like the end of the world. The last thing that crossed Beth's mind before she blacked out was that Bill had kept his word. He had gotten her. And now she would never be able to tell her story.

When Beth woke she was lying on the dirt outside. She had no idea how long she had been unconscious. Smoke poured through the charred door of her house. Nick crouched over her, his face stained with soot.

"It's okay, Beth," he was whispering. "Just hang on. They're on their way."

She heard a siren and tried to sit up. Her head hurt, and she felt dizzy. She began to cough, calling, "Dodger! Dodger! Nick, where's Dodger?"

But the look on Nick's face was a clear enough answer even without words. Distraught, she sank back against the ground.

"Hang on," he said. "An ambulance is coming."

She became gradually aware that he wasn't simply touching her to reassure her, but rather that he was pressing hard on her chest because she was bleeding. She closed her eyes, feeling nauseous. The fire truck wailed toward her house, getting louder and louder, and she opened her eyes just in time to see it jerk to a halt and the fire crew leap off and begin unwinding the hose. Behind the fire truck came an ambulance, and two EMTs rushed to her. Nick moved aside as the two began to check her vitals.

In minutes, she was in an ambulance racing to the hospital.

When the ambulance reached the hospital and she was whisked inside, she again saw Nick's worried face as he jogged along beside the gurney. Then darkness closed over her.

In the waiting room, Nick stood at the window, staring out at the pond they had sat at just last night. How could he have let her open that package? Why hadn't he realized what it was and snatched it out of her hands? Why hadn't he been clued by the return address of the dead woman?

Smoke inhalation, burns, a chest wound—but Beth could have been killed. If the puppy hadn't knocked the box off the couch, if she'd had it in her lap as Bill Brandon had intended, she would have been. Instead, the dog was blown apart, and she'd been knocked back.

He had dived toward her the moment the bomb had exploded, had dragged her out of the fire started by whatever incendiary device Brandon had included in the box. Then he had scrambled to her car where he knew she kept a phone. He'd been shaking so hard he almost hadn't been able to dial 911.

Thank God she was alive.

The sliding doors to the emergency room opened, and Lynda and Jake burst in, with Jimmy on their heels. He had asked a nurse to call them, for he hadn't had the composure to do it himself.

"How is she?"

"She's in surgery," he said. "She has a pretty bad chest wound. I don't know . . . how bad it is."

"I got hold of Larry Millsaps in his car," Lynda said. "He's heading out to Beth's house with a bomb inspector, and he's determined to get definitive evidence against Bill Brandon. He'll need it—he said they tried again today to get an arrest warrant for Brandon, and Judge Wyatt refused again."

"What is wrong with that judge?" Nick shouted, slamming the heel of his hand against the windowsill. "If he'd issued it last night, there wouldn't have been a fire at the paper, and Beth wouldn't have . . ." He stopped, unable to continue.

"I don't know, Nick. Judge Wyatt is really hard-nosed. I always try to avoid him in the courtroom if I can. He's not the most reasonable man in the world."

"Then what's he doing on the bench?"

"He's a lifetime appointee. Plus, he's the presiding judge. There's no one higher to appeal to unless they go to the prosecutor. He has great job security."

"Even if he's an idiot?"

She sighed. She was still trying to find an answer when the doctor came out and looked around for Nick. "Mr. Hutchins?

She's out of surgery, and she looks good. We were able to clean all the fragments out of her wound—it wasn't as bad as it looked, and her stitches should heal quickly. Thanks to you, her blood loss wasn't bad, nor did she inhale much smoke. You just may have saved her life."

"The dog saved her life," he said.

Jimmy's eyebrows rose. "Dodger saved her? Where is he?"

Nick swallowed. "Jimmy, I'm sorry, but Dodger's—" He stopped, gesturing hopelessly, trying to think of a way to break the news.

Jimmy's face fell. "He's dead, isn't he?"

Nick looked at Lynda and Jake, wishing for someone to say it for him. But there were no takers.

"I'm afraid so. If he hadn't done what he did, Beth might be the one dead instead."

Jimmy tried to plaster on his tough-kid look, and nodded stoically. He turned away from them and went to look out the window. Jake followed him, laying a hand on his shoulders, but the boy shrugged him away.

Nick turned back to the doctor. "When can I see her?"

"In a little while. We've put her in a room, and she should be waking up soon. We'll be keeping her until we're satisfied that there aren't any complications. Maybe she can go home tomorrow."

Home, Nick thought. Her home was in bad shape. She wouldn't be going there.

Lynda patted his back. "We'll wait here, Nick. You go on in and see her."

Nick was grateful that they didn't make him wait.

There was a nurse standing over her bed when she woke up. "Beth, how do you feel?" the nurse asked.

Beth had to think for a minute. "Okay," she whispered, but realized instantly that that wasn't exactly true. "Where is this?"

"The hospital," the nurse said. "You were in an explosion. Do you remember it?"

It started to come back to her in film-clip images . . . the package . . . the tape that was too tough to tear . . . Dodger getting it away from her . . .

"You've had some injuries, but you're going to be fine. I'm going to run out for just a minute and let the doctor know that you're awake, okay?"

She watched the nurse leave the room, and lay there for a moment, looking around at the cold, barren room, with nothing in it that belonged to her, and realized how alone she was. Just like Tracy.

She closed her eyes, her mind moving slowly through disjointed images until it called up a time when she was ten, when she'd broken into a huge home of a wealthy businessman. No one had been home, but he'd had a bird that she hadn't been told about. The bird had fluttered in its cage, spooking her, and she'd taken off running. She'd been so spooked that she had run through the sliding glass door to his patio. It had shattered around her, knocking her out and cutting her in a million places. The other kids had quickly carried her out and thrown her into the van.

Bill had refused to take her to the hospital because he was afraid someone would make the connection between the glass door shattered in a robbery attempt and the little girl covered in glass fragments. Then they'd be caught for sure. So he'd kept her in a room by herself at the home, where he had tweezed the fragments out one by one. It had been a slow torture, one he had seemed to enjoy, and he had followed each withdrawal with a swab of alcohol that had stung worse than any pain she'd ever felt before or since. She still had small scars in some places to remind her.

She'd had bruises all over her body from that incident, and must have had a concussion as well, for she'd slept at least three days following the accident.

Lying here in this room alone reminded her of the week she'd spent in bed in that room at SCCH as a child, wondering if anyone out there cared at all about her, wondering if anyone even gave her a thought.

Bill had told her as he picked glass out of her that they had ways of identifying the blood on glass shards, and that he expected them to arrest her at any moment. It was her fault she was in this position, he'd told her, because she shouldn't have panicked. He was trying to protect her by keeping her here, he'd told her, but Bill's kind of caring wasn't the kind she craved. His was a sick, self-centered concern that frightened her to death.

Funny that Bill was behind this injury, as well. He had almost succeeded at keeping her quiet. He had almost killed her along with her story.

Tears rolled down her face. Lying here, alone, she felt like a wasted, discarded, useless body—the way Tracy probably felt. Was God really there, watching out for her, or was he just disgusted by her?

She thought of the lies she'd told about this story, the anonymous confession, the sneaky way she'd tried to get Maria to confess so that she, Beth, wouldn't have to. She thought of the secrets she'd kept from Nick, from Phil, from the law enforcement officers who needed to know the name of the only available adult witness. The secrets she had kept from little Jimmy, who needed to know that there was someone who truly understood his plight as no one else could, someone who had been there and suffered as he was suffering, someone who had survived it—maybe even grown through it.

Could God see through those sins and walk with her now? The consequences of confessing those sins loomed ever bigger in her consciousness, reminding her that there would be a price to pay. But all those children were still paying. Paying and paying, and they would continue to pay as they grew older and broke free of Bill Brandon. They would pay like she was paying until someone broke the cycle.

And that's what she'd been trying to do. But she'd been trying to do it the easy way, the cheap way. Maybe there was no cheap way. Maybe the only way was to accept the possibility of losing her job and her reputation, and to tell the truth. Maybe then she could have a chance with God.

To do that, she'd have to forget the story she'd written so neatly and remotely, and instead offer herself as a witness who could put Bill Brandon away for life. The buck had to stop somewhere, and it was going to stop here. Unless he stopped her first.

She heard a knock on the door, and then it opened. Nick stood there, looking as fragile and shaken as she'd felt lying out on the dirt with her house burning behind her. He tried to smile, but she could see that the effort was almost too great for him.

He came and leaned over her. "Are you all right?" he asked.

Her voice was hoarse, weak. "Yes. Amazingly, I am. I wasn't supposed to be, though. He intended to kill me."

She could see that Nick agreed with her.

"If I could have just gotten the package away from you before you opened it," he whispered. "I should have realized right away . . . I should have taken it and—"

"Shhh," she whispered, reaching up to touch his lips. "Don't. He set us up. He knew I wouldn't be able to resist a package with Marlene's name on it. He's smart, Nick. I told you how smart he is." She closed her eyes, fighting the tears. "Poor Dodger. He didn't know what hit him."

Nick clearly didn't know what to say. He just stroked her hair back from her face, and she closed her eyes.

A memory, white-hot and miserable, came back to her, a memory of another little dog they had found at the home. It had wandered up onto the lawn one day, and they had played with it, then asked Bill if they could keep it. He'd told them no.

She wasn't sure why that little dog had created such a fierce longing in them, why the children had wanted him badly enough to risk Bill's wrath, but someone had suggested that they hide it and keep it anyway, that they could keep it a secret from Bill. They had all agreed.

They had hidden the little dog in a storage shed at the back of the grounds at night, then moved him wherever he was least likely to be found during the day. He had been a kind, gentle secret that bound the children, so unlike the dark, ugly secrets they had shared before.

But one night, when they'd come in from robbing the home of the president of the local college, Bill told them that he'd discovered the puppy, and that he realized how much they must love the dog to work so hard to hide him for so long. He told them that they had worked hard for him, too, and that they deserved something of their own for their labors. He told them they didn't have to hide the puppy anymore.

Eagerly, they had all run out to the shed to get the puppy and bring him in, each of them arguing about which one of them the dog would sleep with that night. They had reached the shed, thrown open the door, flicked on the light—

The puppy lay dead on the floor, shot through the head.

Bill had taught them a valuable lesson.

She wondered how many more "valuable lessons" he had taught to Jimmy and Lisa and all those other children at the home—lessons that might twist and scar them for life. How many times over the years had she fantasized about a rescuer who would come and save them all from Bill. Maybe that was why she had suffered the childhood she had. Maybe God was grooming Beth to be the rescuer of these children. Maybe she was going to be their Esther, groomed "for such a time as this."

"I have to go," she said weakly, trying to sit up. "I have to get out of here."

"You can't leave, Beth. You have to stay, at least overnight."

"No, I can't. I have to talk to Phil, my editor. I have to tell him what happened. I have to tell him some other things."

"I've put too much pressure on you," Nick said, his eyes misting over. "I've made this seem like the most important thing in the world, and you almost got killed. It's not worth it."

"Of course it is! Until I get that story printed, I'm in danger. Once the story's out, it would be too obvious if anything happened to me. He wouldn't dare try anything." She looked up at him. "Nick, tell them I'm okay. That I can go. Please?"

"No," he said. "You're not as strong as you think. You have to lie still, Beth. You have to stay here."

"Then make Phil come to me," she said. "And call Lynda, and Larry Millsaps and Tony Danks at the St. Clair Police Department."

"Lynda's already here," he said. "With Jake and Jimmy. But I'll call the others. I'll tell them to come tomorrow."

"No, not tomorrow. Now! I have something I have to tell all of you, Jake and Jimmy, too. Something important, Nick. Please. It really can't wait."

"Okay," he said finally. "Just calm down. Be still. I'll go call them now."

CHAPTER THIRTY-NINE

The doctors were at first strongly opposed to having such a group in her room so soon after her injuries, but when Beth convinced them that her long-term safety depended on a quick arrest of the one who'd injured her, they finally allowed it.

Phil was the first one in when the group came quietly into her room. "Beth, are you all right?" he asked.

"Yes, for now," she said. "But I need to talk to you. All of you."

Lynda rushed forward and hugged her. "I'm so glad you're okay. And what a miracle that Jimmy wasn't there."

"Yeah," she said. "Where is he?"

"I'm right here," Jimmy said from behind Lynda. He came up to the bed, hands in his pockets, and glanced awkwardly at her. "Bill did this, you know."

She swallowed hard and nodded. "I know."

"But he'll get away with it. He always does."

"Not this time, Jimmy."

Jake bent over the bed and pressed a kiss on her cheek, and she saw Tony and Larry coming in. Nick was last to enter the room, and she held out a hand to him. He came to the bed and held her hand, lending her support he didn't even know she was going to need.

"Thanks for coming, everybody," she said. "I won't keep you long. You've probably all figured out by now that someone's trying to kill me, to keep me from finishing the story I'm working on, about the St. Clair Children's Home. Last night, the *St. Clair News* building was burned down, and this morning, the explosion—Bill Brandon doesn't want it printed." She cleared her throat and looked at her editor.

"Phil, you kept saying you wanted one more quote. Yesterday, I gave you one, but it was from an anonymous source." She hesitated, then forced herself to go on. "But it's time to tell who that source is. The reason this story is such a passion for me is that . . . I was the anonymous witness who grew up at SCCH."

Nick looked more stunned than anyone. His mouth fell open. "You what?"

Jimmy gasped, then narrowed his eyes and studied her closely. The others looked first at one another, then at her, shock evident on their faces.

"I didn't want to tell anyone because . . . being in Bill's home brings with it some degree of . . . guilt."

"Wait a minute," Phil said, scratching his head. "Are you telling me that you've seen these abuses firsthand?"

She closed her eyes again, and Nick tightened his hold on her hand. "I'm telling you that I've been involved in them."

Larry and Tony got up from their chairs and came closer to the bed. "So you were one of the kids in his crime ring? He actually used you to break into homes and steal things?"

"That's right. From the time I was eight years old until I left the home at eighteen." She lifted her chin high, to fight the tears pushing into her eyes, and met Nick's stunned gaze. "I'm sorry, Nick. I should have told you—"

Nick took a few steps closer, his face twisting as he tried to understand. "You were in that home? But I worked for HRS then. I would have seen you."

"No, Sheila Axelrod is the one who processed my release when I turned eighteen. And actually, we did cross paths a couple of times. But I've changed my hair color and cut it, and I changed my name. But I came to you when I decided to expose Bill, because I knew you seemed like someone who would listen. I knew that from the way you treated some of my housemates."

Nick was still gaping, disbelieving, and she turned back to Larry and Tony. "I realize that this confession could get me into trouble, and that's why I've tried not to expose myself in this story.

But Bill Brandon has got to be stopped. An old friend of mine from the home told me yesterday that if I wouldn't even talk, what made me think anyone else would? Well, now I'm talking." She looked at Phil. "You wanted a reliable adult's word? Well, here it is. She's got a name and everything."

"Awesome!" Jimmy said. "No wonder you knew so much about Bill. No wonder he knew so much about you!"

"Wow." Phil slumped back in his chair. "I can't believe this."

"Believe it. It's true. Bill Brandon trained me to be a thief, and for ten years, that's what I was. And as we speak, he's training other kids to be thieves. Maybe worse. Kids were involved in the arson last night. They could have been killed."

"There's more," Tony said, glancing back at Larry. "After the explosion at your house, Nick told us where the package was postmarked, so we went by that post office to see what they could remember about the package. Turns out that one of the postal workers saw a little girl bringing it in."

"A little girl, delivering a bomb?" Beth asked.

"He described her as six or seven, reddish-blonde, shoulder-length hair, big eyes, very polite."

"Lisa," Jimmy said. "It's Lisa."

Nick clenched his jaw. "Tony, Larry, you've got to get this guy. Somebody else is gonna get killed if you don't."

Jimmy's face was reddening, and his lips trembled. "You've got to get Lisa out of there. She doesn't know any better. She's just seven. He's so mean . . ."

"All right," Larry said. "We have ample evidence now to arrest Bill Brandon. If Judge Wyatt refuses us a warrant this time, we'll go over his head to the prosecutor. We'll have Brandon locked up by the end of the day."

"I wish the article hadn't been destroyed," Phil said.

"It wasn't," Nick said. "She has a copy in her car, with a disk."

"I was taking it to the *St. Petersburg Times.*"

"Good idea. They'll print it, if we can't. If you'll give it to me, I'll make sure of it, Beth."

"I want to make some changes, first. I want to put my own name in there, and write down what I just told you."

"You can dictate it over the phone. I'll call you here when I get to St. Pete."

"What about me?" Jimmy's rough voice surprised them all. "What about Lisa, and all the other kids? Are we gonna go to jail?"

"You leave that to me," Lynda told him. "I'll take care of everything."

"Can either of you lead us to where he warehouses all of the things he steals?"

"No," Beth said. "He never shared that part of the business with us. He just gave us our orders, and we followed them."

"Do you know who else was involved?"

"All of the adults who work for him, according to Marlene. But not all of the kids. Sometimes I didn't even know what other kids were involved. He seemed to pick out the ones he could control the best. The ones who would fear him and try to please him."

"Was there physical abuse involved?"

"Yes. Always. That was how he controlled us."

"Sexual abuse?"

She shook her head. "No, thank God. I was never molested, and I didn't hear about it happening to anyone else. I think Bill considers himself a fine, upstanding, normal citizen who happens to have an unusual hobby."

"How about you, Jimmy? Has Bill ever molested you or any of the other kids?"

"Not me, and not the others as far as I know."

"Just beatings."

"Yeah, and other things."

Other things. She thought about the plate-glass window, and the alcohol, and the puppy with a bullet hole through his head. Bill's cruelties knew no bounds. She wondered what horrors Jimmy had experienced.

"What other things, Jimmy?"

He looked down at his worn sneakers. "One time, Keith Huxtin fell from a ladder when he was breaking into a house, and he broke his leg. We didn't think anybody was home, but somebody was, and they came out and saw us. We had to carry Keith down the street to the van, running as fast as we could to keep from getting caught. Bill wouldn't take him to the hospital because he knew they were looking for a kid who'd been hurt. He made him sweat the pain out for two days. Then he took us to school early and made us carry him in and lay him in the hall. We had to pretend he had fallen at school, so Bill wouldn't be blamed and it would seem like it had happened two days after the break-in. Those idiots bought the whole story, even though his scrapes had already scabbed over."

"This van. What does it look like, and where does he keep it?"

"In the shed at the back of the campus. It's dark green."

Larry's eyebrows rose. "Can *you* take us to the warehouse?"

"No. I don't know where it is. It was always dark, and I was always in the back of the van. Sometimes there was a truck there, loading up. I don't know where they took all the stuff. Somewhere to sell it, I guess."

"There are a lot more people than Bill and the kids involved," Beth said. "I don't know who they are, but there are others."

"All right," Larry said. "We need to take Jimmy down to the station to make another statement, and we'll send someone in here to get Beth's. We'll also post a guard here for protection."

"I'm going with Jimmy," Lynda told Beth. "I'll be back as soon as they're finished with him."

"Nick, we need everything you've already compiled about the home," Tony said. "We're going to throw the book at this guy, and make sure no one drops the ball. We also need you to be there for Jimmy's statement. As long as a representative of IIRS is with us, we won't have to get any other bureaucrats involved."

"All right." Nick's voice was distant, and he seemed distracted, preoccupied, as he looked down at Beth. "I'll be back as soon as I get them what they need, okay?"

"Yeah," she said, touching his face. "Just one thing."

"What?"

"Are you disappointed in me?"

"Why would I be disappointed?" he asked.

"Because I lied about my interest in the case. And you didn't know that I was raised breaking into people's homes. You thought I was a normal, healthy woman."

"Hush," he said, stroking her hair back from her face. "Enough of that. You are a normal, healthy woman. And you're courageous. You could have let it all go. But you cared enough about those kids to tell the truth."

"Took me long enough."

He leaned over and kissed her forehead, but she could still see the troubled expression in his eyes. "I'll be back."

When the room had cleared out, Beth lay on her back, staring at the ceiling and wondering what would happen next. Wouldn't there be consequences? Wouldn't the media ask when she'd been old enough to know right from wrong, and to do something about it? Why she hadn't turned Bill in years ago? Maybe the media wouldn't ask—but *she* still had those questions. She pictured that little boy, Keith, who'd broken his leg and suffered for two days. The plate-glass-window incident could have been the last time, if she had found some way to turn Bill in then. Then Keith wouldn't have had to suffer. But no, she'd kept her mouth shut, and gone along, and even after she was out, she'd been so grateful and relieved to be away from Bill Brandon that she hadn't thought much about the kids she'd left behind. Jimmy had come only shortly after she'd left. Because of her silence, he'd suffered.

Now she wondered what her own personal consequences would be. While Nick was too kind to condemn her, did this revelation change the way he felt about her? It wasn't as if she was looking toward marriage, but the thought that Nick might reject her because of this filled her with despair. What if Nick, who dealt with troubled pasts and presents all day every day, decided that he didn't need all her baggage—that she just wasn't the one for him?

She wouldn't blame him at all if he did.

CHAPTER FORTY

Jake was in the Police Department waiting room when Jimmy, Nick, and Lynda came out of the interrogation room. Jimmy had just spent two hours answering questions, and he looked worn out.

Jake stood up as they approached. "How'd it go?"

"Okay, I guess," Jimmy said. "I think I told them what they wanted."

"All they wanted was the truth."

"Well, that's what I gave them." He looked up at Nick. "What now?"

"Nothing yet. We just have to keep you safe until we get Brandon off the streets and start moving the kids from the home. I'll spend the rest of the day trying to line up places to relocate them."

"You'll keep me and Lisa together, won't you?"

"Of course. I'll move heaven and earth to do that, Jimmy."

"Hey, Nick," Jake cut in. "Since you'll be so busy, and Lynda needs to go to the office, how about letting Jimmy spend the afternoon with me? I have some errands to run, and he can help me."

Nick looked down at the kid. "Want to, Jimmy?"

"Sure," he said. "It's better than nothing."

Jake chuckled at the under-enthusiastic response. He kissed Lynda good-bye and ushered him out to his car.

"So where are we going?" Jimmy asked.

"Someplace really important," he said. "Remember I told you I was going to try to get my medical release so I could get my pilot's license back?"

"Yeah."

"Well, it's this afternoon. I thought you might like to come with me."

He shrugged. "Yeah, okay."

"You can't go into the examination room, but you can wait outside, and if they turn me down, you can help carry me out to the car. I'll be too depressed to walk."

"Nervous?" Jimmy asked.

"Were you nervous in there with the cops?"

Jimmy nodded.

"That's about how nervous I am," Jake said. "I have a lot riding on this. I have a flying job lined up that I really want. But no license, no job."

"And you won't ask Lynda to marry you?"

He thought that one over for a moment. "I'm not sure, Jimmy. All I know is that I want to get back on my own two feet before I ask her."

"They'll give you your license back. Why wouldn't they?"

"Well, one of their concerns is my reflexes. Whether my legs have healed enough to react as they should. I think I've got that one in the bag. But the eye thing . . . Sometimes they'll overlook a false eye, if the pilot can convince them that his vision is fine anyway, that he can compensate with the other eye. But it all depends. Sometimes they decide it's just too risky, and they ground you for life."

Jimmy just looked up at him. "I hope you get it, Jake."

"Yeah, me too."

Jimmy sat by the window in the Federal Aviation Administration offices, staring down at the parking lot just in case Bill managed to find him and come after him here. If Bill only knew what he'd told the police, he'd kill him for sure. And if he couldn't kill Jimmy, he'd kill Lisa.

The door opened, startling him, and Jake came out, his face solemn and pale. Jimmy got to his feet. "They turned you down?"

A slow grin stole across Jake's lips. "No! They gave me my license back!"

"All right!" Jimmy said, jumping up and slapping Jake's hand. They both danced a little jig, and then Jake pulled him into a tight hug and almost knocked him over. "I'm glad you were here to share this moment with me, buddy. I don't think I could have done it if I hadn't known you were out here for moral support."

"I didn't do anything."

"You did plenty. You were here!"

Jake practically floated back out to his car, alternately walking fast, then punching the air, then dancing again.

"Wait till you tell Lynda," Jimmy said.

Jake shook his head as he got into the car. "No way. I still don't want her to know. I want to spring the whole thing on her when I ask her to marry me."

"So when will that be?"

"Soon, my boy. Very soon. Let's just hope she says yes."

"She'd be stupid not to."

Jake laughed. "You're a good friend, pal-o-mine. And just as a reward, I think I'll take you for my first post-crash flight without another licensed pilot tagging along. Are you up for it?"

"Yes!" Jimmy said. "Let's go."

At the airport, Mike, the owner, celebrated with Jake over the return of his license, and offered him free use of a rental plane for the afternoon. Jake took Jimmy up, and they flew out over the Gulf, where Jimmy had a bird's-eye view of St. Clair.

The familiar serenity washed over Jake, calming his spirit and making him feel close to Jimmy. "Isn't this beautiful?" he asked.

"Yeah," Jimmy said. "When I grow up, I want to be a pilot."

"I'll teach you myself," he said. "The job I'm hoping for is as a flight instructor. I'll do that part-time, and fly for several ministries around this area on the side. But I'm sure I could make time to teach a bright kid like you how to fly."

"It depends," Jimmy said. "I don't really know where I'll be. I may not even be in St. Clair anymore."

How pressing this worry must be for Jimmy, Jake realized. The low hum of the engine accompanied the thoughts going through both their minds.

"Tell me something," Jake said quietly. "Tell me about your parents."

"They're dead," Jimmy said quickly.

Jake knew that wasn't true, but he wasn't sure that Jimmy knew it. "Do you remember them?"

He shrugged and looked out the window. "My dad was a spy who was killed in France during the war," he said. That was impossible, Jake knew, but it didn't matter—it was a fantasy he could identify with. He'd never known his father either, and had made up similar stories.

"I didn't have a dad," Jake said. "Never knew him." Jimmy didn't change his answer, so Jake pressed on. "What about your mom?"

Jimmy took a little longer to answer that. "She died almost three years ago. That's why they put us in the home."

"What did she die of?" Jake asked.

"Cancer," Jimmy said. "She had cancer."

"I'm sorry, Jimmy. What kind of cancer?"

Jimmy thought for a moment. "Prostate cancer, I think it was."

Jake's eyebrows shot up. "Prostate cancer, huh?"

"Yeah."

"Oh." He almost smiled. "That's rare in women."

"Yeah."

"Do you remember much about her?"

"Sure. She was the greatest mom in the world. She made our lunches, and cooked these great suppers, and we'd all sit at the table and talk about our days. And we always had plenty to eat and warm beds to sleep in and clean clothes . . . and she loved us."

Tears came to Jake's eyes. The memories were sweet, yet the boy thought his mother was dead. What if he found out that she was alive? What if they reintroduced him to her?

He looked at the boy, and saw the solemn, dreamy look that had passed over his face. "Do you ever miss her?"

Jimmy swallowed and shrugged. He couldn't seem to answer, so he only nodded. "Lisa misses her most," he said. "She can't remember her too good. I tell her stories about her. Good stories, about all the things she used to do."

Jake had heard enough from Nick to know that none of those stories were true. But maybe they could be, if they reintroduced the boy to his mother . . .

The thought wouldn't leave his mind, and after they landed, he left Jimmy alone and made a couple of phone calls—to Lynda first, and then to Nick.

Jake didn't mention his phone calls to Jimmy when they got back into the car. Instead, he told him that they were going to the hospital to check on Beth, and that Nick would meet them there. But as he drove, he prayed silently that he was doing the right thing.

CHAPTER FORTY-ONE

Tracy had been moved out of ICU, Jake learned when he got to the hospital and found Nick waiting for him. Nick spoke to Jimmy, then stepped aside with Jake. "Look, if he gets upset or anything . . ."

"He's out of there. No problem."

"All right."

They went back to where Jimmy waited, and Nick leaned down to Jimmy. "Jimmy, before we go see Beth, while you're here at the hospital, I think there's somebody here you might like to see."

His eyes widened. "Lisa?"

"No, not Lisa. Someone else. A patient who's in here with pneumonia. I found her real sick the other day and brought her here."

Jimmy hesitated. "I'm not too good with sick people."

"It's okay. You don't have to do anything. You don't even have to say anything."

"Then why am I going?"

The elevator doors opened, and Nick led him on. "You'll see. Just wait."

Jake was quiet as he followed Nick and Jimmy off the elevator.

They reached the open door, and Nick peered in. It was a semiprivate room, but the other bed was unoccupied. Tracy lay in bed, IVs still attached to her and an oxygen mask over her face.

Jake touched the back of Jimmy's neck, and followed Nick in. As they came closer to the bed, Nick leaned over her. "Hi," he said. "How're you feeling?"

"Okay," she said weakly.

He looked back at Jimmy, who stood awkwardly back. "Recognize her?"

Jimmy shook his head. "No. Do I know her?"

Nick shot a concerned look at Jake. "I have someone here I wanted you to see, Tracy," he said.

Jimmy froze at the name. "No. Not her." His mouth tightened, tears sprang to his eyes, and he began to back out of the room. "I don't want to see her."

Tracy rose up slightly and saw her son. "Jimmy?"

"No!" he shouted, and the nurse came running. Jake grabbed him, but he shook free and fled from the room. Jake followed him out.

"Jimmy, wait!"

The boy ran to the elevators and began punching the down button, waiting for one to open. His face was crimson and covered with tears, and he turned his face away so Jake couldn't see. Jake squatted in front of him and held him by the shoulders. "Son, you don't have to go back in there. It was a bad idea, okay? We didn't know it would upset you. We thought you'd be happy. Will you forgive us?"

"So you proved I lied. You coulda just told me you knew!"

"I didn't know you lied, Jimmy. I thought you might really think she was dead."

"I know what you're all up to. You're gonna take Lisa out of the home and give us back to her. And it'll be even worse than it was at the home." His voice broke off, and he bent over, weeping, and covered his face with both hands. "I should have known."

"Jimmy, nobody's giving you or Lisa back to your mom."

"Lisa's better off where she is than with that sorry excuse for a mother in there!" Jimmy raged. "At least she has a chance where she is. I can take care of my sister better than *she* can. I was the one who did it, anyway, when we lived with her."

"Jimmy, you've got to trust us."

Jimmy's eyes flashed. "I don't believe anything you say. You're all a bunch of liars! You don't care who gets stuck with who, or what things are like there."

"Jimmy, listen to me, please—"

"I'm not listening anymore," he said. "Just let me go, and I'll handle things myself."

The elevator doors came open, and Jake grabbed Jimmy's shoulder and followed him on. *What a terrible move*, he thought. *What a mistake.*

"Look, son, you don't have to talk to me, but you do have to come with me. And you can just listen, okay?"

Jimmy didn't answer.

"We'll go for a ride. Maybe out to the beach."

Jimmy didn't respond.

The doors opened on the first floor, and Jimmy darted off. Jake caught up to him and grabbed his shoulder. "This way, little buddy," he said, and directed him to his car.

Back in Tracy's room, Nick tried to apologize to her, but the sight of her son had shaken her. She was crying and gasping for breath, and he wanted to kick himself for making such a stupid error in judgment.

"I'm sorry, Tracy," he said. "I thought—I don't know what I thought. That it would help Jimmy to see you, I guess. To know that he still has a mother. That he's not all alone in the world."

"I'm not his mother," she wheezed. "The state took him away. He hates me, and I don't blame him, 'cause I hate myself."

"Don't say that, Tracy," Nick told her. "How can you hate someone God loves?"

"God doesn't love me," she said. "Why would he love me?"

"Because he created you."

"Yeah, and then I destroyed myself."

"Not yet. It's not too late to turn around, Tracy. It's not too late to make your kids love you again, either."

She turned her head to the side and wiped at her eyes. "You don't even know what you're talking about," she said. "Just leave me alone."

Nick started to protest, then thought better of it. "All right," he said quietly. "Listen—if you decide you want to talk in the next hour or so, call me up in Beth Wright's room."

She didn't answer, and he felt a deep self-loathing. He shouldn't have tried it. So stupid. Defeated, he walked out of the room.

CHAPTER FORTY-TWO

Tony didn't even bother to sit down when they returned to Judge Wyatt's office. All he wanted was to snatch the warrant and run as fast as he could to SCCH so he could arrest Bill Brandon. "The evidence is overwhelming and conclusive, your honor," he told Judge Wyatt. "We have an adult who was raised in the home who has given us a statement. We have a child who's been participating in Brandon's crime ring recently. We have the murder of Bill Brandon's sister, and we have two attempts on Beth Wright's life—including a package bomb that almost killed her, and we have the arson at the newspaper the night before the article exposing Brandon would have come out."

Judge Wyatt adjusted his glasses and looked over the charges, a deep wrinkle clefting his forehead. He seemed to study it too hard, as if it required much thought, and Larry, who was sitting, shot Tony a disturbed look.

The judge started to get up, almost distractedly, as if he'd forgotten they were in the room. "I'll spend some time looking over these charges tonight," he muttered. "I'll take all of it under advisement and get back to you tomorrow."

"Tomorrow?" Larry sprang out of his chair. "Judge, tomorrow's too late. He's a killer, and he's trying to take out our main witness. She's in the hospital as we speak."

"She'll be safe until tomorrow," the judge said. "No idiot would attempt murder in as public a place as a hospital."

"Give me a break!" Tony cried. "What is the deal here? You've stood in the way every step of this investigation!"

The judge banged his fist down. "It's my job to ensure that you do your job within the bounds of the law, so that my court-room doesn't fill up with a bunch of lawyers who waste my time with technicalities and loopholes. I will not issue arrest warrants for every Tom, Dick, and Harry you *think* may have committed a crime!"

"Think? What does all this evidence spell, Judge? Witnesses, bodies—what do you want? You want him to come after you? Would you give us an arrest warrant then?"

The judge's dagger eyes pierced Tony. "Get out of my office. Now, or I'll hold you in contempt!"

"We're not in court, Judge!"

The judge snatched up the phone. "I'm calling security."

"No need," Tony said, jerking the door open. "I get the pic-ture."

Larry covered his face. This was going from bad to worse. "We need this warrant," he said, in a voice he hoped would appease. "There are children in danger, your honor. Every minute counts. Brandon knows we're bearing down on him, and he's going to get desperate. Please let us know the minute you decide to issue the warrant."

"You'll hear from me."

Larry followed Tony out, and Tony slammed the door behind them.

"Good going," Larry said. "That ought to change his mood."

"He's either senile or dirty," Tony said. "He doesn't want us to arrest Brandon, and there's a reason. We're going to the prose-cutor's office right now. We'll get the warrant from him."

"Whoa—we can't just go over Wyatt's head without talking to the captain," Larry said.

"Fine. Then let's do it."

An hour later, they sat in Captain Sam Richter's office at the police station, watching him pace, clearly disturbed, as he processed the facts they had given him. "Did he say why the evi-dence wasn't sufficient?" he asked. "Did he tell you what he would need to give you the warrant?"

"No," Tony said. "He's not interested in helping us on this, Captain. If we handed him videotapes of Brandon beating and maiming the kids, the man would still have to take it under advisement. Something stinks."

"Yeah, I'd say so. But I don't like making enemies of our judges. There's got to be another way."

"What, then?" Tony asked. "We need to get this guy locked up tonight!"

Sam sank into his chair and leaned back, staring at the ceiling. "But if we go to the prosecutor, and it turns out that Judge Wyatt has just taken a conservative turn and isn't really doing anything wrong, we'll have made an enemy out of the person who's supposed to be our number-one ally in this game."

"He's a judge because he's supposed to have good judgment," Larry pointed out. "If he's lost that judgment, for whatever reason, then he needs to be removed from the bench."

Sam opened a drawer and dug around, then came up with a roll of antacids. He broke the roll of tablets in half and put four into his mouth. As he chewed, he leaned forward on his desk, studying both men. "Here's what I want you to do. I want you to follow Judge Wyatt tonight. Just tail him and see what he does. If he's dirty, maybe you'll get evidence of that. Tomorrow, if he still hasn't issued the warrant, you can go to the prosecutor's office— I'll even go with you—and we'll try to get the warrant from them."

"What about Brandon?" Larry asked. "Captain, he's a killer, and there are people that he needs dead."

"You follow him, Larry. Watch every move he makes. Don't lose him for a second. In fact, we might be able to set up a stakeout in that hardware store across the street from the home."

Larry shot Tony a frustrated look. "Captain, that may not be good enough."

"It'll have to be," Sam said. "I'm not willing to bring a judge down until I know for sure that I have an excellent reason. It sounds like somebody tipped Brandon off about the article, right after you showed it to Judge Wyatt. Maybe it was the judge."

"I'd bet my life on it," Tony said.

They went back to their car, then just sat there for a moment before Tony started the ignition. "How do you do it, Larry? How do you stay calm when the top of your head is about to blow off? This whole Christianity thing is new to me, I know, but I don't think I'll ever get to the point where I don't want to throw a man like Judge Wyatt against the wall and beat some sense into him."

"It's not a sin to be angry, Tony. Christ got angry."

"It wouldn't be so bad if I could trust that the work we do out here, on the streets, is going to count for something, that it was a partnership. We nab the bad guys, and the judges and courts put them away. Now the courts won't even let me nab the bad guys."

"What do you think Brandon's next move will be?"

"Whatever he wants," Tony said, throwing up his hands. "He can blow up the police station, for all Judge Wyatt cares. Get an automatic weapon and mow down every kid in his home. You think Wyatt would give us a warrant then?"

"He'd take it under advisement."

Tony's face reddened as he jabbed the key into the ignition and cranked the old car. "Sometimes I think I need to find another job."

"You couldn't leave this, even if you wanted to."

"Don't count on it. It sounds better and better every day."

He headed out into traffic. "You can take this car tonight. I'll use my car to follow Judge Bozo around."

"Take your cell phone so we can stay in touch."

"Nick and Beth are gonna keel over and die when they find out that we can't get that scumbag today. Not to mention Jimmy."

"We'll just have to do the next best thing."

"What's that?"

"Make sure no one else gets hurt before we can get him behind bars."

CHAPTER FORTY-THREE

St. Clair beach was busy this time of year, but Jake found a parking space. Jimmy got out before Jake could say anything and headed for the long pier shooting out into the Gulf.

The wind blustered through the boy's hair, making him look small and vulnerable. Jake followed him down the pier.

When they got to the end, Jimmy leaned over the rail and looked out toward the horizon. Jake sat down on a bench next to where Jimmy stood and looked up at him. "Want to talk now?"

"No."

"Then will you listen?"

Jimmy ignored him.

"Jimmy, I know how you feel."

"No, you don't."

"Yes, I do. There was a time when I pretty much despised my mother, too. And I was embarrassed by her, and I never wanted to see her again."

Jimmy gave him a reluctant glance. "What did she do to you?"

He sighed. "It wasn't so much what she did. It was more what she didn't do. She wasn't exactly June Cleaver."

"Who?"

He regrouped and tried to find a more modern reference point. "She wasn't a storybook mom. She had a lot of problems. She caused me a lot of problems. And while I was growing up, I remember always thinking that the minute I was old enough, I'd be out of there and never look back."

"I didn't have to wait that long."

"No, you didn't." He looked up at the kid. "What did she do, Jimmy? Did she hurt you in some way?"

"Hurt me? No. She didn't pay enough attention to hurt me. Unless you call leaving us without food for three days hurting us. She was so strung out on dope that she didn't know where she was half the time."

"Pretty messed up, huh?"

"Yeah."

"So when you went to the home, I guess it seemed like an improvement."

He sighed. "I didn't have so much responsibility."

"How old were you?"

"Seven."

Jake thought it over. He almost couldn't blame the kid for hating his mother. No seven-year-old should have responsibility for his home, himself, and his four-year-old sister.

"What about when you realized the home wasn't what it seemed to be?"

"It was okay," he said. "As long as I did what Bill said, I didn't worry too much. He took care of us. And he never touched Lisa. I knew I could take whatever heat there was to take, if they'd just leave her alone. While I was there, they did. Now, everything's all messed up. I don't know where we're gonna live, I don't know if Lisa's all right—and if they give us back to . . ." His voice trailed off. He didn't seem to know how to refer to Tracy.

Jake understood. "Mother" didn't seem to apply, and neither did "Mom." "Jimmy, I want you to understand that when Nick went looking for your mom, it wasn't to reunite you, necessarily. He just wanted to see if she was still in bad shape. He wanted to see if there was any hope there."

"Well, there's not."

"Maybe not. Not in human terms, anyway."

"What's that supposed to mean?"

"It means that when we think something's impossible, or someone's impossible to change, God sometimes comes along and does something really awesome, and the next thing you know, you've got a bona fide human being there with morals and a heart and a conscience."

"You talking about your mother?"

Jake smiled. "No. I'm talking about myself, kiddo."

Jimmy leaned his shoulder into the rail and looked at Jake, grudgingly interested.

"Have you ever heard the term 'morally bankrupt'?" Jake asked.

Jimmy shrugged.

"It's a term used to describe a person who doesn't have any morals. Someone who lives for today, and only cares about the pleasures of the moment. Someone who doesn't care who he hurts or what he has to do to get what he wants." He stood up next to the boy and leaned on the rail, looking out over the ocean. "That's what I was, Jimmy. I may not have been a junkie, and I may not have had a couple of kids to neglect, but I was morally bankrupt. And God taught me a few things."

"I don't know if I believe in God," Jimmy said matter-of-factly. "But if he was real, what did he teach you?"

"He taught me that I was no better than your mom, or my mom, or any other morally bankrupt person out there. Some of us wear it prettier than others, some of us are masters at hiding it, but the bottom line is that sin is sin. We've all got it. And until we trust in someone bigger than ourselves, it'll do every one of us in. Me, my mom, your mom, you, Lisa—"

"We're already done in," Jimmy said.

"No, you're not. Because God can turn things around. He turned things around for me, and made a new person out of the sorry slug I was. He can do that for your mom. He could even do it for you."

"You calling me a sorry slug?"

"No. But I'm telling you that it doesn't matter that you didn't have a father to bring you up and take care of and protect you. I didn't, either. It doesn't matter that your only other parent failed you. It doesn't matter that the adults in your life, for the most part, have been morally bankrupt and even abusive. What matters is that there's someone more important than them, someone who has a lot more authority over you than they do, someone who loves you more than you can even love yourself—even more than you love Lisa."

The little boy considered that as the wind ruffled his hair. "Well, you can believe that if you want to. I'm not gonna make fun of you. I just don't believe it."

"That's fine, kiddo. I'm no preacher, and I'm not trying to shove a sermon down your throat. But take it from me, one homeless, fatherless guy to another: God is taking care of you, whether you believe in him or not."

"I don't want him to take care of me. I'll be all right. I want him to take care of Lisa."

"Her, too. If I'm lyin', I'm dyin'. God loves you both."

"We'll see," Jimmy said.

Jake smiled and messed up his hair. "Yeah, we'll see. What do you say we go back to my place and chill for a while? See what Lynda's found out."

He sighed. "Whatever."

"Okay. Come on." He started walking back up the pier, and Jimmy followed behind him a few paces. After a moment, he caught up. "Jake, why'd you say 'one homeless guy to another'? You have a home."

"Not really. It isn't mine. See, when I was where you are, homeless and broke, feeling like I didn't have a single soul to love me, with no idea where I would live, God sent Lynda to help me. And she did, man. I've been living in her garage apartment ever since. But it's not really mine, and even though I'm paying rent now, I still feel like I'm mooching."

"When you marry her, you won't be a freeloader anymore."

The choice of words both stung and amused Jake. "I guess not. Listen, I've been thinking. If she says yes, I'm gonna need a best man. You think you might be up for the job?"

Jimmy's eyes widened. "Really? Me?"

"Yeah, you."

"Well, I guess so."

"Good. But I may be jumping the gun. Maybe I need to wait until the bride says yes before I start planning the wedding, huh?"

By the time they got to the car, Jimmy's mood had lifted, and he was a kid again.

CHAPTER FORTY-FOUR

Beth didn't know if it was sheer boredom or genuine concern that made her decide to slip out of her room to visit Tracy Westin. Without asking permission of the nurses, she pulled on the robe she had borrowed from Lynda and walked weakly to the elevators.

It was only one floor up. Fortunately, Tracy's room wasn't far from the elevators, so the walk wasn't long.

Tracy was sitting upright in her bed, still weak, and still connected to an IV and a monitor.

Beth knocked lightly on the door and went in.

Tracy looked up. Her eyes were red, wet, and swollen, and it was clear that she'd been crying. Something about that fragility touched Beth.

"Hi," she said. "I'm Beth Wright. Do you remember when I was here yesterday, with Nick?"

Tracy nodded, her expression holding more than a little suspicion.

Beth looked down at her robe. "As you can see, I'm a patient here, too. I had a little accident, but I'm okay."

She was babbling, she thought, and so far the woman hadn't said a word to her. She wished she hadn't come. Tracy wiped the wetness from her face, and Beth wondered how to comfort her. "Want to talk about it?" she asked.

Tracy shook her head.

"Okay." Beth pulled up a chair and gingerly sank into it. "You look better. You have more color in your face." She realized, kicking herself, that that might only be because she was crying. Didn't everyone's face turn red when they cried? She looked down at her hands. "Look, I know you don't know me from Adam. And you probably don't feel like spilling your guts to a complete stranger. I don't blame you. So if you want me to, I'll just go back to my room." She started to get back up.

"What kind of accident?" The woman's question startled her, and she turned back around.

"What?"

"What kind of accident did you have?"

"Oh. I was kind of in an explosion. Somebody sent me a package bomb, and I made the mistake of opening it."

Tracy's face twisted. "Really?"

"Yeah, really. Pretty awful, huh? You think I look bad, you should see my house."

Tracy drew in a deep cleansing breath, and wiped her face. "No wonder there was blood on Nick's shirt."

"You saw him?" she asked.

Tracy nodded slightly, and tears filled her eyes again. "He brought Jimmy."

Beth stepped closer. "He brought *Jimmy?* He didn't tell me he was going to do that. He came by a little while ago, but I was sleeping, so he just left a note."

"Apparently it was . . . spur of the moment. It turned out to be a . . . really bad idea."

"Why?"

Tracy's face twisted again as she relived the scene. "My kid took one look at me and took off running. I told you, he hates me. He has every right."

"I'm sorry." But Beth didn't know if she was sorrier for Tracy or Jimmy.

"Yeah, me too. Too late."

Beth stood there awkwardly, watching her cry for a moment before it occurred to her to hand her a tissue. "I wondered why they didn't bring Lisa," Tracy said, wiping her nose. "Is she dead?"

"Dead?" Beth asked, surprised by the question. "No, she's not dead. She's just . . . she's still at the children's home."

"Does she hate me, too? I was hoping . . . that she was too little . . . when she left . . ."

"I don't know," Beth whispered. "I've never met Lisa. Just Jimmy."

"Ohhh," Tracy moaned on a weak breath. "Why didn't I just die when I had the chance?"

"Maybe it wasn't your time."

"Why not?" she asked. "I've seen it all. I've done it all. I'm just so tired."

"There's lots more, Tracy. And just because Jimmy doesn't want to see you now doesn't mean there won't be a chance later. And speaking of chances, Tracy, you've got another one yourself—to pull your life back together."

"Yeah, right." She looked Beth over. "Easy for you to say. You have people you can trust. You probably have a job, money—and you don't have a monkey riding your back, so hard that no matter how you fight him, he's still there, reminding you, threatening you, pulling you . . ."

"Addictions can be overcome, Tracy. Think about it—it's been weeks since you've had any drugs. You could walk out of here and never touch the stuff again. Nick found you for a reason. Someone up there was looking out for you."

"Why now? He never has before."

"Maybe he was, but you just didn't notice."

"Yeah, right." She looked up at the ceiling. "If there's a God in heaven, he wouldn't waste his time on somebody like me."

Beth understood that sentiment. She had uttered it herself. "Nick wasted his time on you. Do you think God isn't at least as compassionate as Nick?"

"I don't know," she whispered.

"He is, Tracy."

"I abandoned my kids. I was a lousy mother. I shouldn't have even been allowed to have kids."

The old bitterness from childhood reared its head in Beth's soul, and she tried to argue. "Don't say that."

But Tracy had more to say, and she sobbed out the bitter words. "You want to know what I was thinking that last time I left them alone? I knew they were there without any food or anyone to watch them. But all I kept thinking was that I needed a fix. That was the most important thing. And I did whatever I needed to do to get one." She shook her head and covered her eyes. "I don't even think I was that upset when I got home and found them gone. I was too high by then, and I didn't want to come down. Somebody told me a few days later that the state had taken them, but I never did anything about it. I let them take my kids, and the truth is, I didn't even care."

Tears stung Beth's eyes, and she wondered if her own mother had had the same attitude. Had anyone cried when she'd been taken from her home? Had anyone felt any remorse? Did it change anyone's life, one way or another?

"So don't tell me about God loving me," Tracy went on. "If God loved me, he would have let me die before Nick found me. Then it would all be over, and I wouldn't have to deal with all this."

Beth tried to harden herself, so she wouldn't fall apart. "I'll see that Jimmy isn't brought back up here. Then you won't have to deal with him."

"No, that's not what I mean!" Tracy cried. "I *want* to see him. It just hurts . . . The past . . ."

The past did hurt. Beth knew that more than anyone. And it was hard having compassion for a woman who had left her children to be cared for by an indifferent and impersonal bureaucracy, to be turned over to a thief and child abuser.

"Tracy, you can change if you want. But you have to want to. Nobody can force you."

"I *do* want to. I just don't know if I'm strong enough."

Beth sat there for a long moment, wishing she had some strength to give her. But she didn't think she could spare any. Her throat tightened until she felt as if she were choking. She had to get out of here. She had to go somewhere where the memories didn't rush up to smother her. She had to get away from Tracy Westin. "I've got to go."

Tracy accepted that without a response.

When Beth reached the door, she turned back. "Maybe I'll come back by tomorrow. See how you're doing." But she had no intention of doing that, and she suspected that Tracy knew it.

CHAPTER FORTY-FIVE

L ynda was home when Jimmy and Jake pulled up. She came outside to meet them, looking a little apprehensive, and Jimmy realized that Nick must have filled her in about the fiasco at the hospital. He hoped they all felt real bad about it.

He got out of the car. "Has Bill been arrested yet? Can they get Lisa out?"

Lynda shot a look to Jake. "Uh—no, Jimmy. Not yet."

Jake stiffened. "Why not?"

She sighed. "Judge Wyatt is still giving them a hard time. He's taken the matter under advisement."

"You're kidding me!" Jake said.

"What does that mean?" Jimmy asked.

Lynda didn't want to say it, but she bent down to get even with his face and tried to find the words. "It means that it may be tomorrow before they're able to arrest Bill."

"Oh, man!" Jimmy cried, backing away as his face darkened. "No way! *No way!* They can't wait."

"Larry and Tony are tailing him tonight, Jimmy. They'll make sure he doesn't do anything. They'll know where he is at all times."

"But they can't see into the home!" he shouted. *"If he beats Lisa, they won't know!"* He was crying now, and he hated himself for it.

Lynda reached out to hug him, but he shook her off. "I told you! I told all of you!" He ran into the house and back to his room.

He threw himself on the bed and cried into the pillow, cursing Bill Brandon, cursing the police, cursing his mother, cursing

Lynda and Jake. His little sister's safety depended on them, and they were stupid, all of them.

He had to talk to her. He had to call Lisa and make sure she was all right. Wiping his face, he sat up on the bed and tried to calm himself so that he could talk clearly. He reached for the phone and started to dial the number, then thought better of it. He'd tried that before.

The computer. He hadn't checked to see if he had any messages from her or Brad.

He heard Jake and Lynda in the kitchen, and he went into the bathroom and blew his nose, splashed water on his face, and dried it off. He went into the living room, and they both saw him through the door into the kitchen.

"Jimmy? You want to talk now?"

"No," Jimmy said. "Can I play on your computer?"

The question seemed to surprise them, but he knew it was partial relief he saw in their faces. They thought he'd be playing games or something and were glad for the distraction. "Sure, Jimmy. That's fine."

He went to the computer and turned it on, navigated his way to the network, registered himself as a guest user, and signed on. In moments, the computer told him he had mail.

Lisa had gotten his message!

He clicked "read incoming mail," and found Brad's screen name posted at the top.

He opened the letter, and read as the color drained slowly from his face.

> Lisa's hurt real bad from the beating Bill gave her. Jimmy, you need to come get her before he kills her. I'll leave Stella's window unlocked so you can get in. Please hurry!

Jimmy stared at the words, his heartbeat slamming against his chest. Then he sat back and closed his eyes in horror, trying to think. He'd known this would happen. He'd tried to tell them all, and they hadn't listened, because they didn't know Bill Brandon. He couldn't depend on them. He had to do something. He had to do something *now*.

His heart pounded so hard that he almost couldn't think. He had to get Lisa out of there. But he needed a weapon.

Beth's gun. He knew just where she kept it.

He navigated his way on the network to a game that had sound effects, and started it running. The sound would make them think he was still in there.

Then, leaving the computer on, he went to the back of the house. He knew that one of the bedrooms had an outside door. Quietly, he unlocked it and slipped out.

The backyard was fenced, but he climbed it and leaped down. Night had fallen, and no one was around to see him. Lynda's closest neighbors lived on the other side of the cluster of trees up the street. He ran through the woods until he came out on the street that ran parallel to Lynda's.

He was home free. All he had to do was figure out how to get to Beth's house to get the gun, and then get to the children's home from there without being caught. Then he had to figure out how to get Lisa out. He didn't know how he would do it, but whatever he did, it would be better than what all these grown-ups were doing.

CHAPTER FORTY-SIX

W hen Nick got to Beth's hospital room, she was standing at her window, peering out. For a moment, he didn't knock, just stood at the door without letting her know he was there. She must be doing well, he thought with a rush of relief, to be standing and walking without help. This morning, after the explosion, he had wondered if she'd even live to see another day.

He knocked lightly on the wall, and she turned around.

"Hi," he said.

"Hi." She had more color in her face than she'd had earlier, but the light was still gone from her eyes.

"Are you okay?"

"Yeah. They said they would probably let me go home as soon as the doctor came by one last time."

"Really?"

"Yeah. The thing is, I don't *have* a home."

"That's just temporary. You can rebuild."

She turned halfway back to the window and gazed out again. "What do you think of me now, Nick?"

He came further into the room and joined her at the window. "What do you mean?"

"Now that you know I'm a criminal." She couldn't look at him as she uttered the words.

"You're not a criminal. You're a hero."

She breathed a mirthless laugh. "Yeah, right."

"You are. If it weren't for you, no one would have ever figured out what Bill Brandon was doing with those kids."

"You would have. You already had a feeling."

"Feelings don't change things. They don't give you evidence. You came up with that."

"I *am* the evidence."

"That's not your fault."

She sat down on the edge of her bed, and Nick grabbed a chair and pulled it up to her bedside. Straddling it, he got close to her. "Beth, you can't blame yourself. You're a good person, no matter what Bill Brandon spent years trying to make you believe."

She didn't want to face him, didn't want to meet his eyes, but she forced herself to. "I'm not really a good person," she said. "I went up there to visit Tracy today, and I've got to tell you, Nick. I have a hard time with her."

Nick waited, then prompted her. "Tell me."

Beth sighed. She got up and went to the window, putting her back to him. "She brings back a lot of memories, Nick. A lot of really bad ones."

"Your mother?" he asked.

She closed her eyes.

"You know, I'd really like to hear about her," he said softly. "I want to know everything about you."

"My mother was like Tracy," she said, "only she wasn't a junkie. She was an alcoholic. My father got disgusted and left her—and me, too. I guess the Invisible Daughter wasn't important enough to take along. Eventually, the state took me away from her and put me in Bill Brandon's home."

He was quiet for a moment, then asked, "Have you heard from your mother since then?"

She gazed out the window for a moment, one side of her face cast in shadow, the other side in light. "She died a couple of years ago. Those distant relatives who were nowhere to be found when the state took me into custody managed to get in touch with me to tell me about the funeral arrangements. I didn't go."

Nick looked down at his hands. As many kids as he'd taken out of homes himself, as many as he'd seen neglected or abused by their parents, he would never have guessed that Beth had been one of them.

"All my life I kept thinking that something would happen, that she'd sober up and remember she had a child and come back and get me. She'd be this wonderful, perfect mom. But she never did. And then one day she was dead."

Nick got up from the chair and came to stand behind her. He touched her shoulder and leaned his forehead on the crown of her head. "Beth, I'm so sorry."

She swallowed back the emotion in her throat. "It wasn't that hard. It wasn't hard at all. I hardly knew the woman, and what I did know of her, I hated." When she turned around to face him, her eyes were blazing with tears. "I know we're not supposed to hate, Nick. I know that with all my heart, and I've asked God to help me with it. But I can't help it, I still hate. And the worst part is that the person I hate is dead, and there's nothing I could ever do to change it."

"You can forgive a dead woman, Beth."

She shook her head. "I don't think I can. Maybe after I've read through the whole Bible and learned all the things that I'm supposed to learn, maybe then I'll have the strength to forgive my mother. But right now, it doesn't seem possible. She doesn't deserve forgiveness."

"Probably not," he agreed. "But you do. You deserve to be able to let it go. Sometimes forgiveness does more for us than it does for the ones we forgive. Besides, God told us to forgive."

She shook free of him and walked across the room again, picked up a water glass from the bed table, turned it over in her hand, then set it back down hard. "You don't know anything about it, Nick. You've never been thrown away like a piece of trash. You've never been dumped into an orphanage under someone who's going to turn you into a thief for his own selfish gain."

"No, you're right. I never have."

"That's the thing with Tracy. Her life—her attitude—it reminds me so much of my mother's."

"She had some bad breaks, Beth. Maybe it's not too late for her."

"Bad breaks?" she asked with an angry laugh. "She *chose* to abandon her children. She got herself hooked on drugs. She was a junkie, and probably a prostitute, and you're telling me that she just had some bad breaks?"

"You don't know what her life was like, Beth."

"I know what *my* life has been like, Nick. I know that if everybody turned to drugs because of a horrible past, then I'd be the worst junkie in town."

"You're right. You have more strength. More character. You've risen above your past. There's something about you, Beth, that some people just don't have. It's what's so attractive about you."

She looked as if she didn't know how to respond to such a compliment. Nick sighed and rubbed his eyes. "But God's grace covers people like Tracy, too. When I found her, she was lying there helpless, almost dead. I don't know why God put it in my head to go look for her that day, of all days, but I did, and if I hadn't, she'd be dead now. That means that God loves her, for some reason that you and I may not be able to fathom. And she has the same opportunity for heaven that we have."

"That's absurd," she said. "God doesn't send junkies and child abusers to heaven. Tracy Westin has never done anything for God or anyone else. Even if she were to repent now and turn into Mother Theresa for the rest of her life, all the junk in her life up until now would still outweigh any good she could do. Even God's grace couldn't balance all that out."

"But that's the great thing about grace. It doesn't have anything to do with a balance sheet," he said with a smile. "How do you think that thief on the cross came out when God looked at his balance sheet?"

Beth tried to think. "I don't know. I still say he hadn't done that much wrong."

"He was *crucified*, Beth. Whatever he did wrong was bad enough to get him executed. The Bible calls him a thief."

She was getting confused. "But God wouldn't take someone like Tracy—or even me, for that matter—and give us the same reward he gives someone like you or Lynda! You've done good things all your life, Nick. You've probably never really done anything displeasing to God."

"Don't bet on it," Nick said. "In God's eyes, there's no real difference between your life and mine. The only thing either of us has ever done that would win us admission to heaven is to believe in and trust in Christ."

Her face paled again, and she sank down into the chair. "That's not enough. Not for someone like me. It wouldn't be fair to people like you."

He knelt in front of her, his eyes riveting into hers. "Yes, it is." He grabbed the Gideon's Bible off her bed table and flipped through the pages. "Here," he said. "Matthew 20:1." He read to her the parable of the landowner who paid the same wages to those hired at the end of the day as he paid those who had worked all day. Those who had worked all day complained.

Nick read, "'I want to give the man who was hired last the same as I gave you. Don't I have the right to do what I want with my own money? Or are you envious because I am generous?' So the last will be first and the first will be last.'"

He handed her the Bible so that she could see it for herself.

Tears came to her eyes. "But what about redemption? I'm not stupid, Nick. There's a price for the secrets I've kept all these years."

"Christ redeemed you when he gave his life for you, Beth."

She just couldn't buy it. Not the Messiah, dying for her, leaving her blameless. It was too unbelievable. "I'm not sure I agree with your theology, Nick."

"All right," he said. "Just promise me you'll think about it. Pray about it, too."

"I will." She took in a deep, shaky breath. "Faith is a hard thing for me, Nick. Sometimes I feel like I've got holes punched in me. If I walk carefully, I can keep everything in, but if the slightest thing shakes me, it all comes pouring out. All the putrid, ugly things about me that I don't want anyone to see."

"Well, we'll see what we can do about patching up those holes."

CHAPTER FORTY-SEVEN

Darkness seemed inviting to Tracy Westin. She watched lethargically out her window as the sun went down and twilight overwhelmed the sky. It would be night soon. But she needed more darkness than this; she needed enough to hide in.

She looked around her cold, sterile hospital room. It was better than anything she'd had in a long time, but she hated it. She didn't belong here. She didn't belong anywhere. Her life was hopeless, futile, and she didn't know where she had gone wrong.

Liar, she told herself. That was just one of the myths she'd been clinging to for years. She knew where she'd gone wrong—she'd gone wrong the first time she'd taken crack. It wasn't as if she hadn't known better. She had just wanted to be a part of things. She had wanted to fit in, to be a part of that group of people she admired who seemed so glamorous and exciting.

She'd never forget her first experience with the drug. It had been a high like she'd never experienced, yet afterwards she'd felt so low, so hungry for more, that it had changed her thinking. While she was pregnant, she had managed to stay off it, though she had occasionally smoked marijuana. She had told herself that she would clean up her act as soon as the baby was born. But it hadn't happened either time.

For years, she had blamed Jimmy and Lisa's fathers, the men who had wooed, then abandoned her when she'd needed them most. For years, she had told herself that she wasn't really to blame; she was just a victim, after all. But right now she didn't feel much like a victim. She felt like a monster who had ruined two young lives for no good reason. And that was hard to live with. So hard, in fact, that she really didn't want to live at all.

She was angry that Nick had found her lying in her room. If he'd just left her alone, she'd be at peace now. Or would she?

Was there really an afterlife? Was there a god cruel enough to prolong what she wanted so desperately to end? Would she pay the price for the sins she'd committed during her unhappy life? No, she told herself. If there was a god, he couldn't be that cruel.

Desperate enough to gamble that death meant an end to her existence and peace at last, she tore the IV needles out of her hands, peeled off the monitors glued to her chest, and threw down the oxygen mask that was making it so much easier for her to breathe. She didn't need this. She didn't need life. She didn't need another moment of it.

She pulled herself to the edge of the bed, sitting, trying to balance. If she got on the elevator and went straight up, would there be a window at the top from which she could hurl herself? It would be so easy. Just one step, and there would be an end to it all. And she couldn't get in anyone's way again, and she couldn't hurt anyone else, least of all herself. It would be the greatest act of kindness she had ever done for herself.

She touched the floor with her bare feet and tried to stand. Her legs wobbled beneath her, and she remembered how weak she had been when Nick had found her. She had thought she'd been getting stronger during these days in the hospital, but she knew now she was mistaken. She took a step, reached out to hold onto the bed table, then another step. She began to sweat and grow dizzy. How would she ever make it all the way to the elevator?

Finally, she backed up to the bed and sat again. She was too weak to kill herself, she thought bitterly. Wasn't that the way it always went? Finally had the courage, and now she didn't have the strength.

She wilted into tears and pulled her wobbly, bony knees up to her chest and hugged them tightly. She was sickened by her own frailty.

"What are you doing?" came the voice at the doorway. It was a stern nurse, and Tracy didn't have the energy to argue. "What do you mean taking that IV out of your hand? Girl, get that mask back on your face and get back under those covers!"

Tracy did as she was told. She didn't want to talk. She just closed her eyes, wishing to shut out the reality around her. The voices. The guilt. The demands.

She lay still as the woman reinserted the IV. It hurt—but that was fair. It was comfort that she couldn't endure. Never comfort.

"Where were you going, honey?" the nurse asked.

Tracy still couldn't talk, and as the woman put the mask back over her face, she felt sleep pulling her under. But not far enough.

CHAPTER FORTY-EIGHT

I t was already six-thirty, and Judge Wyatt hadn't yet left the courthouse. Tony sat at the wheel of his car, tapping his fingers impatiently.

The telephone on his seat rang, and he picked it up. "Hello?"

"Tony, it's me." Larry sounded excited.

"You got anything?"

Larry, who had been staking out the children's home from the hardware store across the street, began to chuckle. "He just came out and headed to a storehouse at the back of the campus. He opened the door, and voila! Inside sits a green van. I'm in my car; as soon as he hits the street, I'll be on his tail."

"Up to no good?" Tony asked.

"Definitely no good."

"Any kids with him?"

"No," he said. "He's alone."

The door to the side of the courthouse opened, and a cluster of people spilled out. At the back of the group, he saw Judge Wyatt walking regally, carrying his briefcase. He wondered if the briefcase contained the evidence they had given him, and if he indeed planned to "take it under advisement."

"Well, guess what. Our boy just came out, too. Call me if Brandon does anything."

"Yeah, you do the same," Larry said.

Tony clicked off the telephone and cranked his engine, waiting inconspicuously as the judge got into his Lexus and backed out. Tony waited until two or three cars got between them, then pulled out and followed the judge out into the downtown traffic. He had looked up the judge's home address, so he knew his likely route home—but that wasn't the direction that Wyatt headed. Curious, Tony followed at a distance, keeping a mental record of their exact route.

The judge slowed as they came to a gas station with a convenience store attached. Tony braked as the Lexus pulled into the parking lot next to a pay phone. He didn't follow, only pulled to the side of the road far enough away that the judge wouldn't spot him, and watched as Wyatt got out of his car and stood at the pay phone.

Who was he calling? Tony wondered. There was a cellular antenna on Wyatt's car, so Tony knew the judge had a car phone. The only reason he would have for calling from a pay phone was that he didn't want any record of the phone call—or didn't want it traced. Tony grabbed his phone, punched out the number of the police station, and asked for one of the cops that he knew would be around this time of day. "Hey, Mac, I need you to do me a favor. Find out the phone number for a pay phone on the corner of Lems Boulevard and Stone Street, and see if you can get a record of the last few numbers called from that phone. There's a call taking place right now; I want to know who's on the other end of the line."

"Okay, Tony, I'll try."

"Call me back on my cell phone. I'm keeping my radio off so my cover isn't blown."

He hung up as Judge Wyatt finished the call and jumped back into his car. When the judge pulled back onto the street, Tony let a couple of other cars get between them before he began to follow.

He still wasn't heading home, and he wasn't going back to the courthouse. Tony recorded every turn; the route had gotten too complicated to remember, so he scribbled the information without looking on a piece of paper on the seat next to him.

The phone rang, and he clicked it on. "Yeah?"

"Tony, I got the number of the latest phone call from that phone. It was a cellular phone number. 555–4257. It's registered to the St. Clair Children's Home."

Tony's heart tripped. "Are you serious?"

"That's right."

He watched the judge make another turn, and he followed. "Then my hunch seems to be right on the mark. Thanks, Mac."

The Lexus turned down a road that looked as if it was rarely traveled. Tony waited until the judge had rounded a curve before he turned in behind him. The road curved like an S, cutting through a dense forest. Tony passed an abandoned warehouse here and an old, dilapidated structure there. He started to get suspicious—was this some kind of trap? Had the judge spotted him?

No, not likely. Whatever Wyatt was doing, it had nothing to do with Tony. But Tony suspected that it had everything to do with Bill Brandon.

As he slowly rounded the final curve, a big warehouse came into view. Adrenaline pulsed through Tony, and he pulled off the road and into a cluster of bushes where he wouldn't be seen. He got out and pushed through the brush until he had a clear view of the warehouse.

"Bingo," he muttered. "Just what we've been looking for!"

Tony peered through his binoculars and read the sign on the building. He wrote down the name Winrite, Inc., along with the address, and waited for the judge to come back out.

He would look up the owner of the building when he got back to the station to determine what kind of business operated from here. A light went on in one of the rooms. After a few minutes, the light went out, and the judge reappeared in the doorway, locked up, and got back into his Lexus.

Tony got back in his car but kept his engine off as the judge pulled out of the parking lot and back onto the street.

Again, the judge headed away from home, and Tony found his heart beating faster as he tailed him. His gut told him something was going on. The judge was going to lead him someplace that he didn't want anyone to see.

The Lexus turned onto a street that took them near the underside of a bridge on the outskirts of town. It was hard to stay close enough to the Lexus without losing him and still not be seen, but Tony was good at this; he'd done it often enough.

When the judge pulled his car over near the bridge, Tony pulled his car off the road behind a grove of trees. After a minute or two, he saw another car approaching. It pulled alongside the Lexus and idled there a moment.

The phone rang again.

"Yeah?"

"It's me," Larry said. "Looks like Brandon's meeting with somebody. It's a light-colored Lexus."

"A Lexus?" Tony's heart pounded.

"That's right."

"Larry, I've been following the Lexus."

"You *what?* Who is it?"

"One guess."

There was a brief silence, then: "Bingo."

"Looks like we figured out why we can't get our warrant," Tony said.

"You were right all along, buddy."

"Wish I could hear what they're saying."

"I'll tell you what they're saying. Judge Wyatt's filling him in on the gory details of our meeting this afternoon. And Brandon's trying to figure out a way to get out of this whole mess. More buildings to burn down. More people to try to kill."

"No," Tony said. "Just one. Beth Wright."

"Don't forget the kid."

"Jimmy's safe. He's with Jake and Lynda."

"Called the hospital lately to see if Beth's all right?"

"I called earlier. She's getting out tonight as soon as the doctor makes his rounds."

"So where's she going?" Larry asked.

"Not sure yet, but I'll find out."

"Do that," Larry said. "I'd feel better if we had somebody watching her."

"We're low on manpower, buddy. With us watching these two, I don't know who's going to do it."

"Somebody'll have to," Larry said. "I'll take care of it."

CHAPTER FORTY-NINE

Lynda and Jake had talked through everything—the injustice of the judge's delays in issuing a warrant for Bill Brandon, the difficulty of Jimmy's reaction to his mother, the feelings of rejection that reaction must have caused in Tracy, their worry for Lisa, still in Brandon's clutches . . .

But they would solve nothing sitting at Lynda's kitchen table, so after a while Lynda went into the living room to check on Jimmy. Although the noise from the computer game had been consistent for the past hour, Jimmy wasn't sitting there. Shrugging, Lynda walked on past the living room, down the hall, and to the bedroom where he had been staying. There was no sign of him.

"Jimmy," she called. "Jimmy!"

When she got no answer, she went to the back door and looked out into the yard. He wasn't there. "Jake!"

Jake came from the kitchen. "What is it?"

"Jimmy's gone!"

"I thought he was playing on the computer."

"He's not." Growing alarm sent her running from one room to another, searching for the boy and calling for him at the top of her lungs, but there was no answer.

"Where could he be?" she asked Jake.

"I don't know. You don't think—"

"He's run away." Lynda headed for the telephone. "We have to call Larry and Tony."

Jake got to the phone first and punched out the number of the St. Clair Police Department. Larry and Tony were out, he was told, so he left a message and hung up. He didn't want to report the runaway, not yet, not until he'd consulted with Larry and Tony, and even Nick, on how to proceed. So far, Jimmy hadn't been officially reported missing. Reporting it now to people who didn't know the case might do more harm than good; if Jimmy were found, he'd probably be taken back to SCCH.

"I'm calling Nick," he said. "Then I'll call Beth. Maybe he went there, to the hospital."

"Do you think he may have gone to see his mother?" she asked.

"Doubtful," he said, "judging from the way he reacted today. On the other hand, sometimes our first reactions aren't what we really mean. Maybe he did go back to finally confront her."

"Why didn't he just ask us to take him? He knew we would."

"He was pretty upset," Jake said. "I guess we underestimated how much."

"But he seemed content in there playing on the computer."

"It was a ruse," Jake said. "He was just trying to distract us so we wouldn't see him when he ran away."

Lynda paced across the floor, running her fingers through her hair. "We should have kept an eye on him. We should have been watching him."

"We thought he was safe, Lynda. Who would have thought he'd leave here, knowing that Bill Brandon is still out there?"

"That's no excuse!"

Sighing, Jake dialed the number for Nick's house, but there was no answer, so he quickly dialed the hospital and connected with Beth's room.

"Hello?"

"Beth, thank goodness you're still there. I thought you may have checked out by now."

"No, I'm still waiting for the doctor."

"Beth, Jimmy's missing."

"What?"

"He's run away. He's gone."

"Weren't you watching him?"

"We thought he was playing on the computer. We were just in the next room. We're thinking maybe he went there to see you, or maybe even his mother."

Beth paused for a moment, thinking. "All right, I'll be on the lookout for him. But aren't you going to call the police?"

"We put a call in to Larry and Tony, but we're reluctant to report this to anyone else."

"Do it anyway!" she said. "Bill Brandon is out there, Jake. If he gets his hands on Jimmy, we'll never see him alive again!"

"But Brandon may have a police scanner. If he hears about the disappearance, he may find Jimmy before we do."

"Call anyway. *Please*, Jake. Maybe the police can find him."

In the hospital room, Beth hung up the phone and turned back to Nick. "He's gone."

"Where did he go?"

"They think he may be coming here. Maybe to see me, or you—maybe even Tracy."

"No way," Nick said. "Not after his reaction today. He wouldn't come to see Tracy."

"But, Nick," Beth said, "what if he thought it over and decided he does want to see her after all?"

Nick shrugged. "Well, maybe we'd better go warn her," he said.

"Yeah, maybe."

They told the nurse where they'd be in case the doctor came, then headed to the elevator. They got off on the floor above Beth's and walked quickly to Tracy's room. Tracy's eyes were swollen and red, and she looked as dismal as she'd looked when Beth had left her earlier.

"Tracy?"

She looked up, but her expression was lifeless.

"Tracy, we need to talk to you."

"About what?"

"About Jimmy."

She closed her eyes. "There's nothing you can say to me about Jimmy."

"Yes, there is. He's disappeared."

"What?" Her eyes came open fully, and she sat partially up.

"Tracy, I want you to listen to me, and I want you to listen carefully," Nick said. "Jimmy's been in trouble. The reason I came looking for you is that he and Lisa were in a children's home and Jimmy was being used in a crime ring. We're about to have the operator of the home arrested, but meanwhile, Jimmy's been hiding with us."

"And you let him run away?" Tracy asked. "How could you do that?"

"He's smart," Nick said. "He duped the people who were watching him by setting up a distraction, and he slipped out of the house without anyone realizing it."

"Well, is anyone looking for him?"

"Yes. But Tracy, we wanted to tell you, in case he comes here."

"Here? Why would he come here?" Tears spilled over her lashes, and she smeared them across her face. "I can't think of a reason in the world he would come to me."

"You're his mother."

"I'm *not* his mother!" she shouted. "He doesn't have a mother!"

Beth moved closer to the bed. "Tracy, you *are* his mother, whether you like it or not. Whether *he* likes it or not."

Tracy fell back on her pillows. "What if something happens to him?"

"We'll find him," Beth said. "They'll find him. He couldn't have gotten far on foot."

Tracy looked skeptical. "Like you said, he's a smart kid. He was smart when he was seven years old. He can go anywhere he wants to go."

"Not if people are looking for him," Beth said. "But Tracy, if he comes here, you have to tell us, okay? You have to call this number." She wrote down Larry and Tony's number at the station and set it on the bed table. "Do you hear me? You have to call."

"What if he doesn't want me to?"

"Do it anyway. He's in danger. The man who runs the home isn't in jail yet. If he finds Jimmy before we do, he may kill him."

"Oh, terrific," Tracy said. "So my son went from a bad situation with me to a worse one with some guy who could kill him, is that what you're saying?"

Nick leaned over her bed and touched Tracy's hand. "Tracy, look at me."

Tracy looked up at him with wet eyes that looked too big for her face.

"Tracy, there's a purpose in all this, whether you believe it or not."

"I *don't* believe it," Tracy said.

Beth felt her cheeks growing hot, and she tightened her lips. "Well, you'd better believe it, because maybe that purpose is to save and protect your son."

Tracy shook her head as if to rid it of the cobwebs. "What about Lisa? Is she in danger, too?"

"We're trying to get her out of the home," Nick said, "but we have to wait until the guy's arrested."

She closed her eyes, taking in the horror of it all. "What have I done to my kids?" she whispered.

More tears ran down the sides of her face, and Beth sat there staring at her for a long moment, feeling the pain that she didn't want to feel, because she didn't want to empathize with this woman who had abandoned her children. She wanted to hate her like she hated her own mother, but something about Tracy's pain touched her, and she leaned over the bed and touched the woman's hand.

"Tracy, it's not too late."

"What isn't?"

"It's not too late to become somebody to your kids. It's never too late until you're dead." Her voice cracked on the last word. "Take it from a kid who's been there."

Tracy brought both forearms up to cover her face. "I don't want to do this!" she cried. "I don't want to be here. I don't want to see my kids. I don't want to face them, and they sure don't want to face me!"

"If Jimmy comes, we'll help you," Beth said.

"And what if he doesn't?" Tracy cried. "What if he gets into more trouble? What if someone grabs him? What if—"

"Shhh," Nick cut in, trying to calm her. "Jimmy's a tough kid. He'll be all right."

"*What if he isn't?*" she screamed.

The silence in the wake of her question lay heavy over the room. "He will," Nick said finally. "Take my word for it. We'll find him within the hour."

214

"What if he went back to that orphanage?" she demanded.

"He would never go back there," Beth said. "He knows how dangerous that would be."

Tracy's sobs were deep, wrenching, soul-rending. "Are you sure I didn't die?"

Nick's own eyes were filling with tears. "What do you mean, Tracy?"

"When you found me lying there on that mattress, are you sure I wasn't already dead?"

"I'm sure," he said, glancing uneasily at Beth. "You're very much alive. Why would you ask a thing like that?"

"Because," Tracy choked out, "this feels like some kind of hell."

CHAPTER FIFTY

I t was getting darker. Jimmy knew that he couldn't hitchhike, since police were probably already out looking for him. For all he knew, his face could be on the screen of every television in St. Clair by now.

So he ran, as fast and as hard as he could, cutting through yards and plowing through woods, trying to get to Beth's house. His body was covered with sweat, and his shirt stuck to him, but he was glad that he had these running shoes. Bill hadn't skimped on shoes for the kids who "worked" for him. They had to be black, and they had to be quiet—for quick getaways.

His navigational skills were pretty good, just as his computer skills were, and he tried to remember where Bill had taken him the night he'd dropped him off at Beth's house. He had turned here, and passed that railroad crossing, then turned again . . .

By the time Jimmy found the long road that connected to Beth's dirt road, two hours had passed since he'd left Lynda's, and it was growing dark. He cut through the woods and hit the dirt road leading up to her house. He slowed to a walk as he headed up the dirt road, trying to catch his breath.

Because there were no streetlights on Beth's little dirt road, Jimmy was on the driveway before he saw that the house wasn't there anymore.

He squinted through the darkness at the gutted structure where he had hidden for so long, where he'd met the first adult who'd really cared about him in a long time, where he'd gotten to know the little puppy. He had known about the explosion, of course, but he had imagined it like one of those cartoon explosions, where one corner of a room gets soot on the walls, but nothing else is hurt. The condition of the house now stunned him, and he leaned back against a tree and slid down to the ground, almost dizzy with the reality of how close Beth had come to death.

And with that chilling thought came another: Bill had probably expected Jimmy to be at Beth's house, too. Had the bomb been as much for him as for Beth?

He felt that familiar pain in his stomach at the thought that his sister could have been killed delivering the bomb or setting the newspaper building on fire. He grew nauseous at the thought of her beaten up and awaiting rescue. He had to hurry.

But first he needed the gun.

There was nothing left of her living room. If the gun had been there, it was ruined now. Then again, she might have taken it with her in the car when she'd tried to go to St. Petersburg the day of the explosion, knowing that Bill was after her.

But where was the car?

He tried to think. It wasn't at Lynda's. It could be at Nick's. Or someone could have taken it to the hospital for her . . .

Yes. The hospital. It wasn't far from here. It shouldn't take long to get there.

He jogged back to the main road again, then cut through the trees skirting the street, hidden by the trees as well as the darkness.

Forty-five minutes later, drenched with sweat and panting, he reached the hospital. He went from one row to another, ducking between cars, until he spotted Beth's car. He closed his eyes and tried to concentrate on the gun being there as he approached it, as if wishing could make it so. Please be there . . . please be there . . .

The car was locked.

He looked toward the front doors of the hospital. Would anyone recognize him if he went in? He had no choice. Sliding his hands into his jeans pockets, the same black ones he'd been wearing since Beth had found him, he ambled up to the doors and slipped into the lobby. There was a coat rack in the corner of the room, so he checked to see if anyone was looking, then went over and grabbed a coat hanger. He shoved it into the front of his jeans, then pulled his T-shirt out to hang over it.

217

Quickly, he headed back out to Beth's car. Just as Bill had taught him, he stretched the coat hanger into the shape he needed, then maneuvered it between the rubber and the top of the window. In seconds, he had hooked the hanger onto the lock and popped it open.

When he opened the door, the light came on, making him feel vulnerable and exposed. He closed the door quickly, encasing himself in darkness.

He felt around on the seat. No gun. He bent and felt under it. Nothing.

Then he saw the glove compartment, and he punched the button and slowly pulled it open.

The gun lay there on its side, filling him with bittersweet relief.

His hands trembled as he took it. Quickly, he pulled his tee shirt up again. He stuck the barrel into his pants, as he'd seen it done on television, then tucked his shirt back over it.

He was ready. He could face a standoff with Bill Brandon now. He could rescue his sister, and maybe some of the others. He was ready to do whatever he had to do. And if he had to go to jail—whether for burglary or for murder—to see Lisa freed from Bill's bondage, then it would be worth it.

He got back out of the car and started walking in the direction of SCCH. His courage rose with every step, until finally he was running again. He knew the way to the home from here. And those who were looking for him would never even think to look there.

218

CHAPTER FIFTY-ONE

The party that Bill Brandon had insisted on having at the home was a first. He had never had one before—though occasionally local churches had given them Christmas parties—but this afternoon, he'd told the children that he was throwing a birthday party to celebrate all of the birthdays that occurred throughout the year. Everyone would be the guest of honor. He had let Lisa out of the back room for the occasion. Though Stella had dressed her up in her newest dress, she was pale and drawn. Weak from the fear of further punishment, she sat in a corner as the festivities unfolded around her.

This was some kind of trick, she thought wearily. He had called the television stations, and cameras went around the room, filming the happy faces of the children as they ate cake or tore into their presents—rag dolls for the girls and plastic race cars for the boys. It was as if he was trying to make the world think that they always did this, that he cared about the children, that he wanted them to be happy. She wondered what the reporters and cameramen would think if they knew where she'd been for the last day and a half, or if they could see the injuries under Brad's clothes. He, too, sat very still against the wall, pale and quiet, as if the effort of speaking might cause too much pain.

She got up, holding her rag doll by one arm, and went to the cluster of boys talking near Brad. She wasn't welcome among them, she knew, especially since Jimmy wasn't here anymore, but she wanted to hear what they were saying.

"I heard Stella say he was expecting someone."

"Someone like who?"

"Somebody from HRS, or cops, maybe. Probably what he warned us of the other day, after Jimmy got busted."

The faces in the circle changed, and Lisa couldn't hold her silence anymore. "Are they gonna arrest us? Did we get caught?"

"Shhhh," Brad ordered. "Are you crazy? Somebody could hear you."

"I told you she was too little to keep a secret."

"I am not too little," she returned. "I have kept the secret. But I don't want to go to jail."

"That's where Jimmy is," Kevin said.

"He is not! They don't have computers in jail!"

"Lisa, shut up!" Brad warned.

"Well, they don't!"

"What's that got to do with anything?" Kevin asked.

"Because Jimmy e-mailed me—"

Brad grabbed her wrist and jerked her to shut her up, when the other boys' eyes widened to the size of quarters. "You heard from him?"

"I'm not saying nothing," Brad said. "And neither is she. Are you, Lisa?" She didn't answer. "I can just tell you that Jimmy's not in jail."

"Well, what if he snitched on us? What if that's why the cops are coming?"

"It might be why," Brad said, looking back over the festive children and the cameras still going. "But I don't think so."

The door opened, and Bill came in, all smiles and laughter. He tried to act as if he genuinely loved all of the children in the home, bending over them and hugging them, wishing them happy birthday for the sake of the cameras.

"Why would Bill want cameras here if the cops are coming?"

"Maybe to show the world that he's really a nice guy, and that we're all happy kids who love it here, so that whatever Jimmy told them won't seem true," Keith said. "I wonder if he told them about my leg."

"He should have," Lisa whispered.

Brad hugged himself around the ribs that were probably broken. "I don't really care what he told them. I don't even care what happens to me. I just want them to get Bill. And I hope he tries to escape and they shoot him, just bad enough for him to hurt and see what it feels like. Then I hope he dies."

The other children only gazed at him, caught up in the terrors they wished on their keeper.

CHAPTER FIFTY-TWO

Weird," Larry told Tony via cell phone. Tony had followed the judge home and was now watching the house. Larry had set up his equipment on the second floor of the hardware store across the street, a vantage point from which he could see most of the buildings on the campus of SCCH. "Brandon just made it back to the home, and it looks like there's a party going on here. Television vans, music . . . I can see into the game room through a window, and I see balloons and streamers. Not exactly what I would have expected from a man who's desperate and knows we're coming after him."

"Sure it is. It's brilliant PR," Tony said. "He's trying to make the press think he's a wonderful guy. Get them all psyched up, so that when they get the real story, they won't believe it. Either that, or he can use it in court. 'Well, to be perfectly honest, Judge, I was just minding my own business giving a party for my beloved children, when the gestapo cops broke the doors down and arrested me in front of all of them. I only hope they're not traumatized for life.'"

"He knows we can't touch him tonight. Not until Judge Wyatt gives us the warrant, and you and I both know he won't do it."

"Well, I've been thinking. What if we went to the judge and told him what we know?"

"Like blackmail, Tony?"

"More like cutting a deal. We tell him that we saw him talking to Brandon, then he gives us that warrant, hoping we'll forget what we saw."

"No way," Larry said. "He's going down with Brandon. No deals."

Tony got quiet for a moment, thinking. "Then call the captain at home," he said. "Tell him about Wyatt's meeting with Brandon. Then try to get him to go to the prosecutor for two warrants tonight—for both of them."

"All right," Larry said. "But I don't want to leave for a while yet. I want to see how this party pans out. It could get interesting."

"At least the kids are safe while the cameras are there."

"Yeah. It's after they leave that I'm worried about. Any word on Jimmy?"

"Not yet. Lynda and Jake are basket cases. They've been out looking for him since he left."

"I hope that kid's all right," Larry said. "I just wonder what he's got up his sleeve."

"I'm just hoping he left of his own free will, and didn't get abducted without anyone knowing it."

"Well, we know Brandon and Wyatt didn't get him. I'd say he's just out there hiding somewhere, trying to figure out who he can trust."

"Let's hope it's not the wrong person."

CHAPTER FIFTY-THREE

Larry's car was the first thing Jimmy saw when he approached the children's home from the woods behind the hardware store. Larry must be in there, watching Bill. The fact that they'd put so much effort into watching him—yet couldn't arrest him—only reinforced the idea that Bill would get off scot-free. Nothing ever happened to Bill Brandon.

Jimmy stayed back in the shadows of the trees, trying to figure out how to get close to the cottages without Larry seeing him. He peered through the trees at the activity building. Something was going on at the home. It looked like a party. And television vans were outside.

He crossed the street a block down the road, then stole through the woods, staying in the shadows so Larry wouldn't see him. He came up on the other side of the building, out of Larry's sight, and peered through the window of the activities building. He saw Stella being interviewed by a local reporter, and across the room, Bill and some of the other employees of SCCH were also talking to reporters, smiling, laughing, gesturing at the balloons, the crepe paper, the happy children.

But not all the children were happy. Jimmy saw his sister Lisa sitting alone, holding a Raggedy Ann doll that she didn't seem interested in. She didn't look good. Near her, Brad sat hugging himself with a pallid, pained expression. Some of the guys around Brad whispered among themselves.

Jimmy turned from the window and looked across the lawn toward the cottages. The lights were all turned off. Maybe if he went in now and hid in the cottage where Lisa stayed, he could get her out tonight before anyone realized he was around. Brad had said he'd leave Stella's window open. He hoped he hadn't forgotten.

Stealing through the trees, he came up on the back door of Cottage B. He went to Stella's room and tried the window. It slid open easily. Quietly, he climbed in, shut the window behind him, and headed farther into the house. A strange mixture of sensations overwhelmed him as he walked through the building he had lived in for so long—homesickness and fear, familiarity and terror. Had any of this been worth it? Maybe everyone would have been better off if he had just found a way to get out of that attic and back to Bill . . .

No, that wasn't right. Eventually, Bill would have used Lisa in his little schemes, anyway. Eventually, Jimmy would not have been able to protect her. Eventually, Bill would have gone too far and killed one of the children. Eventually, they would have been caught. No, he had done the right thing. And what he was about to do was even more right—he had to save Lisa from Bill Brandon.

He went into the bedroom where he and Brad and Keith had slept, along with five other boys, in the bunk beds lined against the walls. Going to the bed that used to be his, he looked under it for the box of his belongings. They were gone; now another boy's shoes were there. Had Bill already replaced him? A sinking feeling began to pull him under. The feeling surprised him. He didn't live here anymore—didn't want to. But he didn't want to be forgotten, either.

He went to Lisa's room. He found his box hidden under her bed, and felt relieved that his sister had protected his things. *She* hadn't forgotten him.

He sat down on her bed, feeling so helpless, so dismal, so confused.

"It's not fair," he whispered to the darkness. "It's just not fair." He had done little to deserve all of this: the risks, the danger, the sadness. And Lisa had done even less. He closed his eyes and wished he had been able to protect her from the past few days. She was tiny, helpless—just the way Bill liked them.

Jimmy hoped he was getting to her in time. He knew she would expect him to rescue her, to make all the evil go away, to set everything right. She had always thought he was some kind of superkid, and he hadn't minded it. She'd looked up to him like he was her father. But he wasn't—and didn't have any more idea of how a father acted than she did.

He thought of the few men he knew that he admired. He admired Nick—the way he had gotten Beth out of the fire after her explosion and taken care of her. Nick had rescued Jimmy's mother, too—although part of Jimmy wished she had died. But then Nick was also the one who had placed him and Lisa in this home.

Tears came to Jimmy's eyes, and he wiped them away. Maybe Nick wasn't the one he wanted to be like. Maybe someone else. Someone like . . .

Jake Stevens. The name came to him with a warmth that burned in his heart. Jake was someone he could look up to. What would Jake do in this situation? How would he get Lisa out?

Lynda had told him how Jake had saved her from some murderer while he was still in his wheelchair. Even that hadn't stopped Jake. And Jimmy didn't plan to let anything stop him, either.

He heard car doors closing outside, and he peered through the window. The television crews were loading up, and Bill was standing outside with them, giving one last interview before they packed their equipment and disappeared. The children were still inside the rec room, and Jimmy guessed that Bill had them all doing cleanup detail before they could return to the cottages.

Just in case someone came back early, he slipped into the closet. He sat down in the corner and closed the door in front of him. It was stifling in there. There was no ventilation, and the hot Florida air was sweltering there where the air conditioner failed to blow. He reached into the waist of his jeans and felt for the pistol. It was there. If he needed it, he would use it. He wouldn't hesitate.

Across the street, Larry watched inconspicuously as the party broke up. Bill seemed to be trying to delay the television crew's departure. It was his last-ditch effort to appear to be a pillar of the community. He wanted to make friends with these people who, tomorrow, would have to condemn him on the news. He was running scared, Larry thought with satisfaction. He only wished he could walk up there right now, while the cameras were rolling, and slap some cuffs on the man's wrists. He wished he could expose him as a murderer, thief, and child abuser, and drag him away in front of all the children. Now *that* would be a party they could appreciate.

He picked up the phone and dialed Tony's car. Tony picked up. "Yeah?"

"The party's breaking up," Larry said. "Camera crews are going home. Has the judge moved?"

"Not an inch. He's tucked safely into his house. Doesn't look like he's going anywhere else tonight."

"Don't take your eyes off him, anyway," Larry said.

"I won't. I'm still trying to track the captain down. Call me if anything happens."

CHAPTER FIFTY-FOUR

J ake pulled his old car into the driveway at Lynda's house, hoping to see Jimmy sitting beside the door, waiting to be let in. They hadn't found him, and their only hope now was that he had decided to come back home.

"He's not here," Lynda said, defeated.

"Maybe he came in through a back door or something. It's possible. He went out one."

Lynda's dull expression didn't change. "He couldn't trust us anymore. I can't believe we let this happen."

"We didn't *let* anything happen, Lynda," Jake said. "It just did. It couldn't be helped."

In the house, Lynda searched every room, hoping, praying that he was there, sitting in the dark, brooding. But he wasn't. "Where could he be?" she asked, fighting tears. "Oh, Jake, he could be in real trouble."

She saw the glow from the computer screen still on in the darkened living room, and went in to shut it off. "If he had just said something—" She realized the computer was still on-line, so she moved the mouse to exit the game. "We could have taken him ourselves, helped him if he needed it . . ."

When the game window closed, the mail window was still on the screen, and she started to close it, too—then froze when she saw the letter on the screen, from someone with the screen name Drab11. "Jake—Jake, this is e-mail! Jimmy's been communicating with someone from the home."

Jake rushed over and read the letter signed "Brad." "You're right. And he didn't like what he heard."

"I don't think we have to wonder where anymore, do you?"

"No, I sure don't. Come on, let's go. Maybe we can stop him before he does something stupid."

"Wait. First we have to call Larry and Tony. Maybe they can get to him before we can." Lynda ran to the phone and punched out the number to Tony's car.

"Yeah?" Tony answered.

"Tony, this is Lynda," she blurted. "We've figured out where Jimmy is."

"Where?"

"He's gone back to SCCH to get Lisa out."

"No. He wouldn't do that."

"He's doing it. I'm telling you, that's where we're going to find him. We're headed over there."

"No way. Let us take care of it, Lynda."

"You said yourself that you aren't authorized to do anything! Tony, there's a child's life at stake here. Somebody has to do something besides sitting around watching!"

"Lynda, we know what's at stake! If you get in the way of what we're doing, I'll gladly arrest you myself. Now stay out of the way!"

Lynda's face reddened. "I'm a lawyer, Tony. You just try and arrest me! I'll drag you into court for false arrest, police brutality, and anything else I can come up with!"

"Go ahead," Tony said, undaunted. "I'll arrest you anyway. It would keep you out of the way tonight while we're trying to get to Bill Brandon. After that, you can do anything you want to me."

Lynda grew quiet, and she covered her eyes with a trembling hand. "So help me, Tony, if anything happens to that kid . . ."

"Let us do our job, Lynda. That's the best way to make sure nothing will."

CHAPTER FIFTY-FIVE

I t was at least an hour before the children began coming back into the cottage. Jimmy heard their voices as they approached the bedroom. The girls who shared a room with Lisa were laughing and talking about their rag dolls, as if they'd been given some precious gift they'd never forget. He couldn't hear Lisa's voice.

He heard the sounds of them getting ready for bed, then Stella's voice barking out orders. He waited until the light went out and everyone had quieted down, then opened the door slightly so that he could see where everyone was. There was Lisa, lying in her bed on her side, still awake, staring dismally into the dark. Her rag doll had been discarded on the floor beside her bed, but she clutched her old teddy bear tightly.

Why had they gotten presents tonight? What was Bill up to?

He felt for the gun again, and it gave him courage to wait. He sat there for what seemed an eternity, hoping the others would go to sleep. But it didn't matter if they didn't. He had the gun, and that gave him power. He could take Lisa anywhere he wanted to, as long as he had the gun.

When silence had prevailed for a half hour or more, he opened the door ever so slightly. It creaked, but no one moved.

He crawled out on his hands and knees, staying down in case anyone's eyes were still open. But they all seemed to be asleep, which surprised him. In his room, which was an older group, that didn't happen. They often argued long after lights out, or they were up getting ready to do some dirty deed of Bill's.

He crawled to Lisa's bed, then got to his feet and bent over her. He shook her shoulder, and her eyes came open with a flash of fear, making him wonder if she'd expected Bill.

He held his finger to his mouth, hushing her, but she couldn't help the gasp that escaped. *"Jimmy!"*

He put his hand over her mouth, but it was too late—a little girl named Jill opened her eyes and sat up. "What are you doing here?" she whispered in surprise.

"Shhh." He waved frantically for her to be quiet. "Come on, Lisa," he whispered. "Come with me."

"Can I come, too?" Jill asked.

"You don't want to go where we're going," Jimmy said.

"I might."

"Just *hush*. I came to get my sister, that's all. And if you tell—" He pulled his shirt up, showing the gun.

She caught her breath and lay back down quickly. "I won't tell."

Lisa shrank back onto her pillow, horrified. "Jimmy, where'd you get that?" she whispered.

He shook his head and put his fingers over her lips. "Come on, we've got to get out of here."

She got up and ran to the shelves where all of their clothes were piled in little cubbyholes. She pulled out a pair of shorts and slipped on her shoes. "Wait," she whispered. "I've got to get the box."

"Leave it," he said. "It doesn't matter. We can't carry it."

"Yes, we can," she said. "We have to. It has pictures of our mama. I don't want to forget what she looks like."

She ran to the closet and pulled out a black backpack—which Jimmy recognized immediately as the kind that Bill issued to all the kids who worked under him. His heart sank. So Bill had gotten to her, too. She stuffed the contents of the box into the backpack, along with her teddy bear, and slipped it onto her small shoulders. "I'm ready," she whispered with a smile. "I knew you'd come to get me, but he told us you were in jail."

"He's the one who's going to jail," Jimmy said. "Not me."

"But we've all broken laws," she said. "He said if we get caught—"

"He lied," Jimmy said. "He's a liar and a murderer and a thief and you can't believe a word he says. Especially all that Bible stuff."

"He said the sins of the brother are visited on the sister. Jimmy, what does that mean?"

"It means that if I see him face-to-face, I might just use this gun on him." He went to the window and tried to open it. It wouldn't budge.

"It's nailed shut," Jill whispered. "Bill did it yesterday."

He breathed out a ragged sigh. "Okay, then we'll have to go up the hall." He turned with a menacing look toward Jill, who still followed them with her eyes, though she lay quietly. "Jill, if you make one sound or tell anyone Lisa's gone before morning, so help me, I'll come back here and get revenge. Got it?"

"Okay," she whispered. "Bye, Lisa. Are you coming back?"

Lisa looked at her brother, and he shook his head no. The little girl's face changed to an expression of deep sadness, and she lay back down. "Are you sure I can't come?"

"Yes," Jimmy said. "Not right now. Maybe later."

He took Lisa's hand and tiptoed with her up the hall, desperately silent. He heard Stella moving around in her own room, so he knew that he couldn't go back out the same way he had come in. They were going to have to sneak through the den. He could only hope that no one was there. But he'd been trained in walking through people's homes while they slept and not getting caught. They cut through the dark kitchen, heading for the den, when the sound of the front door startled him. He heard Stella dash from her room into the den to meet her guest.

"I think that was a success, don't you?" It was Bill's voice, and Jimmy almost panicked. He motioned frantically for Lisa to head back to her room, and he followed.

"Absolutely. You've got them eating out of your hand," Stella said.

"Let's just hope they keep eating out of it," he said. "Judge Wyatt is fighting hard, but they may find a way to go over his head by tomorrow. It might be time for me to get out of town."

"And what about me?" Stella asked. "I'll be implicated, too. We all will."

"Just say you didn't know what was going on. That you weren't actually involved."

"But according to the paper, they know that it was a little girl who delivered the package bomb to the post office—and that she was seen with a woman in a pickup truck."

"That was me!" Lisa whispered. She and Jimmy were standing in the doorway to her room now, trying to listen. Jimmy put his hand over her mouth to silence her.

"They can't prove that woman was you," Bill told Stella.

"Bill, I'm not taking the heat for attempted murder. You know I didn't know what was in that package—"

"You knew it wasn't a box of chocolates."

"What about Jimmy?" she demanded. "He's still out there somewhere, telling his story."

Jimmy moved his hand from Lisa's face, and they both listened hard.

"Don't worry about Jimmy," Bill said. "He's not going to be a factor."

"Bill, you'll never get to him without getting caught."

"I won't have to," he said. "He'll come to us, before we know it. Maybe even tonight."

Lisa's eyes rounded with terror. Bill was *expecting* Jimmy!

But Jimmy only stared into space, trying to figure out how Bill had known he was coming—and how he and Lisa would get past him now.

CHAPTER FIFTY-SIX

Larry's phone rang, and he snatched it up.

"We've got a problem," Tony said before Larry could speak.

"What?"

"Lynda and Jake think Jimmy's headed over there."

"Here? To the home?"

"That's what they said. Seen any evidence of it?"

"No," Larry said. "Why in the world would he come here?"

"Apparently, he got a desperate e-mail note from some kid there to come get Lisa out before Bill killed her."

Larry's hand slid down his face. "Tell me you're kidding."

"No, and Jimmy must have taken off to rescue her."

"But he's a kid! He can't take on Bill Brandon by himself."

"Well, let's hope Jake and Lynda are wrong. But just in case, keep your eyes peeled and let me know if you see anything."

CHAPTER FIFTY-SEVEN

B y now, all of the girls in Lisa's room had awakened. They all looked at Jimmy as he and Lisa turned and came back into the room. "Don't anybody say a word," he whispered. He pulled out his gun again, just for good measure, and waved it in the air. "I'm not afraid to use this."

All the girls lay back down, their eyes wide as they watched to see what he was going to do next. Then Jimmy noticed that their eyes darted suddenly toward the door behind him.

"Jimmy?"

Jimmy swung around to see his friends Brad and Kevin standing in the doorway.

"What are you doing here?" Brad whispered harshly.

"Shut up!" Jimmy mouthed. "Bill's out there."

"I know he is," he said. "He came to get us. He wants Lisa, too."

"No," Jimmy said through his teeth. "He's not taking her." He stepped closer to the boys, keeping his voice as low as he could. "Cover for her. Distract him until we get out of here."

"I want to go, too," Brad returned. "Take me with you."

"No! Just Lisa. That's all I can handle."

"But you *gotta* take me, too," Brad whispered, starting to cry, something Jimmy had never seen him do before. "Bill's got it in for me lately. If you don't take me, you're gonna have to come visit me in the graveyard."

"No!" Jimmy cried. He reached out to push the boy away, but Brad winced and doubled over in pain.

Only then did Jimmy notice that Brad was wearing a long-sleeved shirt and jeans, rather than the shorts and T-shirt he usually wore in the summer. He remembered that he had done that, despite the heat, to cover bruises after Bill's beatings. "What happened?" he asked.

"Bill beat him up because of the e-mail," Lisa said.

A sense of dread washed over Jimmy. "What e-mail?"

"The one we sent you."

Jimmy's face went cold as the blood drained from it. "Bill found it?"

"Yeah, and was he mad."

The little girls were all sitting up now, and Lisa was on the edge of her bed, not sure what to do next.

Jimmy touched Brad's shoulder. "I'm sorry I shoved you, man. No wonder you wanted to leave so bad."

Brad wiped the tears off his face.

"The e-mails," he said. "You were the one who told me to hurry because Lisa had been beaten, weren't you? You're the one who left Stella's window unlocked?"

"No, man. That's not what I wrote. Bill must have sent that."

Jimmy felt such rage that his head threatened to burst. "It was a trap." His face grew hot and mottled, and he pulled the gun out of his pocket. "He knows I'm here. He set this whole thing up. Even left the window open for me."

One of the little girls buried her face in her pillow and began to cry, and the others sat huddled on their beds, eyes wide with fear.

"What's gonna happen?" Lisa asked.

"I'm gonna get you out of here, that's what," Jimmy told her. "All we have to do is get out the door. There's a cop across the street. As soon as he sees us, we'll be home free."

"Is that so?" The deep voice startled them all, and Jimmy turned and saw Bill standing in the doorway, leaning indolently against the frame. "Hello, Jimmy. Long time, no see. I've been expecting you."

With shaky hands, Jimmy raised the gun and pointed it at Bill. "All I want is my sister. Let us go, and nobody'll get hurt."

Bill laughed. "You don't know how to use a gun, Jimmy. And even if you did, you wouldn't."

"Watch me," Jimmy said through his teeth.

Bill started walking toward him, his hand outstretched. "Give me the gun, Jimmy, and then we'll go to my office and talk this thing out, man-to-man."

"Yeah? Like you talked to Brad?"

"Brad knows he deserved what he got. Don't you, Brad?"

"Yes, sir."

Bill got too close, and Jimmy shouted, "Don't take another step or I'll shoot!"

Bill laughed again. "Go ahead, Jimmy. You're not even holding the gun right."

Jimmy trembled as his finger tried to close over the trigger. It didn't budge. He squeezed harder. It was locked, and he didn't have a clue how to release it.

"Just give it to me," Bill said calmly. "I'm not mad at you, Jimmy. In fact, I've missed you. Things haven't been the same around here without you."

"Yeah? Is that why you've already put somebody else in my bed?" It was a stupid, irrational thing to say, and Jimmy knew it.

Bill shook his head. "Your bed is still empty. I put another kid's shoes there in case of an inspection. I didn't want them to know you were gone. I was afraid they'd come after you, lock you up. I was just protecting you." He leaned over, still reaching for the gun. "Jimmy, give me that thing."

"No." Jimmy backed away, and Brad backed with him.

"You have to cock it," Brad mumbled. Suddenly Bill's hand came down across Brad's face, knocking him down. The little girls screamed, and the others came running from down the hall to crowd around the door. Bill jerked Brad up off the floor and flung him back against the wall, and his fist came back to deliver another blow.

Jimmy cocked the gun and fired it.

CHAPTER FIFTY-EIGHT

Beth was watching Nick load her things onto a cart so that he could roll them out of the hospital when Lynda and Jake came in.

"Did you find him?" Beth asked the moment she saw them.

Nick swung around. "Is he all right?"

"No, we didn't find him, but we think we know where he is," Lynda said.

"Where?"

"We think he went back to the home to try to get Lisa out."

"No!" Nick cried.

"Apparently, he did." Lynda quickly recounted the story of the e-mail.

"Well, we've got to get over there!" Beth said.

"No, Tony and Larry are working on it. They made us promise to stay away."

"But we *can't* stay away. What if they mess things up?"

"They won't. We just have to have faith. Tony's been trying to track down the prosecutor to get a warrant. As soon as he gets it, we can go in there and get Jimmy and Lisa out. Until then, Beth, you can come back to my house. Your things are there from the other night, anyway. You can stay until your house is rebuilt."

A few minutes later, as Nick started the engine of Beth's car in the hospital parking lot, she looked uneasily at the shadows around them. "It's getting down to the wire," she said.

"Yeah, it's getting pretty hairy."

"He's going to kill somebody tonight," she said. "Might be Jimmy. Might be me." Beth closed her eyes. "What in the world have I started?"

"You didn't start it. Bill Brandon did."

"But I could have let it go. And the worst those kids ever would have been guilty of was robbing people's houses and businesses. They might have been beaten a time or two, but they wouldn't have been killed."

"Stop it. You're believing the lie that you did the wrong thing. You did the *right* thing, Beth."

He pulled out of the parking space and shifted into drive. They drove slowly past a van, and she jumped as she noticed someone standing on the other side of it. *Just a hospital visitor*, she realized with relief—but it could just as easily have been Bill, or one of his cohorts. He could ambush her at any second, and he wouldn't hesitate if he got the chance.

She was trembling now, and she reached into her glove compartment to get her gun.

"Oh, no."

"What?"

"My gun. It was here, but it's gone. Somebody's taken it."

"But the doors were locked. It didn't look broken into."

"Jimmy," she said. "Bill taught us how to break into cars as well as buildings. Sometimes there were valuable things in cars. Laptop computers, stereos, cellular phones, money—guns. Jimmy knew I had the gun. He came after it. He was here."

Nick braked and sat there for a moment, staring at her. Then he drove to the other side of the parking lot, where Lynda and Jake were standing and talking near Nick's car, which Jake had agreed to drive home for him. Nick rolled his window down.

"Jimmy was here," Nick told them. "And he's got Beth's gun."

CHAPTER FIFTY-NINE

When Nick rushed through Tracy's hospital room door, panting and sweating as if he'd run all the way up, she knew that something was wrong.

"I started to leave, but I thought you should know," he said. "We figured out where Jimmy is. We think he went back to the home to rescue Lisa."

She sat up abruptly and jerked the oxygen mask off her face. "Somebody's got to stop him."

"That's what we plan to do," he said. "I just thought you should know. He could still come here, if we're wrong, and if he does, you have to call us, okay?" When she'd promised, he nodded and ran out.

It took Tracy less than a minute to get the IV out of her hand and pull off the other monitors and cords. She got to her feet and wobbled to the window. Down in the illuminated parking lot, three cars caravanned out—probably Nick and his friends. What if they couldn't stop him?

She stood there for a moment, feeling totally helpless, completely alone, realizing just how badly she had failed her children so many years ago. But she hadn't been herself then. She hadn't understood what was happening. She hadn't cared.

She cared now.

In the closet of her room, she found the dirty clothes she had worn into the hospital. They were filthy, but they were all she had, so holding the counter to steady herself, she pulled them on.

When she'd dressed, she sat abruptly on the edge of her bed because she was so dizzy. It didn't matter. She was determined to get out of here. She had to find her son and her daughter and save them if she could. Maybe then she could redeem herself with them. Maybe for once in their young lives, they could believe that their mother cared about them.

How she would get there she had no idea, but she made her way to the elevator, punched the button, then flopped against the corner and waited for it to hit the first floor, feeling as if she would pass out at any moment. Her lungs felt as if a great weight sat on them, keeping her from breathing, but she pressed on. When the doors opened, she stumbled off and walked out into the parking lot.

Where would she go? How would she get there?

She looked around at the hundreds of cars lining the parking lot and wished one of them was hers. She did have one, sitting out in front of her apartment, though all but one seat was torn out and it had a rusted fender and was missing a door. If she could just get to it, she could drive it. The engine was one of the few things that still worked.

She saw two people walking out to their car, and she made her way toward them. "Excuse me," she said, then had a fit of coughing, which caught their attention. She struggled to catch her breath, supporting herself against the fender of a car.

"Are you all right?" the elderly lady asked her.

"Yes. I've just got a cold," she said, breathless. "Listen, I have a flat tire, and I really need to get home. Could you give me a ride?"

The woman set a maternal hand on Tracy's forehead. "Honey, you're burning up! Have you seen a doctor?"

"Yes, just now. I'm fine, really. I just have asthma—probably the stress of the flat tire brought it on. I have to get home. I don't live that far, I don't think."

"Certainly we can give you a ride," the man said.

"I don't have any money."

"We don't need any," he said. "Come on, dear. Let's get you out of this night air."

She tried to look stronger than she was as she sat in the backseat, but they kept looking over their shoulders with concern. They were nice people. Grandparent types. She wished Jimmy and Lisa could have people like them in their lives.

She gave them directions until they came to her corner, and she started to get out.

"Thank you very much."

The old man reached back across the seat to stop her. "Miss, are you sure you want me to let you off here? It doesn't look very safe."

"It's better than it looks," she said. "Bye now."

She closed the door and headed for her apartment steps.

The couple sat in their car, watching her. She knew they wouldn't leave until she had gone in. But she had no intention of trying to climb those stairs. Instead, she just stepped into the shadows and stood still until, apparently assuming she was safe inside a downstairs apartment, they pulled away.

She made her way slowly and with great effort down the block to where her car was parked on the road. The key was where she had left it, hidden between the vinyl and foam rubber of the torn visor. She pulled it out and jabbed it into her ignition. It coughed, then died. She tried again; finally, on the third try, it caught.

She sat behind the wheel, trying to wait out the dizziness. *Jesus, help me. My children need me. Let me act like a mother just once in this pathetic life of mine.*

The vertigo seemed to clear, and she pulled the car forward, trying to remember where the children's home was located.

CHAPTER SIXTY

The gunshot still rang in the air, and everyone froze. Jimmy had shot at the floor, but now he raised the gun toward Bill. "I told you I could do it," he said in a high-pitched voice that sounded as if it came from someone else. "Next time my aim is gonna be better." He looked down at the boy lying on the floor of the girls' room, half-propped against the wall where Bill had dropped him. "Are you all right, Brad?"

Brad stumbled to his feet, holding his ribs with one hand and his face with the other. "You gotta take me with you, Jimmy," he pleaded. "Please!"

Visibly shaken by the gunshot, Bill pointed at Jimmy with one hand and with the other gestured around the room at everyone else. "Everybody out," he said quietly, his voice trembling slightly. "Now!"

The ones clustered in the doorway scattered, and the girls in the room slid off their bunks and ran crying into the hall. Lisa stayed in her room hunkered behind her brother, and Brad stood next to Jimmy, facing Bill.

Jimmy kept the gun trained on the man who had exploited and abused him.

"You know, Jimmy, you may think I'm some terrible person," Bill said, trying to speak in gentle, soothing tones, "but that's only because they've brainwashed you, wherever you've been. Probably Beth Wright has been working her evil on you. But there's something you should know about Beth, Jimmy. That's not even her real name. She's really Beth Sullivan, and she killed my sister. But her wickedness will catch up with her. The Good Book even describes her in detail. It says, 'She has haughty eyes, a lying tongue, hands that shed innocent blood, a heart that devises wicked schemes, feet that are quick to rush into evil. She is a false witness who pours out lies and stirs up dissension among brothers.' She's like that, Jimmy, and the Lord finds those things detestable. But he knows my heart, and so do you. I forgive you for straying, Jimmy, because you're young and easily influenced. But in your heart, you know I've always thought of you as a son. My son."

Jimmy's cheeks mottled red, and he kept the gun aimed. Bill took a step toward him, but he backed up.

"Jimmy, if you do this, every child here will be farmed out to foster homes. Some of those homes are bad, Jimmy. Really bad. And those of you who have committed crimes will be locked up until you're so old that you'll never have kids of your own, or families. There won't be any hope for any of you. You kids are spoiled by all the nice things here, but you won't have that there. You and Lisa will be split up, for sure—since they don't jail men and women together—and you may never see her again."

"No!" Lisa cried. "Jimmy, is that true?"

Jimmy held his breath for a moment. "I don't know."

"But Jimmy! I thought we were gonna be together! I thought you said—"

"Listen to her, Jimmy," Bill cut in. "Do you want to hear your sister's screams as they drag her away from you? Do you want to wonder every night whose care she's in—and just what they're doing to her?"

Jimmy swallowed. He was getting confused. The thought of Lisa being placed in some foster home—or worse, a juvenile detention center or jail—where he didn't know who would be taking care of her, made him sick. Sure, Beth and the others had assured him that he and the other kids wouldn't go to jail, but he couldn't really trust what they'd said. They'd been wrong about other things. Still—"At least she won't be raised a thief or an arsonist or a bomb smuggler," Jimmy said. "Or even a murderer!"

"You've been watching too much television, Jimmy. You have a very loose grasp on reality."

"Like Beth?" he asked through lips stretched thin. "You almost killed her! And you did kill her dog. Dodger never did anything to you."

"It was just a warning, son," Bill said. "It wasn't meant to hurt anyone. I just wanted to put a scare into her to keep her from telling those lies." He bent over, his face too close to Jimmy's. "Jimmy, listen to me. All this time you were gone, I didn't report it, because I didn't want you to have to go to jail. Now you can just come back and pick up like you never left. No one will know. We'll just go on like we were . . ."

Bill's voice was mesmerizing, and Jimmy wanted so much to believe that he meant the things he said. Suddenly all that was familiar about Jimmy's life at the home began to call out to him— spending time with Brad and Kevin, his own bed, being able to watch over Lisa and protect her . . .

He lowered the gun slightly . . .

Bill lunged for him and wrestled the gun from his hand as Lisa screamed. He flung Jimmy to the floor, then turned the gun on them and laughed. Jimmy, Lisa, and Brad shrank back.

"I'm going to call a news conference tomorrow," he said, "and I'm going to tell the world that you three were responsible for the murder of my sister, the arson at the paper, and a hundred other crimes that haven't been solved. I'm going to tell them that you had a twenty-one-year-old cohort named Beth Wright who drove you, and every night you sneaked out to wreak havoc on the town. They'll have you locked in a cage in no time." He laughed cruelly, then regarded them tauntingly for a moment. "Or maybe I'll just decide to kill you first and dump your remains off a bridge somewhere. They'd never find you, not until the sharks had gotten their fill."

Lisa pressed herself into the corner of her room, trying to get smaller and farther away from the man who looked so natural with a gun. Brad stood next to her, a defeated, desperate look on his bruised face. Jimmy got up and stood in front of them both. "You'll have to kill me to get to them."

"I can do that." Bill backed to the doorway of the room and called out to Stella. She waddled into view, looking a little frightened herself.

"Go to the shed and get my Buick out," he said. "I'm gonna take these kids for a ride. After I get the stuff in the warehouse shipped and collect what's due me, then I'm going on a long vacation."

Stella dashed out, and they heard the door close behind her.

No one spoke until the car pulled up to the front door of the house and Stella came back in. "It's there, Bill. Just one thing before you go. What about us?"

"What about you? You're on your own. I'm getting out of here."

CHAPTER SIXTY-ONE

I'm exhausted," Beth said, getting slowly to her feet. She looked around Lynda's living room at Lynda, Jake, and Nick, who looked back at her with sympathy and understanding. "I need to lie down for a while."

"We'll wake you up the minute we get any word from Tony," Lynda said, with a weary smile.

Beth nodded and plodded down the hallway, apparently barely able to put one foot in front of the other. But as soon as she got into the guest room, her eyes brightened and her movements became quick and sure. She slipped out the back door of the guest room onto the patio and stole around the house to her car.

She prayed, as she started the car and pulled out of the driveway, that the others wouldn't hear her; she breathed a sigh of relief as no one followed. Then she headed for the children's home, determined to do something to keep Jimmy from getting killed. Even with a gun, she knew the boy was no match for Bill Brandon. Neither was she. But she might at least be able to distract Bill long enough for Jimmy and his sister to escape.

Her bandaged chest hurt as she drove to the home as fast as she could, knowing that Nick or Lynda or Jake might discover at any time that she was gone and come after her. She took every shortcut she knew to cover the short distance to the compound where she had grown up. After she pulled up to the front of the compound, she sat for a moment, letting the car idle with the headlights off as she stared up into the buildings where all those children slept at night, trying to forget the heartache and terror of their pasts—even though the present might be worse. Tears came to her eyes, and she covered her face with her hands. She hadn't seen Bill face-to-face since she'd walked out of the home on her eighteenth birthday. Just seeing him now would bring back a flood of despair and resentment and hatred. In truth, she might not come out of this alive. Bill wanted her dead, and wouldn't be likely to just sit back and watch her walk out.

She wished she had her gun. She couldn't go in there to face her enemy unarmed, not if she expected to help Jimmy.

She scanned the cottages. She wasn't even sure which one to try. And what would she do? Break in? Knock? What would she say when she came face-to-face with Bill? Was she really as tough as she thought, or would she melt in fear, as she had done as a child, the moment Bill's angry eyes had turned on her?

Hatred so real and vibrant that it seemed to have a life of its own welled inside her, and she suddenly realized that she didn't need a weapon. Her hatred of Bill Brandon was enough. It would propel her, drive her, protect her ...

She wilted. That was a lie. Hatred wasn't going to get her anything. There had to be another way.

The words of an old favorite passage of Scripture came back to her, and she chanted them in a whisper. *The Lord is my shepherd, I shall not be in want. He makes me lie down in green pastures, he leads me beside quiet waters, he restores my soul.*

Her soul didn't feel restored yet, but that was her fault. There was a price that had to be paid, a sacrifice that must be offered ...

He guides me in paths of righteousness for his name's sake.

She didn't feel righteous, either, but she wasn't finished trying.

Even though I walk through the valley of the shadow of death, I will fear no evil, for you are with me; your rod and your staff, they comfort me.

This was the valley of the shadow of death—it always had been for her. Now she tried to imagine walking into this valley with that rod and staff as her only weapons—and found confidence that they would be enough.

Armed with new courage, she got out of the car and slammed the door, not even caring if Bill heard her. She *wanted* him to see her, wanted him to forget whatever he was doing and come out to confront her. That might give Jimmy a window of opportunity to escape with Lisa.

As she entered the compound, she saw a cluster of crying children standing in front of one of the cottages, huddled together. The Buick that had tried to run her off the road days ago was parked in front of the door with the driver's door open. Across the compound, she saw Stella hurrying into a shed. The big woman backed a van out of it, and sped through the yard and away.

Beth approached the kids. "What's going on?" she asked.

"Bill's gonna kill them!" one of the children cried. "We heard a gunshot, but Bill's still in there yelling. He must have shot Jimmy or Lisa or Brad!"

Beth thought she might faint, but she forced herself through it. "Are there any other adults on the campus?"

"There were, but they all left!"

"Go over to the rec room," she ordered. "Get down on the floor and don't come out until I tell you. Do you hear me?"

She watched as they fled to the building across the campus.

Taking a deep breath, she tested the knob, then opened it. "Your rod and your staff, they comfort me," she muttered under her breath as she stepped inside.

She heard voices in the back room. Taking a deep breath, she held it for a moment, marshaling her courage and steadiness of mind. This was it. Then she yelled: "Bill Brandon!"

The voices stopped. "That's right," she called. "It's me. Beth Sullivan. You wanted me dead. Well, now's your chance."

CHAPTER SIXTY-TWO

The moment he had heard the gunshot, Larry had called Tony, explaining even as he pounded down the stairs and out the door what he'd heard. As he rushed across the street and toward the home, he said, "What the—Tony, you're not going to believe this."

"What!" Tony prompted.

"Beth. She's heading onto the compound—too far away for me to stop. Her car's out front here. Looks like she's heading for a group of children."

"What's she thinking of? If Brandon finds her, he'll kill her—he's already tried it twice."

"I'm right behind her," Larry said into the cell phone. "Send me some backups."

He tucked the phone into his belt pouch as the children fled to the rec room. As he rounded the corner, he could see Beth heading into the cottage where a Buick was parked out front. He pulled his gun out of his shoulder holster. Praying under his breath, he ran in a crouch the remaining distance to the cottage, went to the window, and looked through. Bill stood with a pistol pointed at three children—Jimmy and two others. The little girl had to be Lisa. The gunshot he'd heard hadn't wounded any of these people, apparently.

He heard Beth call out. Bill swung around . . .

CHAPTER SIXTY-THREE

Bill stepped slowly into the hallway, grinning at Beth. Then he motioned with the gun in his hand—her own gun, Beth realized—and Jimmy and two other children stepped out into the hallway with him, huddled together. Beth choked back her fear. "Let them go, Bill," she said. "Let it be just you and me, face-to-face."

He chuckled. "Well, well. Been a long time, darlin'. How are you?"

"Better than you expected," she said. "I'm just fine."

"Well, it was nice of you to drop in tonight. You missed the party, though. It was a good one. Made me some friends, I'll wager. You can never have too many friends in the media."

"Let them go, Bill," she said again. "You don't need them."

"Oh, I need them, all right," he said, slowly herding the children down the hallway toward her. "And as much as I'd like to finish the job I started a couple of days ago, I need you. I'm not stupid. I know the cops have been trying to get a warrant. I know that as soon as they do, they'll be out here to arrest me. But I won't be here. And neither will you. We're gonna be taking a little trip. I'll take all of you along for insurance."

"Just me," she said. "Let them go and take me."

"Let them go?" He threw his head back and laughed. "Beth, Beth, you know better than that." He was almost within arm's reach now. Could she grab the gun? No, too dangerous. If it went off and hit one of the kids . . .

"There are too many of us," she said. "We'll be too conspicuous. If it's just me . . ."

"Just you and me, Beth? Think about it. They'd shoot us as soon as look at us. You're nothing but trash, and you don't have family that'll sue them later. They'd be safe taking risks with a hostage like you. But with these cute little kids, they wouldn't dare take a chance, or they'd have the whole country coming down on them the minute they pulled the trigger. No, the kids are my ticket out of here."

"Where will you go?" she asked through her teeth. "Somewhere to ruin more lives? Are you going to keep killing everybody who gets in your way?"

"I might," he said with a grin. He grabbed her hair by the roots, and swung her back toward the door. "But right now, I need to keep you alive." He scowled at the three children huddled together. "Come on, kids. Into the car. All of you."

Jimmy held his sister close to him; tears ran down both their cheeks. "Beth, I'm sorry. I shouldn't have taken your gun. Now he's got it and—"

"It's okay, Jimmy," she said, her face reddening with pain as he jerked her by her hair. "Just do what he says."

Bill kept the gun trained on them as the children climbed into the backseat of the car. He shoved Beth into the passenger seat and said, "Scoot over. You'll do the driving."

He was just about to climb in after her when a voice cut through the night: "*Freeze!*"

Bill froze, then slowly turned to see Larry with his gun trained on him.

"Drop the gun and get down on the ground!"

Bill leaned down slowly, the gun still in his hand. His arm swung out, apparently to toss the gun, but instead he raised the pistol and pulled the trigger.

The children screamed as Larry dropped to the ground.

Bill dove into the car. "Let's go!" he told Beth. "Turn that key and get us out of here! Move!"

"You killed him!" she cried as she cranked the car and pulled across the lawn. "You killed him!"

"Yeah, and you're next! Now shut up!"

The children tried to muffle their sobs of horror as Beth tore down the dark street.

"Where are we going?" she asked.

"We're just gonna drive," he said. "Until I get far enough away that I don't need you anymore."

"And then what?"

"Then I'll find a bridge to throw you over. Every last one of you."

CHAPTER SIXTY-FOUR

Tracy was nearly to the children's home when she was overcome with dizziness. She pulled the car to the side of the road and tried to gather what little strength she had left. She was almost there. She had to make it.

Just when her head seemed a little clearer, a coughing fit hit her. It was getting harder to breathe. Her lungs felt heavy and full of fluid, as if they didn't have room for anything as mundane as oxygen.

She was still struggling to catch her breath when she saw a car race across the children's home lawn and shoot the curb onto the street.

The car sped toward her, and as it passed under a streetlight she saw Jimmy sitting in the backseat with a little girl next to him.

A little girl! Was it Lisa? Tracy sucked a huge gulp of air, despite the pain. Her kids were in danger. She was their mother; it was her job to stop him. Ignoring her weakness, she shoved her car into a tight U-turn, tires squealing, and followed the other car until she'd caught up with it. Then, stepping on her accelerator, she pulled up beside them and tried to pass.

The other car began to zigzag, to keep her from staying on the road next to it. But she wouldn't give up. Tears streamed down her face as she urged the old rattletrap ahead and, finally, almost through sheer force of will, she inched ahead of them. *This was it*, she told herself. Her last chance to do something for her children. Something important. Something that mattered. It was her last chance to show her children she loved them.

She cranked the wheel as hard as she could, throwing her car into a power turn, spinning out of control just a few feet in front of the other car.

Tracy felt the impact of the collision almost immediately, heard the crunching metal. She only hoped Jimmy and Lisa were wearing their seatbelts. Her car had none, nothing to hold her in, and the last thing she was aware of before she lost consciousness was the sensation of being thrown out of the car into the night air.

CHAPTER SIXTY-FIVE

There was a moment of shocked silence just after the two mangled cars ground to a halt. Then the inside of the Buick erupted in frightened screams. But the loudest was Jimmy's—because he had seen, behind the wheel of the rusty old car that had passed them and then pulled spinning in front of them, the face of his mother.

With no regard for Bill or any further danger, Jimmy bolted from the Buick and ran to the other car, which now lay on its side. But there was no one in that car. He looked up then, frantic—and saw his mother, several yards ahead, lying motionless on the concrete like a discarded rag doll. "Mom!" he yelled through his tears. "Mom!" He fell down beside her, wailing at the sight of the blood oozing from her nose and mouth.

But she opened her eyes slowly and looked up at him. "Run!" she whispered. "Take your sister and run!"

Jimmy was crying so hard he could barely speak. "Why did you do it?" he asked. "Why?"

"Because I . . . love you," she whispered. "Run, Jimmy! Please run . . ." Her voice trailed off, and Jimmy watched her eyes go dead and empty.

He wanted to stay with her, but her words echoed in his mind: *Take your sister and run.* He looked back toward the car. Lisa and Brad had gotten out, too. Bill had hit his head, and was holding it with one hand as he tried to crank the car with the other. Jimmy couldn't see Beth.

Jimmy ran to his sister and took her hand. "Come on, Brad," he whispered. "Let's hide in the woods."

He pulled Lisa after him, and Brad followed in a painful, stumbling run. Then he heard a yell. Looking back over his shoulder, Jimmy felt a surge of panic as he saw Bill throw open the car door and leap out. But with Bill's first step toward them, Beth dove from the car, landing on Bill's back, and wrestled him to the ground.

"Come on!" Jimmy urged, and pulled Lisa toward the safety of the trees.

It only took Bill a moment to regain his equilibrium, throw Beth off of him, and get the upper hand, but by then, the children were gone.

He grabbed her by the throat and lifted her to her feet. "Back in the car," he said through gritted teeth.

He threw her in on the driver's side, then pushed her across to the passenger seat. She gasped in pain as she moved, and he saw blood seeping onto her blouse from some wound he couldn't see on her chest. He jumped in beside her, cranked the car, and it started. He'd noticed some significant damage to the front of the car, but it looked driveable.

"Are you just going to leave her on the road?" Beth screamed.

"Shut up!" he shouted, bringing his fist hard across her jaw. "Don't say another word or it'll be the last thing you'll say!"

Furious, he drove around the wrecked car and the body lying in the street, and flew as fast as he could out of the area.

CHAPTER SIXTY-SIX

J immy urged Lisa and Brad through the woods at a run, trying to make it to the road on the other side where they might find help. Maybe a police car would come by, and they could flag it down.

Not long ago, Jimmy realized suddenly, a policeman would have been the last person he would have turned to when he was in trouble. For that matter, he wouldn't have trusted any other adults, either. But since then, he'd learned something: Adults weren't all bad. Beth had come here tonight, despite her fears of Bill, for the sole purpose of rescuing the children. And then there was his mother. A lump rose in his throat again, and he swallowed it down.

He still didn't understand why she had done it. She had already proven she didn't care about them. She had let the state take them and dump them somewhere. Why come back now, sick and weak, and risk her life to stop Bill from taking them away?

It didn't make sense. But it changed things, somehow.

"Why are you crying?" Lisa asked him breathlessly as they fought the vines and bushes in their way. "Aren't you happy we got away?"

Jimmy wiped his face. "Yeah, I'm happy. I was just thinking about the cop and that lady in the street." He couldn't tell her the lady had been her mother. Not yet. Maybe someday.

Brad was panting and wheezing, and Jimmy wondered if he was going to make it through the woods. He needed to get Brad to a hospital; they couldn't just hide someplace. Somehow, he needed to find help. Besides, they had to get help for Beth. They were the only ones who knew that Bill had taken her.

And he had to get help for all those children back at the home, who wouldn't know what to do or what was going to happen to them next.

The trees thinned, and suddenly they came to the road. Not far away was a gas station with a convenience store attached. Jimmy reached into his pocket for the change that Jake had let him keep when they'd gone for a Coke earlier. He fished out a quarter. "Come on, let's go call for help."

"Who are we gonna call?" Lisa asked.

He thought about it for a moment. "Jake," he said. "We'll call Jake."

Lynda answered on the first ring. "Lynda Barrett," she said.

"Lynda, it's me. Jimmy."

"Jimmy! Where are you? We've been worried sick—"

Jimmy cleared the emotion from his throat and tried to speak clearly. "I need to speak to Jake," he said.

"Oh . . . okay." Lynda gave the phone to Jake.

"Jimmy, are you all right?" he asked.

"I'm okay," he said. "But Bill's got Beth."

"What do you mean he's got Beth? Beth's here," Jake said. "She's asleep in the guest room."

"No. She came here. Bill's got her in a car, and he's taking her away. I think he's gonna kill her! Jake, you've got to stop him!"

"Jimmy, where are you?"

Jimmy was crying again. He stopped and wiped his eyes. "At the gas station about a mile from the home. I think it's called Quik Stop. It's on—" He checked the street signs near the phone booth. "The corner of Jefferson and Third Street."

"Jimmy, we're coming after you. You stay there. We'll be there in ten minutes."

"No! Don't worry about us! Lisa and Brad and me will be okay. You gotta worry about Beth. He'll kill her. And there's something else."

"Yeah? What?"

"My . . . my . . ." Jimmy lowered his voice to keep Brad or Lisa from hearing.

"What? I can't hear you."

"My m—" He choked on the word, then tried again. "Tracy. She needs an ambulance. And so does that cop—Larry, I think it was. He was shot."

"Shot? Are you sure?"

"Hurry, Jake! They may not be dead yet."

"But Tracy's in the hospital, Jimmy. You're confused—"

"No!" he shouted. "She came here, too. We'd still be in the car with Bill if she hadn't. But first he shot Larry, and then he ran over her, and she's lying in the road . . ." His voice broke off, and he couldn't go on.

"Jimmy, stay right where you are. We'll be there in ten minutes."

J ake drove faster than he'd ever driven in his life. In the passenger seat, Lynda was on the cellular phone, trying to locate Tony or Nick. She heard sirens, but they were coming from the opposite direction.

She found Nick in his office. "Nick, it's Lynda."

"Hi. I've been working on what to do with all the children. It's not going to be easy, but I think—"

"Nick, listen to me," Lynda said. "Jimmy just called."

"Oh, that's great! You've found him?"

"Yes. He went to the home, and something went wrong. We're headed to get him. He says that Bill's got Beth."

She heard something crash on Nick's end. "He can't. She's at your house! She was asleep—"

"No, she snuck out to go to the home to rescue the children. But apparently it backfired, and he's got her now."

"Oh, no."

"Nick, you've got to—" Her voice stopped as Jake slammed on the brakes and skidded to a halt. Lynda dropped the phone and looked through the windshield.

The headlights shone on something in the road, and Jake whispered, "Oh, God, please don't let this be."

"Tracy," Lynda whispered.

CHAPTER SIXTY-SEVEN

T he police radio report of an officer down at the St. Clair Children's Home stunned Tony, but before he could call in to ask for details, his cellular phone rang. He grabbed it as he turned a corner on two wheels, on his way to SCCH. "Larry?" he asked.

"No, Tony, it's Lynda!" She was choked and could hardly speak. "I'm sitting on Tenth about a mile from the children's home. Tracy Westin is lying in the middle of the road—she was thrown from her car. I checked her pulse, but there isn't one—she's dead, Tony. Bill Brandon ran her down. And Jimmy said he shot Larry!"

Tony went cold. "Larry?"

"Yeah. I don't have details, but I hear sirens. They may have gotten to him by now, but they're coming from the other direction and they don't know about Tracy. Jake's gone to get Jimmy. Apparently Bill had him, but Jimmy escaped. Bill's still got Beth, though! Jimmy said he's in the Buick. Tony, he's holding her hostage!"

Tony's heart lurched. He longed to check on Larry, but he knew that Beth's safety had to come first. "Lynda, I'm on my way."

It took only a few minutes to put an all-points bulletin out on the Buick, and soon roadblocks had been set up on the outskirts of town, and the policemen in other parts of the county were alerted. Additional ambulances and squad cars were dispatched to the children's home. As soon as the prosecutor had been informed of the circumstances, officers were sent to check out the warehouse. When they tallied over a hundred thousand dollars' worth of stolen goods, the prosecutor issued warrants for the arrest of Judge Wyatt, Sheila Axelrod, and her husband—in whose names the warehouse was listed—and all of the employees of the children's home, who had fled.

At the home, Nick paced the lawn in front of the cottages as they loaded Larry into an ambulance. He was still alive, thank God; Nick had no idea how badly he was injured. All he knew was that Beth was in danger of the same fate. In a few moments, when he saw Tony's car barreling into the parking lot, he bolted toward him.

Tony got out of the car and met him halfway. "How's Larry?"

"Alive," Nick said. "But unconscious. He's lost a lot of blood. It doesn't look good."

Tony fought the panicked rage and the furious despair threatening to smother him, and looked toward the ambulance, on its way off the property with its lights flashing. He was halfway back to his car, intending to follow it, when a cop shouted, "They've spotted Brandon's car! It's heading up Highway 18 toward St. Pete. There's a high-speed chase underway." Tony hopped behind the wheel and cranked the engine, knowing there was nothing more he could do for Larry, but maybe he could help save Beth.

"He's going to kill her!" Nick shouted. "Please, Tony, let me come with you."

"Who'll take care of placing these children for the night?"

"My colleagues," Nick answered. "I've already called in every social worker in the county. They're on their way. They can handle it."

"Nick, listen—we just learned that Sheila Axelrod is involved. She's probably being arrested as we speak. That leaves you. You're the only one who can take care of these kids right now. We're counting on you."

"*Sheila?*" he asked, then backed away, trying to sort it all out. He shook the information from his head and decided he could only deal with one thing at a time. "But what about Beth?"

"We'll take care of Beth. That's our job."

Nick kicked at some invisible wall in the air. "How could she do this? How could she confront him? She's *terrified* of him—and she *knew* he would kill her!"

"She did it for the kids," Tony said. "And right now she would want you to think of the kids, too."

Nick hesitated. "All right," he said. "I'll stay. But call me the minute you hear anything!"

CHAPTER SIXTY-EIGHT

In the Buick, Bill cursed as the flashing lights grew closer behind him. He turned off onto a little country road, then slammed his accelerator to the floor, flying around corners and curves. But the police stayed close behind him.

He kept one arm clamped around Beth's neck, with the cold barrel of the gun pressed against her cheek. Beth sat as still as she could, frightened that the slightest provocation might cause him to pull the trigger. He had nothing to lose. Nothing except his hostage.

As he drove, she prayed. Prayed that he wouldn't lose the police. Prayed that they would manage to set up a roadblock ahead of him. Prayed that she would find an opportunity to escape. Tears streamed down her face, born of all the confusing emotions whirling through her heart.

"You've sure caused a lot of trouble," Bill said through his teeth, clamping his arm tighter. "Unbelievable."

Beth tried to lift her head enough to see the squad cars in the rearview mirror, but Bill let go of the wheel, grabbed a handful of hair, and jerked her head back against the seat. "Be still," he said. "I didn't tell you to move. I'm not ready to kill you yet."

Only then did he notice the tears running down her face. "I've never seen you cry, Beth, darlin'," he mocked, his eyes back on the twisting road again. "Tears become you."

She stiffened her lips, determined not to shed another tear in front of him.

"Funny how scared you are now," he said. "You weren't scared at all when you were coming after me with both barrels for that newspaper of yours, hiding Jimmy from me, putting the police on my tail, turning HRS against me. But you know what? It didn't matter. I have friends in high places. Nothing you did could have gotten me. Even now, I'll probably get out of this scot-free."

"If they don't kill you first," she muttered.

"They *can't* kill me," he said. "They won't even aim a gun at me as long as I've got this one pointed at your head. You're my ticket out of here."

She didn't respond. And as the road emerged from the woodland and led them through a complex of industrial buildings, she watched his eyes dart, searching for something. "We're gonna find us a building," he said, glancing at the rearview mirror to gauge the distance between himself and the nearest cop behind them. "If I drive up to the front door, we'll have just enough time to get inside before they catch up."

"And then what?"

"Then I can negotiate."

"For what?"

"For a plane. I'm leaving the country, and you're coming with me."

"I'm not going anywhere."

"Yes, you are," he chuckled. "If I have to drag your dead body with me, you're going. Like I said, you're my ticket, and I'm not letting you go."

He swerved into a gravel parking lot in front of a building with light coming through the windows. Through the glass, they could see a man heading for the front window, probably alerted by the sirens. Bill skidded to a stop in front of the door. Grabbing Beth's hair, he pulled her behind him as he bolted from the car and, putting his shoulder to the door, broke through into the building.

The man who'd been working there backed into a stack of boxes, knocking them over. "What the—"

"Get out!" Bill screamed. "Get out or I'll kill you!"

The man stumbled to the door and ran out into the night. By now the parking lot was filling with police cars—skidding in the gravel, sirens blaring, their doors flying open as the officers leaped out to crouch next to the cars, guns drawn.

Bill threw Beth down on the floor behind a desk, reached to the wall behind him to turn off all the lights in the room, and grabbed the phone.

Wincing in pain, Beth looked down. The front of her shirt was spotted with blood where her wound was bleeding through the bandages. She tried to push back the pain and concentrate, instead, on finding some means of escape.

"Now we wait for them to call," he said. "Should be just a matter of minutes."

Beth jumped when the telephone rang almost on cue. He picked it up confidently, wiping sweat out of his eyes with the back of his gun hand. "One wrong move and she's dead," he said.

"What do you want, Brandon?" Beth could hear the voice from the phone's ear piece.

"A plane," Bill said. "I want a plane to take me to Cozumel."

"We're not going to get you a plane, Brandon."

"Then you'd better start calling her next of kin." He chuckled and glanced down at her. "Not that she has any."

"If you let her go, we'll talk about a plane."

Bill laughed. "You think I'm stupid? She's the only reason you haven't killed me yet. I'm not letting her go."

Bill hung up, sat down, and tried to catch his breath. Beth leaned back against a file cabinet. He kept the gun leveled at her, just inches from her face. Desperately, her eyes searched the darkened room, lit only by the flashing lights coming through the windows. This appeared to be a small accounting office. She looked for a knife, a letter opener, anything she could use as a weapon if she needed one. She saw nothing.

Bill got down onto the floor next to her and dragged her face close to his. His breath smelled stale, and she turned her face. "You know, Beth, I always liked you. Sure will be a shame when I have to kill you."

She glared back into his eyes. "Go ahead, Bill. Kill me." But she knew he wouldn't. Not yet.

Bill chuckled. "In good time, darlin'. In good time. How do you feel about being buried in Cozumel? 'Course, we could work out a burial at sea, if you'd prefer that. I could rent a boat and take you out over the Caribbean."

The phone rang again, and he jerked it up. "You got the plane?"

265

"This is Tony Danks," Beth heard the voice say. "I'm a detective with the St. Clair Police Department. I'm on my way over, and I think we can work something out."

"A plane is all I want worked out," Bill said. "I want a plane to get me out of the country. You have one hour, and then I'm gonna kill her."

"The minute you pull the trigger, we'll be on you like fleas on a mutt. I'd think twice before I tried that," Tony said.

"Get me the plane," Bill said, "and nobody else has to die."

Tony punched "end" on his cell phone, then punched in the number of the hospital emergency room. Concentrating on high-speed, one-handed steering down this curving road through the woods, he asked the nurse about Larry's condition. He was put on hold for what seemed an eternity, and finally, the nurse came back on the line and told him that they weren't allowed to give out any information until Larry's family was contacted. Tony slammed the phone down on the seat next to him and kept driving. Was Larry dead? Was that why they couldn't give him any information? He breathed a prayer that it wasn't so, rubbed the mist stinging his eyes, and pushed his car even faster.

Moments later, he skidded into the parking lot of the building where Bill was holding Beth. He grabbed his cell phone, made a quick call to the airport, then called the children's home and asked for Jake, who was still waiting there with Lynda and all the children.

"Jake, I need a favor," he shouted into the phone. "We've found Brandon. He's holed up in a building, holding Beth hostage. He wants a plane and a pilot. We're running out of time, Jake. We've got a plane, but we need a pilot. Do you have your license back yet?"

"You bet I do," Jake said.

"All right, get to the airport as fast as you can. We're trying to come up with a plan."

Suddenly Tony heard Nick's voice on the line. "Tony, where's Beth?"

"He's holding her hostage, Nick. He's demanding a plane."

"Don't let him take her out of the country!" Nick cried. "You've got to stop him!"

"We're going to."

"I'm coming over there right now," Nick said.

Tony thought about that for a second. "The other social workers are there to take care of the kids?"

"They are."

"All right. If you promise to stay out of the way and not do anything stupid, I'll give you the address."

CHAPTER SIXTY-NINE

Less than fifteen minutes later, Nick found himself crouching with Tony behind the squad cars in front of the building where Bill held Beth. Beside him, Tony dialed the number of the phone inside.

"We got you a plane," Tony said when Brandon answered. "And a pilot. How do you want to be transported to the airport?"

Bill hesitated. "My car," he said.

"You know we're not gonna let you drive off without an escort."

"Fine," Bill said. "Escort me. But once I hit the airport tarmac you stay back. I'm getting on that plane and out of here, and if anybody tries to stop me, Beth will be history."

Nick held his breath as the building's front door opened and Bill Brandon stepped out with an arm around Beth's neck. He opened the car's passenger door and climbed in, pulling her with him, then slid across to the steering wheel. He was obviously trying to keep Beth between him and the police, so that they wouldn't be able to get a clear shot at him without endangering Beth, too.

Nick watched as Bill's car started and pulled out on the street. The police jumped into their cars and Nick into his, following at the end of the procession.

"Lord, you've got to save her," he said as he drove. "I don't know why you brought her into my life, but I haven't felt like this about a woman in a long time, maybe never." His voice cracked as he drove at breakneck speed behind the procession of police cars, with a killer at the front of the caravan who seemed to be in control of it all.

When they reached the airport, the squad cars stayed back as Bill headed for the waiting plane. Nick stopped his car back beyond the fence and got out, standing with the cops to watch.

Bill pulled Beth out of the car and dragged her toward the plane. The only way into the plane was to climb up onto the wing and go in from there, but to do that, Bill had to let Beth go for a moment. Nick watched, holding his breath, as he lifted her up onto the wing, then quickly followed her before she could balk and run.

Nick let out a heavy, disappointed breath as the plane began to taxi out toward the runway.

"What now?" Nick asked Tony.

"Pray," Tony said. "Pray hard."

CHAPTER SEVENTY

In the plane, Jake tried to stay calm as Bill panted on the seat behind him, still holding Beth in a wrenching grip with one hand and pressing the barrel of the gun to her temple with the other. Jake didn't know whether she had noticed that he was the one flying the plane. When Bill had searched him after getting on, he thought Beth may have realized it was him. "Come on! Get moving," Bill said, "before they pull something."

"St. Clair Unicom," Jake said into the microphone. "Cessna 3–0–2–2 Delta requesting takeoff."

There was a crackling on the other end. "Cessna 3–0–2–2 Delta, go ahead. All's clear. Runway 3."

It was the same runway where Jake and Lynda had crashed, but he had overcome the fear of crashing months ago. Still, he had never flown at gunpoint before, and he'd never had a man like Bill Brandon in his plane. He glanced back at the couple entangled on the seat behind him. "Cozumel, huh? Nice place. I've been there."

"Shut up and fly the plane," Bill said. "And turn the light on back here. I don't want any surprises."

Jake cut on the dim light over their seats. Instantly, the light cast a reflection of the two onto the windshield in front of Jake, offering him a clear view of the backseat. He taxied the rest of the way to the runway, straightened the plane, and increased power to the engine. Beth wasn't fighting, and Bill had relaxed his hold on the gun. From the expression on his face and the way he was sweating, Jake had the feeling that Bill Brandon didn't like to fly.

The accelerating plane approached the end of the runway and lifted off, and Bill's face seemed to grow paler. His hold on Beth was looser now, and he seemed distracted—as though airsickness was assaulting him now.

Jake met Beth's eyes in the glass, hoping she was thinking what he was thinking. With a little help from Jake, Beth might be able to knock the gun out of his hand.

He thought of that first trip with Lynda, when he'd played the hotdogger and dipped and zigzagged all over the sky like a Thunderbird. Even Lynda, a seasoned pilot, had gone pale at that. A good dip might just push Bill over the edge.

Jake took a deep breath, braced himself—then shoved the control yoke forward, making the plane drop, them quickly pulled it back up.

Bill fell backward against the seat, but Beth was ready. With a quick swing, she knocked the gun from his hand. "You sniveling piece of trash!" he shouted, bringing his backhand across her face as he dove for the gun. She slid to the floor on her knees, and just before he grabbed the pistol, she reached it herself. His grip on her wrist made her drop it, but she managed to knock it with her elbow, sending it sliding under the seat.

"Jake, help!" she screamed as Bill hit the floor, grabbing her hair and banging her head into the floor, while he groped under the seat for the gun.

Jake couldn't abandon the controls and felt helpless as he tried to find something that could be used as a weapon. "Get the gun, Beth. You have to get the gun!" He looked back and saw the blood seeping through the side of her shirt around the edges of the bandage on her chest. Still, she lurched under the seat, reaching, stretching ...

Jake pulled the plane up, made a steep climb, then dove suddenly, making Bill slide toward the front of the plane. "*Now*, Beth!" Jake shouted.

Twisting her body sideways, Beth dropped onto her stomach and pushed further under the seat until, at last, with a desperate, painful lunge, she reached the gun. Sliding backwards out from under the seat, she put her back to the plane's side wall and pushed with her feet until she was as near upright as she could get in the small plane. She pointed the gun at Bill's forehead.

"I got it, Jake!" she shouted.

Jake glanced back at her. Blood was dripping down her temple where Bill had slammed her head into the floor, and more blood soaked through her shirt. Her eyes were venomous as she aimed the gun at the man who had tormented her for most of her life. Her hands trembled as she clutched the pistol in a life-or-death grip.

"Don't shoot, Beth," Jake said. "I'm turning around."

"I won't shoot," she said. "Not until we're on the ground."

There were strings of wet hair plastered to Bill's forehead, and beads of sweat rolling down his face. He looked up at her. "Come on, Beth. You couldn't pull that trigger. You know I didn't raise you to be a killer."

She cocked the hammer and through her teeth said, "You raised me to do what has to be done."

"Beth, don't do it! You may shoot the plane," Jake said. "I don't want to crash again!"

"He'll finagle a way out of this," she said in a dull voice. "He could go free, get off without even a fine. They're all in it with him."

"All who?" Bill asked.

"All your friends. They're all making a mint off what you're doing to those kids. You'll keep on doing it. You'll find a way. Unless I kill you. And I can do that. All I have to do is wait until we touch down, then pull this trigger and watch your whole world end. Then it'll all be over."

"Let him go to jail, Beth," Jake said. "Let him see what it feels like to be locked up in a place he can't leave. Let him see what it feels like to live the way he made you live, Beth."

"It's different," she said. "He's not a child. There's no way to show him how much worse it is for a little, innocent kid who can't defend himself."

"Then let God teach him that, Beth."

Bill latched onto that idea. Breathless and beginning to shake, he said, "That's right, Beth. If I've made mistakes, if I've hurt anyone, the Creator will deal with me. 'Vengeance is mine, saith the Lord.' It's not yours, Beth."

"Don't you dare quote Scripture to me!" she screamed. "I've heard enough of your filthy distortions and your twisted paraphrases. Maybe God will get his vengeance on all those kids through me. Maybe he wants a bullet in your head for defiling his Word."

"Don't believe it!" Jake shouted. "That's twisted thinking, Beth!"

"That's right, Beth, darlin'. You don't want to pull that trigger."

The plane touched down with a bump, and Jake slowed the plane to a stop.

Bill was looking up at her, as though he knew she would never shoot. Her finger trembled over the trigger. She thought of all the ways she'd tried to purify her life, the score sheet she'd been keeping. But all of that meant nothing if she could still contemplate murder for revenge. If she could still hate, after all she'd learned about God, maybe she didn't have it in her to be a child of God. That reality filled her with choking despair, and for a split second, she thought of turning the gun on herself.

But something stopped her. Some still, soothing voice from the center of her soul: *You don't have it in you, but I have it in me.*

She had a quick, fleeting memory of the discussion she and Nick had had about the thief on the cross, and the grace that God had extended to him. For the first time, it made sense.

Beth's law-keeping was worthless. Her good works were empty. It was only through Christ's power that she could have any righteousness at all.

Nick was right.

She moved her finger from the trigger, keeping the gun pointed at Bill Brandon. Murder—even if some would consider it justified—would only destroy it all.

"Radio in and tell them I've got him. Tell them to come get him."

In moments, police had surrounded the plane. Nick jogged up just as they helped Bill Brandon, handcuffed, down from the plane's wing and led him away.

As soon as Beth stepped down from the wing, Nick caught her in a crushing hug. "Are you all right? You're bleeding."

"Not much," she said. "I popped a few stitches, but I'm all right."

"Don't be such a tough guy," he said. "I know you're in pain." He wrapped his arms tighter around her, and in a moment, he felt her body quaking with tears. She stood on her toes and wrapped her arms so tightly around his neck that he felt tears burning his own eyes. She was sobbing now, sobbing out her heart and her soul, sobbing in a way he'd never seen her do before.

Somehow, he didn't have to ask what she was crying for. He knew she was crying for the children in that home who had robbed all night and then studied all day, those children who had been deprived of their ability to trust, those children who would carry the guilt of what they'd done all their lives. He knew she was crying for herself, for the child she had been, the child who'd had no one to protect her from evils such as Bill Brandon. He knew she was crying for a lifetime of loneliness, a lifetime of wishing she could belong somewhere.

And he vowed that, if it was the last thing he ever did, he would give her that place to belong.

He lifted her and began to carry her back, and she kept her face buried against his neck. "Where are you taking me?" she asked him.

"Back to the hospital," he said. "So they can make sure you're all right."

"I don't want to spend the night at the hospital," she said. "I don't want to be alone."

"I have no intention of leaving you alone. I'm going to sit with you all night long."

"Why?" she asked.

"Because I don't think I could tear myself away from you if I wanted to," he whispered.

CHAPTER SEVENTY-ONE

T ony burst through the ER doors and bolted to the desk. Someone was talking to the receptionist, but he couldn't wait. "My partner was brought in here with a gunshot—Larry Millsaps!"

The receptionist shot him an annoyed look. "I'll be with you in a moment, sir."

"No, I have to know now! Is he dead or alive?"

"He's alive," she said. "Now if you'll wait . . ."

Tony sank back in relief, feeling as if he could finally breathe. "Alive? You're sure?"

"Yes, I'm sure."

"I have to see him, then." He started toward the double swinging doors leading to the examining rooms, and the woman stood up.

"Sir, I'm sorry, but you aren't supposed to go in there." When he kept walking, she picked up the phone. "I'll call security!"

Breathing a weary sigh, he turned around and flashed his badge at her. "I'm a police officer, and my partner was shot tonight. I'm going in there, and if security would like to try and stop me, they're welcome to."

She sat back down, and he pushed through the doors.

He went from room to room, looking for Larry, hoping that he wouldn't find him comatose or on the verge of death. His heart pounded as he rounded the corner in the hall, looking into every room—

"Tony?"

He swung around and saw Melissa Millsaps, Larry's wife, looking pale and fatigued, standing in a doorway across the hall.

"Melissa!" he said, stepping toward her. "How is he?"

She nodded without speaking, and led him into Larry's room. Larry lay on a gurney, his left shoulder bandaged and his arm in a sling.

"It just missed his heart," she said as tears came to her eyes—tears that didn't look as if they were the first she had cried tonight. "Angels were watching over him."

"Then he's . . . gonna be all right?"

Larry opened his eyes, and looked up at his partner. "'Course I'm gonna be all right. Takes more than a bullet to stop Larry Millsaps."

Tony began to laugh with such relief that tears filled his own eyes. Larry reached up to take his hand, and Tony grabbed it and squeezed it hard. "Thought I'd lost you there, buddy."

Melissa went to the other side of the table and stroked his forehead gently. "Me, too," she said.

Larry looked up at Tony, his eyes heavy. Tony knew they had probably given him something strong for the pain. "You get Brandon?"

"Locked up tight," Tony said. "Right where he's gonna be for a long time. Him and Sheila Axelrod and the good Judge Wyatt."

Larry grinned. "What about the kids? And Beth?"

"When you're feeling better, I'll tell you about how everything happened. But Beth's fine. They're still processing the kids, though," Tony said. "But they'll be all right. Nick's looking out for them."

Larry closed his eyes and smiled, and Melissa leaned over him and pressed a soft kiss on his eyelid. He reached up with his good arm and held her face against his. "Sorry I scared you," he whispered to his wife.

"It's okay," she said. "I've given you a few scares, too. You owed me one."

Tony told Larry to get some rest, then went back out into the hall. Emotion overwhelmed him as he realized how close he had come to losing his best friend. And how close Melissa had come to losing her husband.

He felt a sudden urge to talk to Sharon, the woman who had meant so much to him for the past several months. He wanted to hold her and tell her that he loved her, to ask her if they had a future together, to take care of her and her children. There was so much ugliness out there, so much horror—and Tony just didn't want to stand alone anymore in a world like that. He went through the emergency room doors, picking up purpose with every step.

He got into his car and sat there for a moment, looking up at the sky as he had done months earlier, when he had opened his heart to Jesus Christ. Tony knew that he wasn't really alone now—his Lord knew all of the weariness in Tony's soul, all the wounds in his heart—and all the reasons that this man who never committed, wanted to commit now.

Tony began to smile as he cranked his car and headed to Sharon's house.

CHAPTER SEVENTY-TWO

Beth slept better than she'd ever slept that night, knowing that Bill was in jail, along with all of those who'd worked with him, including Judge Wyatt, Sheila Axelrod, and a number of others whose names and fingerprints they'd gotten from examining the warehouse.

When she woke the next morning, still in the hospital, Nick was sitting beside her bed, where he'd been when she'd fallen asleep last night. He looked sleepy as he smiled at her. "Hi."

"Hi," she said. "You really did stay all night, huh?"

"Right here in this chair." He handed her the newspaper. "Thought you might want to see this."

"What?"

"The *St. Petersburg Times*. Phil did it. He got them to print your article this morning, along with several sidebars about last night, and the arson at the paper, and the bomb in your house, and even Tracy Westin."

She sat up slowly in bed and read her headline. "I don't believe it. I had given up."

"Whatever Brandon and Judge Wyatt may have planned for squirming their way out of this, it isn't likely to work now—not with all this publicity. I think the media will dive into this story today. Maybe even the national networks. Better get ready to be a hero."

"I'm no hero," she said. "I'll never shake the stigma of being one of Bill's kids." She sighed. "What about Jimmy and the rest of them? Will they be punished?"

"Nope," he told her. "There's a quote right here by the prosecutor. 'We have no plans to prosecute any of the children who participated in these crimes, nor any of those who participated as children and are now adults.' All he wants is for you to be witnesses in the trial."

She closed her eyes in relief, whispering, "Then they aren't presuming we're all guilty until we're proven innocent?"

"Not at all," he said. "You're altogether innocent."

"Not altogether," she whispered. "But I believe in the power of Christ's forgiveness now."

"Wanna talk about it?" he asked.

She swallowed and tried to sort through her feelings. An image of Tracy, weak and sick, trying to stop the car that was carrying off her children, offering her life in exhange for theirs, overwhelmed her. No matter what Tracy had done in the past, in the end, she had loved her children enough to die for them.

Beth closed her eyes as tears streamed down her face. "I can't quit thinking of Tracy," she whispered. "What she did—I think that's the kind of love you tried to tell me about. The kind that could ransom those little kids."

"That's right," Nick said, stroking her forehead. "The same kind of love that could ransom a woman with a painful past."

She breathed in a shaky sob. "And no score sheet can ever outshine that kind of love, can it?"

Nick shook his head, and she saw the tears in his eyes. She covered her face as her tears fell harder, as her soul swelled within her.

"Oh, Jesus, I believe you," she prayed aloud through her tears. "Ransom me. Not just from Bill, but from myself. From all the lies I've believed. From all the pain I've hardened myself to . . ."

Nick held her hand tightly as she prayed, encouraging her prayer with words of his own.

When she opened her eyes, she was smiling, but the tears continued nonetheless. Nick was crying, too. For a moment, they just looked at each other and laughed through their tears. When Nick took in a deep, cleansing breath and began to wipe her tears, her smile faded. "I just thought of something," she said. "You remember how I compared Tracy to my own mother?"

"Yeah," Nick said.

"Well, I wonder—would she have done what Tracy did? I mean, if Tracy had the capacity for that kind of love in her, maybe, in the end, my mother could have cared, too. If she'd been put to the test—who knows?"

"God knows," Nick said. "That's why you're thinking of it right now. Maybe God can help you forgive her."

A light of realization dawned behind Beth's eyes. "Yeah, I think I can," she whispered in wonder. "I think, if God can forgive me for all that I've done—yeah, I can forgive my mom."

Nick pulled her up into his arms and held her as tightly as he could without hurting her. For the first time in her life, she belonged. Right here, in his arms. Together, they cried and clung together until there were no more tears, and laughter joined their hearts.

When he let her go, she reached out and touched his stubbled jaw. "I guess you'll be getting Sheila Axelrod's job, huh?"

He looked thoughtful. "I've had a lot of time to think tonight—about my job, about all these problems we've seen, about how hard it's going to be to place those kids. And I think I've come to a decision."

"What?"

"I want to apply to take over the home. I want to give those kids a chance to see what God's grace is like. I want to bring them to him—to the real Lord, not some perverted version like Bill had. I want to be a father to all those kids."

Her heart burst. "Oh, Nick, you'd be wonderful at it, and you have such a heart for them."

"I'd need helpers," he said. "I was thinking about that nice couple, the Millers, who wanted so badly to be in the foster parent program. Maybe they could be cottage parents, and I can think of other retired couples who'd be good, too. And I thought that, well—maybe you could help."

"I'm too young to be a cottage mother."

"You're not too young to be my wife."

She stared at him for a long moment, stricken with disbelief. He took her hand, kissed it, and set her palm against his jaw. "What do you think, Beth? Would you make me the happiest man in the world and be my wife? Have my children? Let me be your family, and then we can be the family for all those kids."

Beth threw her arms around his neck, too choked up to answer. Somehow, Nick was pretty sure that she was going to say yes.

CHAPTER SEVENTY-THREE

Two weeks later, Lynda bought Lisa a new bathing suit and got special permission to take her and Jimmy out to the beach that morning. But Jimmy and Jake were cooking something up, and they were late arriving.

"What do you think those two boys are doing?" she asked the little girl.

"I don't know," Lisa said. "Can we build a castle while we wait?"

"Of course we can. Come on. Let's go down to the water."

"But we'll get wet."

"It doesn't matter. A little water never hurt anybody." Lynda got down on her knees just out of reach of the waves, and began helping the child pile the sand into a castle.

"When I grow up," Lisa said with a self-conscious smile, "I want to live in a castle."

Lynda laughed. "I thought that, too, when I was a little girl. And when I grew up, I got something just as good as a castle. But you know what? It didn't make me happy."

The little girl hung on every word. "What made you happy?" she asked.

"People," she said. "People I love. People who love me."

"I have people who love me," Lisa said. "Jimmy loves me. And my mom."

Lynda's smile slowly faded. "Do you remember your mom, Lisa?"

She shook her head and looked across the water. The breeze blew her hair back from her face. "Not really," she said. "But

Jimmy's been telling me about her. He told me how much she loved us."

"She did," Lynda agreed.

"She died, though." Her wistful eyes focused on the half-formed castle, and she started patting the sand again. "Do you love Jake?"

Lynda grinned. "Very much."

They heard a plane overhead, and Lisa looked up as Lynda dug up more sand.

"Look, Lynda! What does it say?"

Lynda looked up. It was a skywriting plane, and it was writing something across the sky. Lisa stood up and waved, jumping up and down. "It looks like . . . M-a-r-r-y . . . Marry . . . me . . ." Lisa read. "L-y-n—"

Lynda got to her feet and shaded her eyes as she stared up in disbelief. "Marry me, Lynda." She caught her breath. "It's Jake, Lisa! He's asking me to marry him! What should I say?"

Lisa began to dance and wave her arms with delight. "Tell him yes! Hurry!"

The cellular phone in Lynda's beach bag rang, and she pulled it out and, with a big grin, answered, "Yes, I'll marry you!"

Jake laughed out loud. "Will you, really?"

"Of course I will! Now get down here so I can kiss you!"

CHAPTER SEVENTY-FOUR

That night, after they had taken Jimmy and Lisa back to the home—which Nick was already running on a temporary basis until the state approved him to take it over permanently—Lynda and Jake sat out on the swing in her backyard, moving slowly back and forth.

"There's something I want to talk to you about," Jake said. "Something important."

"More important than marriage?" she asked, smiling down at the ring sparkling on her finger.

"Not really. But maybe *as* important."

"What?"

"It's about children."

"I want them," Lynda said. "Lots of them. And I hope they look just like you."

He laughed. "I'd rather they look like you. But I was thinking of a head start, kind of. I was thinking of adoption."

Her eyes caught his grin, and she sat up straight and cocked her head to look at him. "Jake, you're not thinking what I think you're thinking, are you? Because I've thought it myself, only I didn't think you'd think—"

"Jimmy and Lisa," he said.

"Yes!" she shouted. "Yes! We can be the best parents anybody ever had, and—"

"Let's call Nick," he said. "I don't want to waste any time!"

CHAPTER SEVENTY-FIVE

Six Months Later

The plane Jake had named *Trinity* circled the airfield, to the cheers of the dozens of children—most of them residents of the St. Clair Children's Home—then descended for a landing on the long dirt runway. Nick and Beth watched from a crowd of children as Jake Stevens rolled the plane to a stop, and Lynda Barrett Stevens turned back to the crowd with her bullhorn.

"All right, guys! Who hasn't been up yet?"

"Me, Mommy! I wanna go!" Lisa jumped up and down in front of her, waving her arm in front of her face so she wouldn't be missed.

"You can go anytime!" Jimmy said. "Let Dad take *them*, Lisa!"

"But I wanna go too! I wanna see their faces!"

Lynda laughed and hugged the child that had brought so much joy to the home she and Jake were making together. "All right, sweetie. You're in the next group."

Melissa and Larry Millsaps counted off the next group of kids Jake would take up for a flight, then herded them over to the wing, where Tony Danks and his fiancée, Sharon Robinson, stood waiting to pull them up and help them into the plane.

The children roared and cheered as Jake turned the plane around and taxied back up the airstrip.

Nick slid his arm around his wife and pulled her close. "They're loving this," he said.

Beth laughed and ran her fingers through her hair. She had let it grow out some and had returned it to its natural color. "Yeah, it was a good idea. And you know he's not just showing them the clouds. He's got a captive audience up there to tell them all about Jesus."

"The way things have been going at the home, they might just tell *him* about Jesus. You're a great influence for them, Beth. You never let an opportunity go by—"

"When they lie down, and when they rise up. I wish someone had explained it all to me earlier. Then I would have known that I was loved. That I wasn't just some throwaway kid that nobody wanted."

"Not one of these kids feels like a throwaway," Nick said. "They're happy, aren't they?"

"Yeah, I think they are. Bill Brandon's brainwashing goes deep, but Christ's grace is deeper."

"Way deeper," Nick said. He leaned over and kissed his wife, then pulled her into a crushing hug as the plane circled over their heads, and the burgers sizzled on the grills, and the children laughed and squealed and ran across the grass.

And the joy they all felt was a divine gift that couldn't be doused or destroyed by men, because God had chosen to bestow it on them like a beautiful package under a Christmas tree—

Or a marriage that blossomed brighter with each passing day—

Or an eternity without threat or malice.

Miracles, they were, all shining and bright beneath the warm rays of God's smile.

AFTERWORD

Recently, I was sitting in the Green Room at CBN Headquarters in Virginia Beach, waiting to go on *The 700 Club*, when God taught me one of those lessons that he often teaches when we least expect it. The producer had just come in and told me that I'd be squeezed on at the end of the program, and that I might get six minutes.

My heart sank, because I wanted so much to give my whole testimony about how God had convicted me to leave my career in the secular market and write Christian fiction only. There were so many miracles God had performed in my life, so many things I wanted the *700 Club* viewers to know about. But there was no way I could tell them all of it in six minutes.

The guest coordinator of the show and the executive producer were in the Green Room with me, and when the producer who had delivered the startling news retreated, I looked at the other two and confessed that I was nervous. That was an understatement. The truth was that I was in a state of sheer panic.

Without batting an eye, Jackie, the guest coordinator, began praying for me. She asked God to remind me that he had brought me here for a reason, and that he wasn't going to forsake me now. Immediately afterward, the two were called away, and I was left in the room alone.

Instantly, I began to pray again. I asked God not to let Terry Meeuwsen, the interviewer, waste time with fluffy talk about writing and publishing, but that the Lord would give her the exact questions that would move the story forward rapidly enough that I could get out the most important parts of my testimony. I asked him to give me peace about going out there under such time constraints, as well as a clear head so that my thoughts and my words would flow smoothly. And I prayed for the hearts of those viewers who needed to hear what God had done for me.

Peace fell over me, and when the producer came for me, I was calm. Terry asked pertinent and intelligent questions that jumped the story forward when it needed to jump forward, and I was able to get my testimony out. The interesting thing is that some parts of the story which I might have left out, God saw fit to leave in. Terry's questions prompted me to answer them.

What was the lesson I learned that day? I learned that when we do anything by our own strength, we have the potential of failing. But when we empty ourselves of our own intentions, our own plans, our own goals, God will fill us up with his Holy Spirit. When we're directed by the Creator of the universe, how can we fail?

God gives us everything we need. Christian friends, teachers, churches, pastors, the Bible . . . But if we just use those things to get us to some end—whether it be a successful interview or salvation itself—they're nothing more than tools. Without the Father to guide us, the Christ to motivate us, and the Holy Spirit to empower us, we have the potential to fail.

But thanks be to God, through Jesus Christ our Lord, that "he who began a good work in you will carry it on to completion until the day of Christ Jesus" (Philippians 1:6). And thanks to our Father for giving us not just the tools, but the reason and the power to go along with them. And thanks to him, especially, for giving us the outcome—success, always, pure and divine, the way he designed it.

Terri Blackstock is an award-winning novelist who has written for several major publishers including HarperCollins, Dell, Harlequin, and Silhouette. Published under two pseudonyms, her books have sold over 3.5 million copies worldwide.

With her success in secular publishing at its peak, Blackstock had what she calls "a spiritual awakening." A Christian since the age of fourteen, she realized she had not been using her gift as God intended. It was at that point that she recommitted her life to Christ, gave up her secular career, and made the decision to write only books that would point her readers to him.

"I wanted to be able to tell the truth in my stories," she said, "and not just be politically correct. It doesn't matter how many readers I have if I can't tell them what I know about the roots of their problems and the solutions that have literally saved my own life."

Her books are about flawed Christians in crisis and God's provisions for their mistakes and wrong choices. She claims to be extremely qualified to write such books, since she's had years of personal experience.

A native of nowhere, since she was raised in the Air Force, Blackstock makes Mississippi her home. She and her husband are the parents of three children—a blended family which she considers one more of God's provisions.

PRIVATE JUSTICE

Enjoy this preview from the first book
in the Newpointe 911 Series.

Chapter One

● ● ●

The competing sounds of brass bands, jazz ensembles, and
zydeco musicians gave Newpointe, Louisiana, an irresistibly
festive atmosphere, but Mark Branning tried not to feel festive.
It was a struggle, since he stood in a clown suit with an orange
wig on his head, preparing to make the long walk down the
Mardi Gras parade route. Already, Jacquard Street was packed
with tourists and townspeople here to chase beads and candy
being thrown by drunken heroes. In moments, he and his fellow firefighters, also dressed as clowns, would fall into their
sloppy formation on the town's main drag, followed by the fire
truck that carried even more painted firemen.

It was what promoters advertised as a "family friendly"
parade—unlike the decadent bacchanalian celebrations in New
Orleans, only forty minutes away. But Fat Tuesday was still Fat

Tuesday, no matter where it was celebrated, and it always got out of hand. It was the time of year when the protective services in Newpointe had to be on the alert. Last year, during the same "family friendly" parade, a man had been stabbed, two women had been raped, and they'd been called to the scene of four drunk-driving accidents. It seemed to get worse every year.

Just days ago, Jim Shoemaker, police chief of the small town, and Craig Barnes, fire chief, had appealed to the mayor that the town was better served if their forces remained on duty on Fat Tuesday. Mayor Patricia Castor insisted that the community needed to see their emergency personnel having fun with everyone else. It fostered trust, she said, and made the men and women who protected the town look more human. At her insistence, and to Shoemaker's and Barnes's dismay, only skeleton crews were to remain on duty, while the rest of the firemen, police officers, and paramedics were to dress like clowns and act like idiots. "It's a religious holiday," she drawled, as if that sealed her decision.

Mark slung the shoulder strap of his bag of beads and candies over his head, and snickered at the idea that they would call Fat Tuesday a religious *anything*. The fact that it preceded Lent—a time for fasting and reflection as Easter approached—seemed to him a lame excuse for drunken revelry.

A police squad car pulled up beside the group of wayward firefighters, and Stan Shepherd, the town's only detective—still unadorned and unpainted—grinned out at him. "Lookin' good, Mark," he said with a chuckle.

"So how'd you get out of this?" Mark asked him, ambling toward the car. "I thought Newpointe's finest were supposed to dress like demonic bikers."

"Makes a lot of sense, doesn't it?" Stan asked with a grin. "Pat Castor wants us to show the town how human and accessible we are, so she makes us wear makeup that could give nightmares to a Marine."

"Hey, what can you say? It's Mardi Gras. You still haven't told me why you're not made up."

"Because I refused," Stan stated flatly. "How's that for a reason?"

Mark leaned on the car door and stared down at his friend. "You mean that's all it took?"

"That's all. Plus I read some statute to her about how it was illegal for someone out of uniform to drive a squad car."

"You're not in uniform, Stan."

"Yes, I am. I'm a plainclothes cop. This is my uniform." Stan looked past Mark to the others milling around, waiting impatiently for their chance to ruin their reputations. "Speaking of nightmares, check out George's costume."

"You talkin' 'bout me?" George Broussard asked, coming toward the car. Mark grinned at the Cajun's gaudy three-colored foil wig and the yellow and purple-polka dot shirt he wore. It was too little for him, and the buttons strained over his protruding gut. His hairy belly peeked out from under the bottom hem of the ill-chosen blouse, and someone had drawn a smiling pair of lips under his navel and crossed eyes above it.

"Yep. The stuff that bad dreams are made of," Mark agreed.

"Yeah, and you got lotsa room to talk," George returned. "Just 'cause you don't got the canvas I got to work with . . ." He patted his bare belly again, and Mark turned away in mock disgust.

Mark was glad he had lost weight since he and Allie had split up. The wives gleefully wielding the face and body paint were particularly cruel to those midlife paunches. His costume did, at least, cover all of his torso without accenting any glaring flaws, though he could have done without the flapper fringe that some sadistic seamstress had applied in rows to the polyester shirt.

"Is Allie gonna be here today?" Stan asked Mark.

Mark glanced at George, wishing Stan hadn't asked that in front of him. He hadn't broadcast the news of his separation from his wife and figured there were still some in town who didn't know about it. That suited him just fine. George, who had only been in Newpointe for the past year, wasn't a close enough friend for Mark to air his dirty laundry with.

As if he sensed Mark's discomfort, George wandered off and blended back into the cluster of clowns.

"How would I know what Allie's gonna do?" Mark asked.

"Don't give me that garbage," Stan said. "You keep closer tabs on your wife now than you did before."

"Estranged wife. I don't know if she'll be here. I doubt it. It's not her thing." He straightened, unwrapped a Jolly Rancher, and popped it into his mouth. "Then again, I did kind of think she might swallow some of her self-righteousness today to come help the wives paint us up. It's a power thing, you know. They love to make us look ridiculous. Allie's devoted her life to it."

"At least you're not bitter."

The barb hit home. "Bitter? Why should I be bitter? Actually, I feel great. I love my new bachelor life. Did I tell you that I picked up some great furniture at Kay Neubig's garage sale? Mid-century relics complete with the original stuffing coming out from the tears in the authentic vinyl. And my apartment has ambiance. The building's foundation is going, so the whole place slants. It's hard to keep gravity from pulling the kitchen cabinets open, and I worry a little when the train that comes by at two A.M. every night makes the building sway and vibrate— but like I said, ambiance. You know how I live for ambiance."

"So you're ticked about the apartment. Do you miss your wife?"

Mark was glad his face was painted so the heat moving to his cheeks wasn't apparent. Stan was a good friend, but he was crossing the line. He decided to change the subject. "Let's just say I'm aware that she's not here. I'm also aware that *your* wife isn't here. Why isn't Celia wielding a paintbrush today with the other cop wives?"

"Because we're boycotting the whole makeup idea. She's here. I'll pick her up when the procession gets up to Bonaparte, and she'll ride the rest of the way with me."

"I thought only uniformed cops could ride in the squad cars."

"She's dressed just like I am—in plainclothes." Stan grinned and winked, then put the car into drive and skirted the band and the motorcycles up ahead.

Mark turned back toward the firemen and saw George dancing to the jazz band. That face painted on his stomach gave him a comical double-decker look that had the women among them doubling over in laughter.

"If Martha could see you now!" one of the wives yelled.

"She will, darlin'," George said. "She's bringin' the baby. They're probably in the crowd as we speak."

"Poor kid," Mark muttered with a grin. "Only six months old, and he has to see a thing like this."

•••

The noise of the sirens, revving motorcycles, and brass bands playing three streets over almost drowned out the screams of the six-month-old baby in the Broussard house, but Reese Carter, the old man who lived next door, pulled himself up from his little rolling stool in his garden and wondered why the baby's mother hadn't quieted him yet. The parents—George Broussard, a local fireman, and his pretty wife, Martha—were attentive, and he rarely heard the baby crying for more than a few minutes. But this had gone on since the parade had started—probably more than half an hour now.

Not one to intrude where he wasn't invited, he tried to mind his own business and concentrate on the weeds he pulled from his garden. He wished the parade would end, so that he could have peace again. The conflicting sounds of jazz and marching bands, drum corps from the high school, tapes playing on floats, and sirens blaring were making him wish he'd picked today to visit a relative out of town. But most of his people lived here in Louisiana, and he doubted there was a place in the state that was immune to Fat Tuesday.

Despite the parade noise, he could still hear the baby screaming. He pulled his gloves off with a disgusted sigh, trying to decide whether to go inside where he couldn't hear the baby's cries, or check to see if things were all right next door. His first instinct was to go inside, but then he remembered that last Christmas, after his wife died, when he'd expected to spend the day alone mired in self-pity, Martha Broussard had knocked on his door and invited him over to share Christmas dinner. He hadn't wanted to go—hadn't been in a festive mood and didn't want to pretend he was—but she had insisted. So he had gone, and several hours later he realized that the day was mostly over and he hadn't had time to feel sorry for himself.

If something was wrong next door now, he owed it to them to see if there was anything he could do. Maybe the baby was sick, and he could go to the drugstore for some medicine. Or maybe Tommy just had colic and couldn't be comforted, in which case Reese could show Martha some of the tricks that his wife had used on their children and grandchildren.

He dusted off his hands, then rinsed them under the faucet on the side of his house and dried them on his pants. He caught a faint whiff of smoke in the air. Someone must be breaking the city ordinance about burning limbs in their yard. Fat Tuesday seemed to give people license to do whatever they wanted, he thought with disdain as he headed down his driveway, cut across the Broussard yard, and trudged up the porch steps to the door. He rang the bell and waited. No answer.

Now that he was closer, he could hear that the baby wasn't just crying—he was screaming wildly. Reese leaned closer to the door and called, "Martha? Are you there?"

He knocked hard, hurting his arthritic knuckles, then raised his voice. "Martha! It's Reese Carter, next door. Martha, are you there?"

But all he heard in reply was the baby's gasping wails against the background of jazz music three blocks away.

•••

The jazz band in front of Mark and the other firemen changed tunes, and some accordions launched into a zydeco tune. Trying to keep himself and the rest of the firemen in the spirit as they waited for their turn to march out onto the parade route, Mark led some of the others in an absurd chorus-line kick dance that fit perfectly with their attire. As he clowned, he scanned the other firemen and wondered how much beer they—and the rest of the parade participants—had already guzzled in the spirit of the festivities. It was only ten o'clock in the morning, yet trays and trays of drafts in plastic cups had been doled out to those waiting to participate.

Some of the wives still milled among the firemen, finishing up the outlandish makeup jobs. Jamie Larkins, with a cup of beer in one hand and an eyeliner pencil in the other, was swaying to the beat as she painted Marty Bledsoe's face. Susan Ford, a pretty black woman who wouldn't touch alcohol even if she were dying of thirst, finished Slater Finch's bare back—on which she'd drawn Betty Boop eyes and lips and applied a fake nose. She saw Mark horsing around and said, "You better stop that sweating, Mark Branning, you hear me?" The sweet demand cut through the laughing voices as Susan approached him with her makeup tray. "Look at you. Your smile is dripping. Our king of choreography is losing his looks."

"Me? Never," Mark deadpanned. "You may note that I have the least amount of face paint on. They knew not to mess with a good thing."

"Either that, or you already fit the bill without it."

Mark looked wounded. "Susan, you slay me. I believed you when you said I looked like George Clooney."

"Loony, Mark, not Clooney. And I never mentioned a George."

He grinned as she reached up with a tissue and wiped the smear from his mouth. "You're a mean woman, Susan Ford."

"You bet I am. And don't you forget it." Her smile faded as she touched up his face. "By the way, I saw Allie yesterday."

"Speaking of mean women?" he asked.

She wasn't amused. "She looked awful lonesome, Mark."

Again, he was glad that his face paint hid the heat rushing to his cheeks. He didn't know why every conversation these days seemed to lead directly to Allie. If Allie looked "lonesome," it was because she'd chosen to be alone. They'd been separated for over two months now, and although neither of them had made a move to file for divorce, there was no movement being made toward a reconciliation, either.

Susan seemed to realize she'd hit a nerve. Reaching up to press a kiss on his painted cheek, she whispered, "Sorry, honey. Didn't mean to bring you down."

"It's okay. No problem." A bone-thin majorette passed with a tray of beer, and he eyed it this time, wondering if he should drink just one to keep his mood from deflating completely. But Susan was there, as well as others from his church who would pass immediate judgment. He let the tray pass and wished the parade would hurry up and move so he could get the morning over with.

•••

At Midtown Fire Station on Purchase Street, where all of Newpointe's protective services were located side by side, right across from city hall and the courthouse, Nick Foster paced the bunkroom and rehearsed his sermon for his little church's midweek service. It was tough being a bivocational pastor, juggling practical and spiritual duties. Sometimes it was impossible to separate his ministry from his profession. Today was one of those times. Whenever he dared to buck the mayor's authority and refuse to participate in something he believed to be immoral—as he had today—he risked losing his job as a fireman. Without it, he wouldn't make enough to pay his rent.

… 299 …

Though Calvary Bible Church had its share of supporters, there weren't many families in the body who had much to give. Newpointe, as a whole, was not a wealthy town. Most of the tithes and offerings went to pay for the building they'd built two years ago, plus the missions projects he'd started. There wasn't much left over for him, which was fine as long as he had fire-fighting to keep his refrigerator stocked. He lived in a trailer across the street from the church. "The parsonage," his church called it, even though neither he nor the church owned it.

He got stuck on one of the points in his sermon, went back to his notes, made a quick change, then began pacing again. What did you tell a town whose residents had been brought up on voodoo and Mardi Gras? Even though he'd made it a point to preach a series of sermons on idolatry in the weeks preceding Mardi Gras, he was still astounded at the number of his church members who made themselves part of the infrastructure that upheld the holiday. Half of his congregation was in the parade, and the other half was watching.

He stumbled on the words again and sank onto a bunk, feeling more frustrated than usual. Did it really matter if he got the words right, if no one really listened?

Taking off his wire-rimmed glasses, he dropped his head and stared down between his feet for a moment, feeling the burden of all those souls weighing on his heart. Finally, he closed his eyes and began to pray that God would make him more effective, that he'd open their hearts and ears, that they would see things clearly ...

He heard the door slam shut and looked up to see Dan Nichols, one of the other firefighters holding down the skeleton crew.

The tall blonde man was drenched in sweat and breathing hard, but to Nick's amusement, he went straight to the mirror and checked the receding hairline that seemed such a source of preoccupation to him.

"Has it moved any?" Nick teased.

Dan shot him an annoyed look. He slid the towel off of his neck and began wiping his face. "I wasn't looking at my hair."

Nick forced back his grin. Though he knew that he and Dan were considered two of the most eligible bachelors in town, Dan was by far the first choice of most of the single ladies. He was athletic and physically fit, something no one could say about Nick. And Dan had something else Nick didn't have. Money. Lots of it. He was one of the rare breed of firefighters who didn't have to work a second job to make ends meet. Dan had come from a wealthy family, had a geology degree, and could have been anything he wanted. But all he'd wanted was to be a fireman.

"You been out jogging?" Nick asked, a little surprised that he'd risk being away from the station when they were under-staffed.

"I didn't go far," Dan said. "If we'd gotten a call, you would have seen me as soon as you pulled out."

"So is it crazy out there yet?"

"Gettin' loud, I'll say that." He dropped down on the bunk across from Nick, still panting. "You know—" He hesitated, as if carefully weighing his words. "I know it was right for us to take a stand and not participate in Mardi Gras, but part of me feels like a stick-in-the-mud."

"Sure, I know," Nick said. "It's just a parade, right? No big deal, just a day of fun that's no harm to anybody. Don't buy into that lie, Dan."

Dan grinned. "It's just that everybody's there. I'm human. I grew up on Mardi Gras. It feels weird not being part of it."

Nick fought his disappointment. "Tell you the truth, I was surprised you stood with me on this. Why did you?"

Dan patted his shoulder and grinned. "Because you're right. You know you are." He stood up. "I think I'll go take a shower."

The door opened again as Dan headed for the bathroom, and Craig Barnes, the fire chief, shot in.

"Hey, boss," Nick said. "Thought you were at the parade."

"Yeah, I'm going," he said. "I'm hoping to avoid the blasted makeup. You won't see Mayor Castor prancing down the street with floppy shoes and a big nose. No, she gets to ride in a convertible and hang on to her dignity, and she expects me to hoof it with a bunch of drunken firefighters whose goal it is to make this department the laughingstock of the town."

Nick thought of echoing the sentiment, but in this mood, he doubted Craig would appreciate it. The chief wasn't one to pal around with his subordinates. He rarely vented, but when he did, it was usually meant to be a monologue.

"Where's everybody, anyway?" Craig demanded as he went to his locker and pulled out his cap. "Don't tell me you're the only one here."

"Dan's in the shower, and Junior is sweeping out back. You know, Craig, if you didn't show up, it might make a nice statement."

"With all those other bozos falling all over themselves to be in the parade? Some statement. No, I've got to grin and bear it." He slammed the locker and started out. "If anybody calls looking for me, tell 'em I'm on my way."

"Sure thing," Nick said.

As the fire chief headed back out the door, Nick sighed. So much was being made of so little. The mania itself ought to be a wake-up call to those who made themselves a part of the custom.

But all he could do was preach and pray, and hope that someday, they would start listening.

•••

The city employees' float, decorated like a pirate's ship, pulled into the street several positions in front of the firemen, cueing them that it was time to get into formation. Laughter erupted from some of the wives milling among the firemen, some already tipsy, others sober yet giddy as they prepared their husbands for the parade.

Lonesome, Mark thought with contempt. He couldn't say why Susan's description had ruined his mood.

He remembered another parade: the July Fourth parade last year, when Allie had been there among them, part of the fire family and the other half of himself. She had dressed like Martha Washington, and he'd been Uncle Sam. It had been a fun day, even in the sweltering heat.

He winced as Jamie Larkins, another fire wife, was swept away on a gale of raucous laughter. Cale, her husband, had been stealing sips from her draft, too, and Mark wondered if the effects would wear off before Cale went on duty tonight. He hoped so. A drunk or hungover firefighter was the last thing they needed on Fat Tuesday.

As the parade began to move, the brass band in front of them kicked into a newer, faster cadence and began dancing their way toward Jacquard Street. The firemen all looked at each other with comical dread before following. Some of them were jollier clowns than others, having been siphoning the beer that had been circulating like water since they'd gotten there that morning. It was the one day each year when the mayor footed the bill for something that wasn't an absolute necessity. Nick Foster, Mark's pastor, had protested the use of funds and asked her to spend it on much-needed bulletproof vests for the cops, a new pumper for the fire department, or updated rescue units for the paramedics. But as usual, she paid no attention.

Mark had considered taking Nick's stand and refusing to be in the parade, but part of him *wanted* to join in the fun, even though he'd voiced his righteous indignation just for the record. Part of him felt like a hypocrite—pretending to be spiritually offended by the parade even though, as everyone knew, he hadn't attended church since he and Allie had separated. It wasn't that he didn't want to—it was just that it was too uncomfortable with his wife there, all tense and cold, and with all of the members who had been his close friends offering advice that he neither needed nor wanted. If Mark had chosen to follow his pastor's lead, he was sure Nick would have used their time alone at the station to lecture him, again, about the mistake he was making in letting his marriage fail—as if that were his choice.

In a whirlwind of noise, the siren on the ladder truck behind them went off, and the motorcycles carrying the cops with faces painted like demonic rock stars roared louder. Another siren farther back, presumably from a rescue unit, moaned at migraine-level volume. Mark tried to shake himself out of the depression threatening to close over him; impulsively, he reached for one of the passing trays. He grabbed a draft and threw it back, then crushed the cup in his hand and dropped it to the ground. It did nothing to improve his mood, but he noticed Susan Ford and her husband, Ray—one of Mark's closest friends and the captain on his shift—watching him with sober, concerned faces. He wished they would both just mind their own business.

As the parade moved, the firemen scuffed onto Jacquard Street in their oversized shoes and undersized ruffled shirts, waving and tossing beads and candy to the cheers and pleas of hyperactive children and intoxicated adults, begging, "Throw me some beads!"

For the sake of goodwill in his community, Mark plastered on a smile and tried to have a good time.

Also from Terri Blackstock . . .

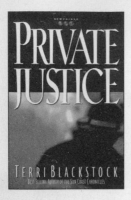

Newpointe 911 Series

Private Justice
Softcover 0-310-21757-1

Shadow of Doubt
Softcover 0-310-21758-X

Word of Honor
Softcover 0-310-21759-8

Trial by Fire
Softcover 0-310-21760-1

Sun Coast Chronicles

Evidence of Mercy
Softcover 0-310-20015-6

Justifiable Means
Softcover 0-310-20016-4

Ulterior Motives
Softcover 0-310-20017-2

Presumption of Guilt
Softcover 0-310-20018-0

Second Chances Series

Blind Trust
Softcover 0-310-20710-X

Broken Wings
Softcover 0-310-20708-8

Never Again Good-Bye
Softcover 0-310-20202-X

When Dreams Cross
Softcover 0-310-20709-6

With Beverly LaHaye

Seasons Under Heaven
Hardcover 0-310-22137-4

Showers in Season
Hardcover 0-310-22138-2

Times and Seasons
Hardcover 0-310-23319-4

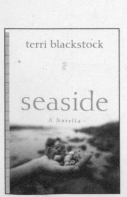

Novellas

Seaside
Hardcover 0-310-23318-6